The descent of the body into hell
And its ascent to the pedestal

Saynt Lachmi

Ivan Arthur

En Route Books and Media, LLC
Saint Louis, MO

Make the time

En Route Books and Media, LLC

5705 Rhodes Avenue

St. Louis, MO 63109

Cover credit: Sebastian Mahfood

ISBN-13: 978-1-956715-19-4

Library of Congress Control Number: 2021953199

Acknowledgements

Saynt Lachmi took a very long time to get beatified into a book and it would still have been coffined on my laptop if not for the encouragement of a few good people. As in any canonization, this Saynt, too, had to pass the test of time: a waiting period, proof of service and miracles.

The waiting period was the author's own silly dithering, I must confess. The miracles came in the person of, first: Bishop Bosco Penha of the Archdiocese of Mumbai, who wrote the foreword for my earlier book, *Pavement Prayers*. I am grateful to him for reading the first draft of the book. Robin Arthur, whose judgement I value greatly, egged me on to get it published. It was he who introduced me to Dr. Sebastian Mahfood, OP. That was the big step forward. Working with Dr. Mahfood was a dream. Encouragement, inspiration, and guidance travelled from his laptop in St. Louis to mine in Goa and later Spain almost every day. The stunning cover design is the halo that he has given the book. Ingrid, my wife, was the one who nursed me through the hospital pages of the book. I am grateful. Very grateful to each one of them.

"... they were naked" and yet "were not ashamed," unquestionably describes their state of consciousness, in fact, their mutual experience of the body. It describes the experience on the part of the man of the femininity that is revealed in the nakedness of the body and, reciprocally, the similar experience of masculinity on the part of the woman.

- Pope St. John Paul II

Part I

THE BODY TALKS

(Notebooks, diaries. Sometime in the 1960s.)

Lachmi's Notebook

munday

see I kan ryt

monika sez shee wood lyk to bee a saynt
    lyk dose nise smol pichers of sweet looking peeples
    holi pichers
    pichers of peeples wid rings rownd de hed
    lyk der woz a lite blub bihind it
    haylos
    hey hello haylo I dont want u
    hee hee hee
    i dont want a haylo
    i dont want dem to put me in a smol picher
    wid my hed folling on wun side
    lyke my nek is broke to look gentil
    an my ands folded namastey ishtyl
    on wich dey wil ryt wid big leters
    SAYNT LACHMI, PAYTRIN SAYNT OF PROSTITOOTS.
    an den to bekum a saynt lyk dat I wil hav to dy ferst
    baap re baap.
    an de pop from rom wil aks me to do sum majik eevin
dho I am ded
    an I dont want to dy no no
    no not now
    i want to bee a saynt wen I am stil alaiv
    to bee klever and look biutiful
    to put on lipstik

hav a nyse hare styl but no haylo
hav lotsa frends
bee appy an mayk evrywun appy
hav big big fun
but no halo

munday nyt

introdoocing mudder supeerier

sister hoo is mudder supeerier toks of dis god
i lyk gods
i seen pichers of lotsa gods on the rodes
in my siti name of bombay
he gods and she gods
smyling gods and angri gods
gods wid meni hands and heds and meni kullers
elefant fayss ganpati
munky fayss hanooman
sad fayss jeezis kryst
a hapy god wid a big stumik
lots an lotsa gods
i lyk dem
dey are not ornery like us
i lyk dat
but sister hoo is mudder supeerier has only wun god
and I say if god is good den dere muss be lotsa gods
undreds an towsans an mor
wy only wun
if der is only wun den he muss be very strong

lyke undred gods in wun

pleesd to meet yoo mister undred gods in wun
nyse to tok to yoo undred gods in wun
god and Lachmi
tok and tok and tok

Fryday

My ryting muss be like cleening rys or dal

i hav lernt how to ryt now
i kan ryt and ryt and ryt
not like ow I was ryting on de rodesyde
wid only leters and no werds
only fethers but no berds ha ha ha
now I kan ryt wid werds
like berds flying
i lyk dis ryting

sister hoo is mudder supeerier sed I must ryt a lot
praktis how to ryt good
i aksed her wot to ryt
shee sed ryt evryting dat I tink and feel
an to ryt de titel
i lyk dis ryting
but I kannot ryt evryting dat I tink an feel an doo
den I will ryt oll dose orrible harami tings
an shee wil reed wot I ryt baap re baap
no no no no no no

my ryting muss be like cleening rys or dal dont yu see
thro out the kachra dat is in my mynd
ryt only good an nys tings in good an nys inglish
shee will reed an say shabaash
or shee will spank de rong ryting
so I will lern
it is not eezee for a gerl lyk mee to ryt good an nys tings
ferst I muss send my thots to de de londri
to de dhobi as we say in bombay
den hang it lyn by lyn in dis book.

i was ferst speeking de werds of the rodesyd
an wen I did de prostitoot werk
I lernt how to speek a litel inglish
a litel french an a litel jermen an a litel rushyan.
but now I speek inglish ferst klaas.
i tok very good werds an I tok dem good
de werds jus fly out of my brane
werds wid wings
dey kiss my throt an my tung an teet an lips
an dey fly out like berds singing
not jus fethers flying
my gramer is good sister sez
like werds wearing tiptop dress
but my speling is terd klaas
not krekt shee sez
nyse but not krekt
i aksed her wich is better.
nyse or krekt
wich is better

shee sez nyse is better
but evrywun lyks krekt
stoopid evrywun
i lyk nyse

Sr. Maria Angelina's Diary

LACHMI.

She was a risk I took.

So did the good Swami when he brought her here. He was not as conscious of it as I was. The paradoxical naiveté of the elevated mind, I suppose; Benevolence blanking out good sense. His gratitude to me for admitting her into the convent fanned his own feeling of having done a good deed.

Blinkered moment. His and mine. Trashing caution in a careless sweep of feeling.

She was not quite twelve or thirteen when she arrived. Her risk-riddled story unfolding over time. Giving us reason to fear the snaky hand of the Law. It could bite the convent at any time.

But Folly is a brave girl sometimes, see?

Or did the morning's Compline engender divine bravado? I was prepared to answer Mother General or anybody for that matter.

Just in case the convent got into trouble.

Lachmi's story is a scarred tale.

She seems to have just strolled through it. As if it had happened to someone else.

Extraordinary child. Among the most intelligent I have ever seen. Street-smart one would expect a girl like her to be, but I see more: the unlikely shades of the scholar and intellectual. Picks up ideas with ease, particularly language.

Vacuum cleaner brain sucking up every single particle. Her cunning, sharpened on the pavement, and more: A rare feeling for aesthetics, visual and verbal.

She amazes me. I find myself trying to hold this amazement in check, conscious of my partiality towards the intellect.

I could easily be biased in her favour. Not right in my position.

Must keep a close watch on her.

She needs encouragement more than guardianship.

Something in her screams potential. She is the most attractive girl in the convent. Her dark, smooth skin exudes a sensuousness that is electric. Just under fifteen, she has an adult body. Not very tall, but shapely, with a longish neck, sloping down into a well-formed bosom. Long hair that tends to get wavy if not oiled and plaited.

The classic female structure.

But her most magnetic feature is her face. Her eyes; dark, shiny pupils in a pool of milk, framed by long dark eyelashes.

Something inside her that's more than just physical attraction. A kind of ESP that I have often sensed in the way she relates to people.

I hope that we can nurture all that with care.

Sr. Maria Angelina's Diary

When did the Word Made Flesh get written down in the Rig Veda?

I LOVE GETTING LETTERS. They are more talkative than talk. They tell more.

Two days ago, I got a letter from the person who sent Lachmi to me. Swami Ram Kumar Mudaliar.

Learned man for whom I have a high regard. Broadminded. Ecumenical. Encourages dialogue between his group of religious scholars and our simple sisters. Keeps in touch with me.

And now there's one more link between us: Lachmi.

Letter from Swami Ram Kumar Mudaliar

Salutations to you, Sister Maria Angelina.

Much happy I was to hear the news that the girl I brought to you, Lachmi by name is doing well. I am grateful to you for taking her because I would not know what to do with her because we do not have the kind of facilities that you have. I wanted to help the poor girl and you helped me to do that.

I was wanting to pen a letter earlier to your respectful self to tell you how much I found interesting our discussion on Predestination we had on the last occasion of my visit to you. It was indeed very stimulating and mind opening. Your reading on many subjects is much, I can see, but more than that, amazed I am at your familiarity with the Vedas and the Upanishads.

I know that you were very cautious in your mention of the

singularity of divinity, but you need not be cautious. The tenth chapter of the Rig Veda sings of a similar unity, omnipotence and infinity.

hiranyagharbha samavartataghre bhutasya jatah
*   patirekasit /*
sa dadhara prithivim dyamutemam kasmai
*   devayahavisa vidhema //*
ya atmada balada yasya visva upasate prasisam
*   yasyadevah/*
yasya chayamrtam yasya mrtyuh kasmai devayahavisa
vidhema //
yah pranato nimisato mahitvaika id raja jaghato
*   babhuva /*
ya ise asya dvipadascatuspadah kasmai devaya
*   havisavidhema //*

In the beginning there arose Hiranyagarbha (the
*   Golden Child);*
at birth itself, he alone was the lord of all that is.
He established the earth and this heaven — Who is the
*   God to whom we shall offer sacrifice?*

2. He who gives breath, he who gives strength,
whose command all the bright gods revere, whose
*   shadow is immortality,*
whose shadow is death —Who is the God to whom we
*   shall offer sacrifice?*

3. He who through his might became the sole king of

the breathing and twinkling world,
who governs all this, man and beast — Who is the God
to whom we shall offer sacrifice?

Do you not hear the echo of your John, Chapter One: *In Principio*
erat verbum. In the beginning was the Word? You may see
Hiranyagarbha as the avatar, Incarnation (the Golden Child), the
Second Person of your trinity or some may see him as the Father of
all creation and life.

So you see, the true Hindu mind is wide like the ocean and it can
take all forms of truth knowing that Truth is one kaleidoscope.

It would be very much my pleasure if we meet more often to share
our views. What do you think? Also the idea of including others in
these meetings? I know some among my swami friends would like to
take part. And you can bring some of your friends also. Yes? What
do you say?

I wanted to intimate you our involvement in the holistic healing
workshop conducted by the Sisters in Daulah Kuan. Our meditation
and yoga centre will be sending some of our instructors to conduct
sessions on basic yoga and meditation. I would strongly recommend
that some of your sisters or even the older girls do the course.

Yours respectfully,

Swami Ram Kumar Mudaliar

My response

Dear Swamiji,

I am pleased to report to you that Lachmi is doing very well. She
is a bright girl. I believe, that if we handle it right, she could turn out

to be a fine young woman of tomorrow.

I would love to initiate a forum to discuss matters of pure philosophy, but I am not sure how attractive these would be to those in my congregation. I must confess that in matters of dialogue with communities, we of the Habit still work within the intellectual allowances of the tightly wrapped wimple.

I would suggest, however, that instead of abstract concepts, if we devote time to examining matters that would help improve the lot of the people around us, we might find more willing participants. Let's look for occasions to engage our hands and hearts and I think our time would be more gainfully spent.

I am interested in the holistic healing workshop being conducted by the Sisters of Daulah Kuan. I will send a few of our sisters and our students for the course.

Warm regards.

Yours truly,
Sr. Maria Angelina

Lachmi's Notebook

wensday nite

ippipooray
do the 4 hands clap with me

my spelling is better now
you will see
mother superior red my notebook
mayed krekshuns in my spelling
krekshuns went from paper to head
then from head to paper
now I can spell all dose words good
yes I am clever thank you very much
i know that
all these yiers my body learnt lessins and not my mind
because the men liked wot I did with my body
not with my mind
but I will tell you about that on one udder day
because it is late now
sleep is pulling the eyelids over my eyeballs
singing soja Lachmi soja
sleep Lachmi sleep
but I wanted you to know that mother superior was
happy with my writing.
    mother superior sister maria angelina
    very clever she
    very clever
    not clever like others are clever

not chalaaki clever
not kunning clever
not wikkid clever
not strikt tite lip skary clever
no no no
she is difrent clever
nice clever
good clever
loving clever
i like mother superior sister maria angelina
i like her so much I want to hold her tite to my brest
but now all this writing is putting a wayt on my eyelids
like the pensil's ledd is dropping on eyelids
insted of on my paper
and there is a soft singing in my ears
soja lachmi soja soja lachmi soja

Sr. Maria Angelina's Notebook

Want to get married?
Join our convent!

Today was beautiful. Our convent was festooned and all. We got Noreen married. Alleluia!

Noreen. Delivered in our maternity hospital. Bombay. Nineteen years ago. Nineteen-hundred-and-I-forget.

Her unwed mother, poor thing. Never came back to see her. Well. Well. Well. That happens.

Christened Noreen; brought to Delhi. Eight years ago. Nineteen-hundred-and-forget again.

This morning wedding bells singing Alleluia! Noreen married Prakash Capoor.

Strangely arranged marriage that. Took eighteen months of convent-sharpened evaluation. Prickly enquiry into this and that. (Oh God! We nuns!) It was a marriage made ... guess where? ... on the way to the bazaar ~ no jokes.

Was like this: But let Sister Mary Helena, groceries-in-charge tell the story. Narrates it with much glee.

Look. I'm on my way to the bazaar
Purse in hand, budget in head.
The boy comes up to me right out of the blue.
Sister, I want to speak with you, he says.
Yes, I say, serious like, imitating Mother General.

What's the name of that girl? He asks.

Which girl? I ask, trying not disturb the budget in my head.

Who goes with you to the bazaar every day?

Why do you want to know her name?

I want to marry her, he says.

Just like that, he said it, I tell you! Just like that!

Can you believe it!

What? You said...what? I ask, the budget gone from head now.

I want to marry her.

You want to marry a girl whose name you don't even know?

(didn't know my voice could squeak so high.)

I want to marry the girl, not her name.

You don't know the girl.

I know the girl. I don't know her name.

You know the girl?

Very well.

Have you met with and spoken to her?

Never. But I want to.

How can you know the girl without speaking with her?

I watch her. Every day.

    She carries your bag to the bazaar, no?

      I see her eyes. Full of life.

        She looks like a good girl.

          I think she would be a very good wife.

Of course, she is a good girl. She will make a very good wife.

    But why should she marry you?

I have fallen in love with her.

    I think she is the most beautiful girl in the world.

        just right for me.

We will have to see about that. I will talk to Mother Superior.

Can you not tell me her name?
Mother Superior's?
The girl's.
I will talk to Mother Superior first.
I will come and meet you again tomorrow, he said.

I'll take over the telling now.

The next day I meet him with Sister Mary Helena. I sense his earnestness. Intuitively I like him. But then. That boor called Good Sense clobbers personal bias. The romantic in me is pushed down. I ask questions. I find out.

He is a graduate. Working in an engineering company as an accountant.

Later. We visit his home. Karol Bagh. A shy, one-bedroom affair. Parents, modest, lower-middle income family folk.

(Terrible Angelina. When did you get so class-conscious?)

Mother looks amazingly young to have such a grown up son. Sari clad; wears a cross on a chain, not the usual *mangal sutra. (Does all this matter, Angelina? Does it really matter?)* Those gilded lines of respectability round her wrists: two thin gold bangles on each hand. Hair neatly tied up in a bun. *(How would I tie my hair if I were not a nun?)*

Father much older, balding a little. That ubiquitous middle-class display of masculinity, the moustache. *(No, you won't find it among the rich or the very poor. The moustache is middle class property.)*

The parents are concerned for their son. Oh yes, they had concerns.

The father, a blunt pencil's question marks.

How? Why? What? When. Who?

Who is this girl? Who the parents? Who? How can we let this happen? What? Our son marrying a girl who does not know her parents?

Expected questions.

Except when you come to the convent to pick an orphan to be your wife.

Yes. I have seen you in this guise. The orphan picker
Seen through you.

You're a second-hand-store-bargain-hunter looking to get lucky, right?

Convent as thrift store.

You as fishing rod.

Convent as fishpond.

With the expectation of a good catch.

You are Patron. With a capital P. *I'm giving a poor girl a chance to be respectable.*

Convent as poorhouse, right?

Then you are that sharp-eyed,
  maybe shy, maybe mature suitor.
Wanting to make your personal choice
    without the whispering gallery
      of family-arranged proposals.
Convent as finishing school.

I've seen you all. However wealthy or educated, you have to go through the same prickly convent enquiry. Sorry. The scrutiny for men is more rigorous than that for our girls.

So, you see, I know.

In answer to the blunt pencil I drew a smile. I am Noreen's mother, I said.

How can that be? From two raised eyebrows, his and hers.

And I am her father, I continued, straightening the eyebrows, but not the knitted brow.

Noreen is one of my many daughters. I am proud of her, I said. Brows unknitted. Slowly.

Match made. Not in heaven. In that shy one-bedroom home in Karol Bagh. Six-month courtship in convent parlour and Karol Bagh.

The marriage today was nice, sweet, warm, pretty and jolly. Heart-warming, for me certainly,

Nice. The ceremony in our chapel, at the request of the bridegroom. Pretty. Ritual, liturgy and event design. Aesthetics of the nunnery's minimalism. Warm. The treble tones of the convent choir singing nuptial blessings. Jolly. The convent band blared out their joy. The young ones stomp their feet. The nuns do it slyly, sitting down.

Looking wistful, wishing for themselves something as beautiful as this. The younger ones, Monica, Christina and Lachmi have stars in their eyes.

God as Matryushka doll

NEW YEAR'S DAY TODAY.

A good day. January 1. The first day of Noreen's new life. Tomorrow will be another day. January 2... then January 3.... And so we stick numbers on to Time. The calendar and the clock. Life's unfeeling metronomes.

Within the measured spaces of this convent, I obey this calendar and clock, cutting up eternity for us into the different coloured labels of Lent, Advent, Pentecost, Ember, Rogation days and even a Liturgy of the Hours, breaking a divine continuity into finite pieces:

Matins, Lauds, Prime, Terce....

Is this what we have done too to that First Infinity, the Creator? Broken Him up into sizes we can handle. God as Matryushka doll?

So we can boast about whose god is bigger. Whose god fits into whose god?

Am I a better, more sanctified person whose soul is saved because of this doll called Roman Catholicism? (Obnoxious label that nails my belief to a nationality with which I have no intellectual or emotional affinity)

Did I have to join this convent to do what I believe are good deeds?

Most times I come up with a Yes for answer, but I keep asking the question.

I say yes because I know me: My pretty intentions do not possess the grit nor find the opportunity to do the "good" I want to do.

It is my Matryushka doll and this convent that pushes me

towards my spirit's trajectory.

The truth is I am happy.
Happy with Here.
Happy with Now.
Happy with my rose garden of thirty-one children.

I wonder sometimes:
Is there some hidden, undiscovered genius-producing gene that inserts itself into the forbidden and clandestine intercourse that produces these children? The divinely naughty rewards of illegitimacy.

I love these fatherless children with an intensity I cannot explain. Is it my own voiceless uterine cry to be part of creation?

Come on, girl, Maria Angelina! Come off those workings of your slippery intellect. You know you have never been an actively sensual person.

Are you okay? Are you normal? Even my good friends asked; just because I was the only one among them who did not have that showcase of boyfriends.

How could they think of me in that way?

I try to disentangle the contradictions within me to align my wild angular, angry ideas with the railroad straight lines of my behaviour.

How can my often vexed, impatient questions to this Matryushka doll be answered by my tame acceptance of things as they are?

How and why do I close my eyes to the huge gaps in reasonableness and good sense between what I am supposed to believe and what I do believe. Between dogma and conscience.

Or even the big distance we have travelled from what I believe to be the Bridegroom's wishes?

As a nun, I find myself examining conscience; asking myself if this intellectual indulgence has not in fact been a sinful vanity pushing my spirituality into a corner.

Would it have been more pleasing to the Creator if I lived the life of a housewife, with conjugal pleasures, a fine home with sons and daughters; with none of these fancy wrinkles in my brain?

Was it this intellectual attraction rather than a spiritual one that prompted my vocation?

Oh Angelina. Angelina!
Thrust these little devils out of your mind.
Surrender to the joy that these children bring.
Your rose garden.
Petals brought here and dumped as in a bin.
Accidents of a censured moment.
They are gifts given to you free.
Allowing you the motherhood you would never have had.
It is the same with the other nuns for sure.
If it were not so,
they would not be able to do what they do.
Because the work is no cakewalk.

Lachmi's Notebook

Monday? Tuesday? ... I don't know

Sentences are like noodles

ENGLISH, ISTRY, JOGRIFY, RITMETIK, SIVIX, GRAMMAR. Can you see those words round my head? Like a halo? Mother Superior is teeching me these subjeks. From big books. They go round in my head, doing the fugree the whole day. Soon she will send me to skool ~ the open skool, not the convent skool. "You are a good lerner," she tells me.

You have notised, haven't you? The long lines. See? Sentences. With capital letters, comas, inverted comas, semi-colens, hyfens, perenthisis and clever punchuation. So I can write in long paragrafs now. Like in the big books. Big book writer Lachmi! No more prostitute, okay?

But, you know what? I do not like punchuation. I have to tie all my thoughts together with these notts they call punchuation. Thoughts with notts. See?
I think big thoughts.
But I like to write in small word-lines
Small sentences.
(Like noodles. Nice to eat it in small pieces.
Put a long one in your mouth.
Not very nice.
You suck it in with a slipry noise.
Your whole mouth gets dirty.)
So then, I get a thought. I like it.
And I put it in a nice, small line.

And then another nice thought.
Another nice, small line.
And another. And another. See?

So how should I write now?
I know.
My thoughts I will put in small lines.
Akshins happenings in long lines.
Okay?

But reading?
I can read long lines in big books.
Eye and brane just run smoothly on long lines.
Like a trane on the rales.
I see thoughts flying past me.
Ideas. Pictures. People. Happenings.
Chug chug chug.
English. Istry. Jogrify. Ritmetik. Sivix. Grammar.
Water for my brane.
Learning for me just goes in.
Look my brane is wet wet wet.
With English, Istry Ritmetik Sivix Fisiology.

But I won't tell you wich body part to use on wich body part.
No I won't

Four hands clap and happiness!
Sister wants to send me to a nersing korse.
I can be a good nerse she says.
I understand peeple's bodys.

Men's bodys and wimin's bodys. My body.
Right she is.
I know my body.
I know what it can do.
Jaadoo mantar choo mantar majik, that's what.
I can make them shayk like a leaf on a tree when the breez is
blowing strong.
Really, I can. And I did.
Choo mantar!
How eezi it is to do choo mantar to men.
From the hare of their head to the tip of their tose.
Big men.
Fat men.
Ruff men.
Gentel men.
Men with big mussels.
Men with no mussels.
Bald men. Hary men. Ugly men. Old men.
Yung men and yung boys too.
Holi men. Moollas. Sadhoos. Preests. Ofisers. Polismen.
I did choo mantar to them all.
It is jaadoo. Magic.
Big men crying. Singing. Skreeming.
Roling their eyes like they are going to die.
Making noises. Bird noises. Animel noises.
Funny words, bad words, no words. Prayers.
Hai ram hai ram hai ram hai ram.

Sister is right. I know bodys.
But only the outside.

From the hare of the head to the tip of the tose.
There is more to lern on the inside.
Inside. There's lots inside.
I can feel it.
Felt it when the dadas carried me to do their begging.
My hands and nose and ears felt it inside their bodys.
Shapes. Trembling. Fire. Music. Fighting. Crying. Laughing
All inside those bodys.
Felt it when scratching Parvati's back.
My fingers saw.
The itch under the skin.
Felt the fire. The trembling.
With all those men.
There is a lot happening inside.

Nersing will teech me all that.
But wait.
I have to pass my bode exam first.

Friday, Saterday... I can't remember

Body parts have nice names

I read the nursing book Sister has given me.
Now I know the good names of body parts.
Not the bad names like... never mind never mind.
Tip of my tongue but they won't come out.
The not so nice names I will bite off and swallow.
Gulp! Gulp. There. Swallowed. Gone.
Only the nice names I will write.

I learnt them when I did sex work.
Now I see them in the nursing book.
Other nice names. I meet and greet them.
Good morning Aunty Clavicle.
How are you Mr. Colon? And Phalanges. And Ulna. And
Appendix.
Names with surnames. Medula Oblangata.
Nice names.
I remember the names and their spellings.
And I know where to find them inside the body.
Body parts like pumps and enjins and lektric wyres
Made of flesh and mussels and bones.
Going dajug dajug dajug dajug all the time.
Without nobody putting on a swich.
Much bigger magic than what I did
I see those pictures in my physiology book.
I say *Wow!* First class work!
So clever. Whoever made it.
Did he or she also put that tremble there?
When body parts touch body parts?
From the hair of the head to the tip of the toes.
Tell me. Tremble inside the head.
Tremble all over?
So strong. Like a diwali atom bomb.
Or sparkler. Or rocket.
So you scream and sing and roll your eyes.
Beg for more and more and more.
And if he-or-she put that jug-jug there, it must be good. No?
But then the police and Sister and everyone say it is bad.
Wicked.

And it is all done in seecrit so nobody should know.
And the police put people in jail
and the sisters put them in hell.
Now suddinly I do not feel so clever.
I feel confused. Very confused.

***

I write better now, I think

Mother Superior's room.
The sound of many rats.
Rats?
I look up.
It is the fan speaking out of turn.
Squeak, squeak with every spin of the blades.
Why does she not have it changed?
Or repaired? She does not seem to hear it.
Nor bothered if she does.
She is busy. Papers. Papers. Papers.

I speak above the fan's squeak.
"*I'm confused,*" I tell Sister.
She does not look up from what she is doing.
But she is listening I know.
"*About what?*" she asks.
The fan now sounds like it could fall any time.
The limping sound of a wheelbarrow with one wheel loose.
"*Why you think our bodies are bad.*"
"*We don't,*" she says without looking up.

The fan limps on. Louder, it seems.
It grates inside my brain.
It interrupts my thinking.
Like an ill-mannered thing.
Why don't they change it?
"You think that the body is the devil."
Am I squeaking now?
"We don't," she says again.

Then she laughs. *"I know what you're talking about. I read your notebook."*
"So then, I'm confused."
"It is alright to be confused." She says.
The fan seems quieter now.
Eavesdropping on our conversation?
A ray of sunshine spills in through a gap in the curtains.
Spreads like a smile across her papers.

She stops what she is doing.
"Often I'm confused myself.
But there are answers to all of them." She says.
"I want to know the answers," I tell her.
"One day we will talk about these things. You're still a child."
Ha ha! Child, she says when my bosom is bigger than hers.
And I bleed every month like a big woman.
I do not know how old I am.
I do not have a birthday.
        (Was I born on no day at all?
        When the world was not looking?
        When the calendar went to sleep?)

Alright. I have no birthday.
But I am big enough.
15 years old. Sister says.
15 years is not a child.
On our roadside, 15-year old girls are feeding babies.
Me? Two years in this home.
Prostitute for more than a year before I came here.
See? I am not a child.

Prostitute. The word is a sharp needle in Sister's side.
I see pain in her face when I say it.
Like a big mosquito has bitten her.
But she won't swat the mosquito;
She has not asked me not to say it.
Even "sex worker." It's the same thing.
A needle in her side.

She is not like me.
She knows what's under a man's skin.
But I don't think she has seen what's inside a man's pants.
I don't think she has done what I have done with men.
I don't think men would want her to do those things to them.
No, I don't think so.
It is because of how she looks.
I think she is a beautiful lady.
Her face. A ripe pear. Smooth.
A nose that is a little long but not too much.
Her lips come down a little at the side of her mouth.
But she does not look sad.
Looks like she is thinking of something.

Men do not like that. She has big eyes.
They look straight at you.
Like she can see inside you.
Men do not like that.
Her skin. Fair and smooth.
Her cheeks get pink when you say nice things to her that she
knows are true,
Like your words were a brush dipped in red.
Yes, she is a beautiful lady.
Wears a white sari like the other sisters.
A long choli with long sleeves.
It hides her small bosom and her body.

No I don't think that she has done things with men.
I asked her about it.
She said that she became a Sister when she was my age.
When you become a Sister with a capital S you do not do it.
You do not get married and have children.
Everybody else's children are my children she says.

She prays to God and to Jesus Christ.
She is a Christian.
I asked her if all Christians were like her.
She laughed.
There are better people who are not Christians she said
People like you.
Can prostitutes be Christians, I asked.
She said that many holy men had married prostitutes.
Prophets from her bible had married prostitutes.
And she told me a story about a man and a prostitute girl.

People wanted to stone her till she died.
This man played a holy trick on them.
The stones froze in their hands.
They all went away.
Like dogs with their tails between their legs, no? I said.
And she laughed. And I laughed.
And raised my hands and did a four hands clap with Sister.
And she laughed and did the four hands clap with me.
I said that this man was a good man.
Hero fellow like Dilip Kumar I said.
I would like to marry him, I said.
She laughed again.
She said she was married to this hero.
All the sisters too.
Brides of Christ, she said.
I asked her if he would take one more wife who was not a convent sister.
One more wife called Lachmi.
Maybe he would, she said.
But that is not important now.
Not important at all.
Think about studying your lessons.
The fan has started squeaking again.

Sr. Maria Angelina's Diary

My cleanest form of expression, my work

THIS DIARY has become my vanity case; my compact mirror.

Is this mirror less sinful than those that we of the order are encouraged to shun?

Is the contemplation of my own physical being more morally corrupting than this Narcissus caressing my brain?

I suspect that I put pen to paper for self-gratification more than for any lofty or pious reason.

This longing for literary finery is a futile conceit, a sin that I ought to have shed with my secular adornments. But it is there still, so help me God.

It dawns on me: my cleanest form of expression is work.

I see that every day. Thought skips the Word and becomes flesh in work. The message is received via aching feet and calloused palms and the message is clear.

A clandestine pregnancy walks into our hospital, and with a new heartbeat is delivered the message that life is beautiful.

A street child is picked up, cleaned, sheltered and fed and the response is: I am precious.

It is perfect language. It satisfies. The spirit smiles.

Why do I not accept the fact that this is my gift; the sign language of work, of decisive action?

Action is more than just talkative; it is persuasive.

Two months ago, Sr. Maria Juanita had come to me and said, "It's no use for Meena and Monica to continue with their schooling. They are not able to cope with their studies."

"What should we do with them," I asked.

"Get them to be more useful in the convent. Maybe they can even help in the maternity hospital."

"I am not so sure," I told her.

"They could even earn some money, working with a good family," she suggested.

"The problem is not with Meena and Monica."

"Then with what?"

"It's with our school," I said.

"What do you mean, Mother? Everyone else says it is a good school."

"It's a good school for everyone else. It is the wrong school for some of our girls."

Vocabulary of action. I took Meena and Monica out of our school. Registered them in the Open School system. Syllabus is sensible, relevant and flexible. Replaces the concept of failure with that of individual capability for Meena and Monica, Christina, Varsha.

For Lachmi too, a glutton for learning, the Open School system is right. The excitement of doing something never done before.

She displays a restless impatience to read and write. Enjoys learning languages more than food and games or anything else.

I have not seen anyone like her.

Lachmi's Notebook

Words are actors.
Our home is a book...

Not written for a very long time.
Strange lethargy.
I don't want to eat.
Or to play. Or to chat. Or to sleep.
Only study.
Snack on words.
I'm in the ideas canteen

Eyes turned into marbles.
The invisibility of things around me.
See only what's in my books.
Words.
History, Geography, Civics, Physiology, English Language.
I see it all.
My brain a TV screen.
Words are my actors.
English Language, my movie.
You keep your Dilip Kumar, Nargis, Pran, Johnny Walker.
I'll keep my words and phrases.
They don't act. They live.
They are my flesh and blood with ideas.
Good. Bad. Funny. Sad. Beautiful. Angry. Gentle.
I like words.

Now I have learnt to use the dictionary.

It fills my head with pictures.
It holds me like a storybook.
What a book!
The dictionary has become my friend.
Reads with me. Writes with me. Sleeps with me.
I see words in my dreams.
Smiling, making faces, jumping up and down.
Fighting for space in the corners of my mind.

Grammar is not such a good friend.
A well-dressed bore with glasses on his nose.
Painfully teaching me to speak the way I already do.
My grammar is good from listening.
To people like Mother Superior.

Hello Wren and Martin! Granma Grammar.
I use it as another dictionary.
Teaching me puffed up words that sound like my roadside abuse.
I like verbal abuse.
Maybe Sister will allow me to use them.
Listen:
Sala gerund! Oxymoron! Tu onomatopoeia!
Nice, no?

Oh, to write like Mother Superior!
Not yet.
My day is one long sentence with bells as semi-colons.
School from morning 7.30 bell till lunchtime bell.
In the evening I am in my books from 6 o'clock bell to 8
o'clock bell.

A little more study and then dinner bell.
Study again till 11.30 in my room.
All commas and semi-colons. See?
And then the Grand Silence Bell.
Full stop.

The convent. Magdalene Home with a big "H".
It's my home with a small "h".
It is not like other homes.
Not like Bombay or Delhi homes.
Bombay homes for me are plastic sheets on bamboo sticks.
You crawl inside only to sleep and to make sex.
You do everything else outside.

Delhi homes are big.
Like well-dressed men. Standing side-by-side in a line.
Looking to see who looks best.
They look handsome, shinysmooth. Not clever.

Our Magdalene Home looks clever.
Not just big. Educated.
A book with a leather cover.
You enter it and you feel you are turning big pages.
The front cover: a long veranda going all around.
Painted blue and white.
Inside, a big page called the parlour.
Another page and you come to the outside again.
This is the courtyard.
So you walk from outside to outside
passing through an inside.

Funny, no?
Like chapters.
All round the courtyard there are rooms and more rooms.
My room is a full page called the dormitory.
The garden is another book. Beautiful.
Lots of flower trees and crotons.
In the cold season, begonia and chrysanthemum
and buttercup and daisy and zinnia and gladioli and exora
and marigold and hibiscus.
Another dictionary for me. Another picture book.
Every morning I look:
a brush has come and painted a new flower.
A new page.

No boys or men in the Home.
Only girls and Sisters.
I have had enough of men in my life.
I have no need for them.
Yet at first, I felt like something was missing.
Like a hyphenated word without the second word.
A coin with only one side.

It took some time for me to get used to it.
I'm comfortable now. Very comfortable.
And happy because of my studies.
The girls are nice.
Some of the Sisters too.
Not all, but most.
Magdalene Home: a footpath or pavement with walls.
The girls here like the children on the street.

Except for a few paying boarders.
Many fatherless, motherless. Orphans.
Some have a mother, but no father.
The roadside babies were brought by the dadas.
Brought or bought from who-knows-where.
For our footpath work.
For begging work.
For pickpocket work.
For shoeshine work.

Our babies come from Magdalene Hospital.
Loud labour pains curse their progenitor
deliver the swaddled bundle and leave.
Leftovers. Say some sisters.
Gifts. Says Mother Superior.
They all stay right up to the time they are young ladies.
Some get married, like Noreen and go away.
Some become Sisters.
But all of them are Lachmis with other names.
So you see, I am at home.

Ten girls in my dormitory. Twelve more in another.
The dormitories are like hospital rooms with no beds.
Mattresses on the floor. I like it.
I don't like beds. I don't.

My prostitute work I did on beds.
I did not like that.
Beds are too high.
Felt like high wire juggling.

I felt I could fall down.
But here in the convent there are no beds. Good.
Beds are idiots. High and mighty idiots.
I like mattresses on the floor.
Sometimes I roll over on to the floor.
Feel the cold stone against my cheek. Nice.

The walls are clean.
Picture of this Jesus Christ and his mother Mary on one wall.
A picture of Mary Magdalene on the other.
Lots of windows with curtains.
Four girls from my room study in the open school I go to.
Christina, Monica and Varsha.
Christina is smart. The others are ...
Let's say just nice?
They are better at their housework. I am not.

I hope you like this book called Magdalene House.
I do.

***

Baby factory

The prostitute story.
The girls in the convent want it.
My words play hide-and-seek.
I try shock as distraction.

I was made in a factory, I tell them.
Premila bursts out laughing.
You're mad. One loose screw. Varsha says,
    I do not have a mother or a father. I offer as explanation.
You donno where dey are. says Monica.
    But I do not have any, I tell them.
"*Impossible*," says Christina.
She speaks very good Hindi. And very good English. Like me.
That is because she grew up in Magdalene Home. Found on
the steps of the Home when just a week old. A *foundling* not a
leftover. There was a small plastic cross on a thread round her
neck. So the Sisters knew that her parents were Christians.
And so they called her Christina.

Surely, you were not made by a machine. She says.
    I must have been, I tell them.
    Like many other small boys and girls on the pavement like
me. They too had no father or mother.
    Christina laughs.
You're crazy. We are not.
    We looked like brothers and sisters.
    Same to same face.
    People would ask if Parvati was my sister. And Durga.

And if Lachman was my brother. Nobody knew.

We all looked the same."

Monica comes up with a thought:

All of you must have had the same mother and father.

Yes, Yes! The girls' eyes light up.

Yes. That must be it.

There! You see? I tell them.

Baby making machine. One father and mother. Factory.

So, how did you come to the roadside?

Somebody must have brought you there? Asks Varsha in Hindi.

Yes. The dadas.

They brought children.

Gave them to the chachas and chachis to do begging work.

But from where?

I don't know.

Parvati. The oldest of us.

Thinks we all have one mother.

Don't know who.

Somebody was hiding her from us.

Paying this machine-mother to make babies.

Making babies all the time.

Cookie cutters of flesh and blood.

What is that? They ask

Girls and boys looking like Lachmi..

Dark. Good looking.

Scattered on the roads of Bombay.

From babies to grown-ups.

Children manufactured by this one mothering machine.

Baby factory, see?

So the dadas have little hands to beg.
All lies. From Monica.
Nothing new. Now everybody knows it. Even the police.
What a story! But I believe it, said Christina.
There were other boys and girls too.
Not like me.
Like Manu and Radha and Gopi and Thambi and others.
We all lived on the roadside.
Slept together on the side of the road.
The big people slept on one side.
The boys and girls on another side.

You slept with the boys? Premila's eyes did a dance.

I slept with Parvati.
Like she was my big sister.
Or my mother.
Made me feel special.
I would look up at the stars in the sky.
Parvati said it was *swarag* up there.
Heaven.
Sometimes I would wake up at night and see that Parvati was not with me.
She had gone to sleep with Lachhman.

Undred percent. She done it. Says Monica.
Very bad of she. Mortal sin.
Did you do it too? So did you let them?
Is that how you learnt to make sex?
No. I told them the truth.

Parvati did not let them do it to me.

Not even once? Premila asks, almost sadly.

Not even once. I told them.
And that was the truth.

Part II

DESCENT INTO HELL

(Police tapes, notebooks and letters)

Sr. Mary Angelina's Notebook

The police finally get to us
The interrogation begins

It had to happen.

No go the convent's folded hands. No go our eyes lifted to heaven. Inevitability pushes through piety.

The search for Lachmi has led the police to our convent.

I knew it was only a matter of time. Stupid me. I had tiptoed across the past couple of years. My vain hope: the celebrated apathy, the wilful indifference of the police force. Shield enough for our protégé, I thought. Stupid me.

Inevitability arrived in the person of Sub-inspector Sharma.

Met me first thing yesterday morning in my office. Tall, potbellied. In his early forties. Handlebar moustache, twirled as a gestural exclamation mark at the end of a sentence.

He sat down on the chair opposite me. Took off not doffed ~ his cap. Placed it on my table, carelessly over some of my papers.

You have a girl child here called Lakshmi? He asked in Hindi.

"Lachmi. Yes." I answered in Hindi.

I may have to arrest you, he said with an unconvincing look of mock threat.

"On what charge?"

Kidnapping. Abetting paedophilia. Obstructing the course of justice.

This is a convent.

Good hiding place, convent.

We are nuns.

So what?

We look after poor and orphaned girls.

So what?

We run a school and a small hospital.

So what?

As a well-informed policeman ...

... Yes ...

I think you ought to know.

Don't tell me what I should or should not know, he said. Moustache twirl.

I knew I had spoken out of turn.

What do you want with Lachmi? I asked.

What do you know about her?

Everything. You can talk to me.

We will talk to you. But we want to see this girl first. And we want to talk to her. Not you.

I will summon her here.

Not here.

Why not?

Have to take her to the police station.

Why?

Interrogation he said.

Did he see me shudder? Did he see the vision in front of my eyes? Quick cuts of police brutality, torture.

I cannot allow that.

Why not?

"She is still a minor."

Madam...

Mother Superior, I interrupted.

What? rudely.

They call me Mother Superior. I can be cussed.

Madam. Superior or Inferior. You're dealing with the police.

I know that.

You know what we can do?

That's why I cannot allow you...

What you saying? Exclamation more than question.

... not outside the convent. You can do it here.

Police station, madam. Police station.
He looked at me with amusement.
You don't know what you are saying. You don't know the police,
Madamji.

Do you have a warrant? I was clutching at straws now.

I don't need a warrant. We are not arresting her. We just need to ask her a few questions.

I will want to be in the same room, then, I said.

You cannot dictate terms to the police," he said as he stood up. We'll call you soon.

***

The interrogation at the police station.
Yippee! Wow and Hallelujah! My expectations of horror. Shattered! The shards glittered with revelations even for me. Saw a side of Lachmi, suspected but never seen.
A bundle of surprises. Cunningly designed. Keeping her audience in mind, turning pavement insights into persuasion.
Brilliant. The interrogation.

Here's how it happened. Phone call this morning.
From Sub-inspector Sharma's senior, Inspector Ms Lata Narain. Soft, refined voice. In English.
Hello. Is that Mother Superior? This is Police Inspector Lata Narain. From the Greater Kailash Police Station.

Call me Sr. Angelina, Ma'am. I said.

She paused. Then with the hint of a laugh, *Sharmaji was rough with you, I gather. But he's a good man, I assure you.*

Perhaps I was being unreasonable, I said as a courtesy exchange.

Would it be possible for us to talk to Lachmi today? she asked.
You can come along.

Sure, I said.

My first time in a police station.
Lachmi and I. Walk a corridor of fear to the office of the
Police Inspector. We see policemen walking arm-in-arm, like
unlikely lovers with their assigned criminals.

My eyes pick out exaggerated expressions of the hate, hurt,
hopelessness, shifty-eyed cunning, defiance and indifference
in this zone of crime, condemnation and punishment.

Inspector Narain stood up to greet us. Beauty queen in
khaki, she. Tall. Shaped for the ramp, not this place. Charm
clothed in authority. Impressive. Police uniform as haute
couture. Could a face like that instil fear in the heart of a
hardened criminal? I wondered.

Learnt later that this pretty face was something else. Eyes
of Mesmer. Her lie detector stare. Charm as torture.
Criminals would rather be interrogated by the Station brute.

Good morning, Sister, she said as she shook my hand.
Putting an arm round Lachmi, she said,
And this pretty young lady must be Lachmi?
She turned to me apologetically.
*Sister, I must tell you that I have broken the rule in allowing you
to be present. I understand your fears as a caring guardian, but we
are investigating a larger case that involves more than just Lachmi.
We need to do all we can to make sure we get the unfiltered truth.*
She paused. *I would have left the process of interrogation to my*

other officers, but I have decided, for personal and other reasons to do it myself.

She turned to Lachmi. *Are you ready to answer my questions, young lady?*

I will try, Lachmi said, ladylike.

Knees together, her hands demurely over them.

I do not mind you being here, Sister, but I request you not to interrupt. Inspector Narain said to me. *I may need to ask you questions separately.*

Lachmi to the Inspector:

Mother Superior knows everything about me. I have told her all.

I need to hear it from you, the Inspector said. *Can you tell me your story from the very beginning?*

I watched Lachmi's face. A study in seriousness.

Eyes pressed shut, she looked up at the ceiling.

Head still tilted upward, she said slowly.

It all happened because of the rain.

Brilliant opening, I thought. Inspector all ears from then on.

The rain?

It was raining. She said, her eyes still shut, as if trying to visualize the scene. **Like a big water tank in the sky went phut, just like that. The road was a river.**

What road? Inspector Narain interrupted her. *Where was*

this road?

Lachmi opened her eyes and looked straight at her interlocutor.

Oh! You don't know Inspector Ma'am? Pause. *I grew up on the roads of Bombay.* Pause. *I was a pavement dweller.*

Which part of Bombay?

Around the Churchgate area.

The road was a river, you were saying. The Inspector prompted.

Yes, a road river that day. I was playing in the rain. Cold rain. My gagra choli was all wet. Sticking to my body like...

Pause.

Yes?

...like another crumpled skin.

Okay. I understand.

I was shivering with the cold.

Yes. Yes.

And Parvati was not there....

Parvati?

My best friend, older than I. She used to take care of me.

Sorry, dear. Go on.

Yes. Parvati was not there that day. Only some big boys.

Did you know them?

No. Boys I had not seen before.

Do you remember their faces?

No. They looked bad bad bad bad bad. Dirtier than

Lachman and Gopi. Dirtier than the other boys on our footpath.

What happened then?

One of the boys pulled me as if I were a buffalo or a donkey.

And then?

He put his hands under my choli. Another hand under my gagra."

How old were you at that time?

Lachmi turned to me. *Sister, how old do you think I was then?*

I turned to Inspector Narain.

May I?

Please.

You are around fifteen now. You've spent around two years with us in the convent and another year-and-a-half before that in the....

Yes? Yes? Where?

...the other place. Well ... the other place. So... you could have been around ... eleven... twelve, I think.

Thank you, Sister, the Inspector nodded in my direction.

Please go on, Lachmi.

I was telling you about the bad boy who grabbed my ...

Yes. Go on.

I ran from him. Other boys came from the other side. Zing zing zing. Like ...

Like?

.... Like ... like flies around rotten fruit.

Fruit, yes. But not rotten, Lachmi!

Alright. Then... Like flies around a ... Lollipop, should I say?

> More like it, the Inspector said smiling.
> What happened then?

They pulled my hair and dragged me behind a tree near the maidan. They pulled off my clothes. They took off my gagra. Then they tore off my choli. My nice choli. Tore it. I was naked.

She looked down at her hands for a moment.
It was almost stage directed.
Looked at me and then straight into the Inspector's eyes.

> Tell me. I am listening.

I ran. I knew about the sex thing: what boys do to girls. I have seen it, Inspector.
Our street boys do it in the night with the girls.
Pause.

> Yes. I know. I know. Go on. Did you do it?

No. Never. I did not.

> I believe you Lachmi.

I did not like these boys. They had a bad look. You know what I think, Inspector Ma'am?

What? Tell me.

This sex thing is like kho kho.

How is that?

When someone does kho to you, it is time to run. Right, Inspector?

I suppose so, Lakshmi.

You don't want to be caught. You can't do it with people you don't like. Unless you are a prostitute. I was not a prostitute then.
I fought. I hit and I kicked and I scratched. I spat out gutter abuse with force. But it was of no use.

She stopped and turned to me.
Sorry, Sister. Then to Inspector Narain. *I am just telling you the truth.*

Very good. Go on. You're doing fine, Lachmi.

They made me naked. I ran.
I found myself in the middle of the road.
The rain was coming down like...

Tell me. Like ...?

... like one big, white plastic sheet dropped from the sky.

You could hardly see through it. Everything looked like a
smudged wet painting done only in white and grey.

I like that, Lachmi. I like that. Just a minute.

The inspector interrupted the narrative. Turning to the
sub-inspector, she asked in Hindi,

I hope this is all being recorded?

"Yes. Yes," he said. *Everything.*

Good. I don't want anything to be lost. You are
doing very, well, young lady, she said to Lachmi,
smiling.
So, you were naked in the rain that looked like a
white plastic sheet, you said.
And in the middle of the road, right? Were there no
people? No cars?

There were motorcars. They looked like smudged
drawings in the rain. They could not drive fast because of
the rain. I ran in between the cars.
I was crying. But no one could see my tears. They were
looking at my naked body. Some of them were surprised.
Some were laughing.
I was shouting bachao bachao. Save me. Save me. The
motorcars had their windows up. They could not hear.
I ran till I came to the red and green lights where the
motorcars have to stop.

Yes. What happened then?

That is where Mr. Kumar and his wife saw me.

Did you know them?

No. I had never seen them before. They stopped at the lights. They opened the car door and asked me what happened.
"Those (I-won't-say-the-word, Sister is listening) boys have taken my clothes,'" I screamed. "And now they want to do (again I-won't-say-the-word-) things to me.' I was very angry.
The bad words came out of my mouth like heavy rain. I was shivering. Cold."

You poor girl!

That's what they said.

What did they say?

"'You poor girl. Get inside the car quickly,"
He opened the back door and I went in. Just then the green light came on. He drove away. They took me to their house...

Do you remember the place?

No. The car went past Marine Drive and up a hill.

Malabar Hill?

*I think so. I don't know. Big house. Like a museum.
Sofas and chairs I would not like to sit on.*

Why, Lachmi?

*They were too beautiful, like works of art. There were big
and small pictures on the wall. Frames beautifully carved.*

I can see you like works of art. What then?

*I was taken inside the servants' room. Lachmi became a
statue, another work of art.*

What do you mean?

*They washed, wiped and dried my naked body. Ooh!
Nice hot water. I had never had a hot water shower before.
Ooh! It felt good. Until then I was shivering.*
*Pavement baths start with a shock. Like icy electric
current through your body. The body goes gada-gadda-gada.
Until the third or fourth mug. Like it is punishing itself in
public for having got dirty.*

So, you enjoyed your bath? Tell me more.

*Ooh! Water like warm fingers running down my body.
Caressing my head and face. Massaging my shoulders.
Running down between my thighs down to my feet.*

I closed my eyes. I saw my body looking good and happy. Truly I did. Tried to follow each little watery finger all the way down to my toes.

Nice! Nice! Nice!

Then the girls' hands were all over my body. I didn't like that. But I let them.

Long pause.

Yes, go on. I am listening.

First I felt the watery fingers. Then the girls' hands. Then something else.

Tell me. You are doing it well, Lachmi. Go on.

Eyes. Big and round, hotter than the water. They slipped down my face, neck, breasts and thighs Down to my toes. Mr. and Mrs. Kumar looking me up and down. Their eyes hotter than the water.

Go on Lachmi. Go on.

Then he spoke. From outside the bathroom door. "More shampoo. More shampoo... the ears, the ears ... armpits ... rub well ... between the thighs ... come on ... nicely .... nicely... yes. There. There."

Showering and soaping over. Wiped with a towel.

Who did all this? The maids? You?

I just stood there. Did nothing. Like a baby. Or a puppy dog.
They gave me clothes to wear. Clean, smelling nice. Did not
fit me. Too big.

Must have been the maids' clothes.

Mr. Kumar's wife asked me to sit down. On the floor.
Looked inside my hair and screamed.

I can guess why;

Animals in my hair, she said. Faces around me feigning
fright and amusement.
Scissors. Haircut. Not enough.
Shave. My head is the top of the shivaling now. Smooth.
Another bath. Stronger smelling medicine this time.
Dressed up again.
Mr. Kumar's wife: arms round me.
"We will make you into a beautiful lady." She says. Her
palms around my face.
A good face, she said; a very good face.
Mr Kumar smiled, "Yes, she has a pretty face. A very
sensuous face."

Mr. Kumar and his wife both have good faces too.
Mango faces both. Mr. Kumar's the bottle mango. His wife's
the roomali aam. He has no beard or moustache. No hair
on his face. He has long hair like a girl's. His wife short hair
like a boy's. He ties it at the back like a horse's tail.

I know. I have seen pictures of the two, the Inspector said.

Yes. Go on.

They were very nice to me. The wife held me close. She did not smell like a human being. No smell of sweat, fear or sickness, the smells I got from Damodar chacha, Parvati and the others.

Mrs. Kumar smelt of crushed petals. I had never smelt perfume before.

They gave me food. Good food. In a beautiful plate. I ate it quickly. They asked me if I wanted more. Yes, I said. Give me more. They gave me more. Good food.

All that is fine, Lachmi. What happened after that?

Some days later, they told me to do a very dirty thing. Chee! Very dirty!

The inspector leaned forward and asked:
What dirty thing? What thing?

They gave me two clean empty bottles. One with a big opening. The other a smaller bottle.

Two bottles?

The next morning. The toilet.

Oh! I see.

I did not know how to do it. But I did it. Chee! I felt bad bad bad. What dirty things rich people do, I thought to myself. On the pavement we did nothing so dirty. Here I did this chee-chee thing in this very nice house.

The Inspector looked at me and laughed.
                    Go on, she said

I closed the bottles very tight. Like there were genies in the bottles trying to escape.

Inspector giggles. Poor you. What happened after that?

They took me to a doctor's clinic. Took blood.

The next day they gave me a new dress to wear. Pretty. Very pretty. Mrs. Kumar's dressing table mirror said nice things about my body. It said Meena Kumari. Vyjantimala. Helen. It was the first time I saw my whole body in a mirror. Fully dressed. Excitement inside me. I wanted to see myself naked. I thought I would look better than those naked ladies on the wall.

A few days later.
Mrs. Kumar looking happy surprised. "'The tests are clean,'" she said. 'You don't have any bad sickness. You have worms,' she said. 'But they will all come out with one little tablet, don't worry.'"

They were surprised. Mr and Mrs Kumar. They thought

I would be a bundle of germs. Bad sicknesses. And the tests were good.

I would be surprised too. Wouldn't you, Sister?
I can tell you now what her next question would be...

'Did you do it?' She asked me.
Do what? I asked.
'That,' she said, pointing to my genitals.
'That,' she said again, pointing there. 'With any boy or man?
I said nothing.
Did you or did you not?
I said no. I did not.
With any boy or girl or man or woman.
I said no. I did not.
She shook her head.
'I don't believe you. How can ...' "
Parvati would not let anyone do it with me.
'Not once?'
Not once. She would fight with them. Would let them do it with her instead.

Mrs. Kumar kept shaking her head. Held me by the shoulders. Looked at me and said, 'Lachmi, you are a very beautiful girl. Love your dark skin. Suits your features.' A white face would look peeka, bland. Like dal without tadka, I said laughing. 'Yes. Yes.' She laughed loudly. 'Like dal without seasoning.'

She turned me round and round. Like I was one of those big round jars with paintings.

'Beautiful.' She said. 'Beautiful. Beautiful. Beautiful.'

She took me in front of her long mirror. "Look at yourself," she said. My hair had still not grown. It was short, like a boy's hair. She put her hand on my head She clapped her hands like a toy doll.

A few months later.

My hair had grown long and black and strong and beautiful. I had never seen it looking so black and so beautiful before. It used to be dirty and thin and not so black. Now it was like black silk thread. Ruby would apply oil before I went for a bath. Then they would comb my hair and try different hairstyles.

Mr. Kumar came in and looked at me when they were combing my hair. He sat behind me on a stool. He took my hair and made plaits. He made plaits on both sides of my head. He asked for red ribbons, rolled up the two plaits and tied them up with the ribbons. He looked at what he had done and said that it was just right.

Inspector Narain said: You must mean, Mrs Kumar. It was she who plaited your hair.

No. It was Mr. Kumar. He sat down at a table. Called for pencil and paper. He then asked me to stand a little away from the table. He looked at me and started drawing.

When he had finished, all of us went to see what he had done. I thought that he was drawing me, but it did not look like me. He had drawn only the body. The face, an oval with no eyes, nose or mouth. On the body he had drawn a dress. A school uniform that schoolgirls wear.

Tailor summoned. Measurements taken. Two days later, my dress: Three school uniforms. In three different colours.

They tailored school uniforms for you? the Inspector asked.

Yes. They made me wear one of the uniforms. They all smiled and said it was good.

A week later.
Mrs. Kumar said she had good news for me. They were going to Delhi and they were taking me with them. Flying there. Flying!

So you flew to Delhi?

Heart flew with my body that day.

Lachmi paused and asked for a glass of water.

What a story!" Inspector Narain said.
And how well you tell it.
Where did you learn to speak English so well?

Lachmi looked in my direction.

I have the best teacher in the world.

"Not entirely true." I said. *Lachmi spoke a fairly good English even before she came to us. Also a number of other European languages. But that is a whole other story in itself, Inspector."*

I think we can stop here for today, the Inspector said. I have a few other things to attend to.

This has been very good. Thank you, Sister.

Lachmi's Notebook

How begging helped me read and write

The girls want to know how I learnt to read. I tell them.

I tell them.
White man and lady sitting on a bench. I go to them. Finger in mouth. They speak to me in English. I do not understand or answer them. They give me a ten-rupee note. Big money for me. Paper not coin. But better than paper money they teach me to write the alphabet. Every day to the bench, finger in mouth. Gave me paper money and ABC.

I liked the ABC better. They showed me 1,2,3 up to ten. I showed Parvati and Dada and Damodar chacha my writing. Wrote letters all mixed up. No words. Just letters.

BGYOK LUITNMKZ KFSDWQ VXAST OLEWCN
LPGT OUIT MGAZ ASOLP BDLKRAPDLDF LSULA
SLDKURLDNL DLDIEL
MDIDLCNOIE;N LODKIOEN NOKLIEG
ITYUEK DIKDNVHGO MITHGSKO HSGFT KLOGN

Read, they would say. Read. Finger out of mouth, pointing to letters I say:
"Please sir, I am hungry. Give me money. You are very kind. Thank you."
And their eyes would become big. Like fugrees. Damodar would say, "Kamaal hai." Parvati would say, see how educated

I was.

English is a good begging language, I tell you. Some white people did not speak English. They spoke French and Italian.

Bonjur musier mersi musier Chiao bonjiorno and graziey sinyoree.

Listen now.

Lachmi speaks English, French and Italian with white people. Also with my friends on the roadside. Just to show off. Like acting on a stage. I like to do writing. And reading. Old newspapers full of letters to read, one by one. Letters not words like I am doing today. Only letters. I wanted very much to know how to read and write.

I would close my eyes and see myself writing and writing.

Parvati's heaven. Swarg.

Night time. I read the stars.
ABC to Z and back to A.
Count One to hundred and back to one.
Parvati sleeping near me.
Says scratch my back.
"Lachmi! Aiee! Kujli! My back's itching."
Scratch. Scratch Scratch.
Nails doing ABC to Z and back to A on her back.
ABC in the right places between her ribs.
My hands under her choli.
Fingertips not thinking, searching for feelings.
"Ooh!" she would say and *"aah!"* feels good.
Back scratching. Every night.
I feel *her* itch on *my* back.

So fingers know where to scratch.
My nails gently catching the *kujli*. The itch.
I play *chor-police* ~ thief-police ~with that itch,
chasing it all around her back.
"*Woh harami kujli! Pakdo saleko.*" she says.
"Catch that rascal, that Itch."
"Oooh Aah! Oooh Aah!
"*Ha wah. Pakad liya.*: "Wow! You got him?"
Arrey ab bhag raha hai! "Oh no! He's run away."
Harami! Daye bajoo ko. "The rascal has gone to the right."
Pakad lo. Catch him
Wah! Pakad liya! Wow! You got him.
Tu kamaal hai, Lachmi. You're amazing Lachmi.
Magic, says Parvati.
I know just where her body needs scratching.
She asks me how.
I say my fingers have eyes.
They can see the kujli.
Ooh aah and ooh and aah!

" *Aah! Yeh swarag hai.*" She says
This is heaven.
"*Yeh suchmooch swarag hai!*
This truly is heaven!"

The girls stare. Eyes glazed.
Am I making it up, they wonder.
I wasn't. Cross my heart. Swear.

Sister Maria Angelina's Diary

The clever body and another session with the police

READING Lachmi's notebook. She insists that I do.

Amazed. I am. Grammar almost textbook-proper. Spelling rapidly taking on the stupid rightness of the Oxford dictionary.

Miss her earlier writing, the near-accuracy of her written phonetics. Her English better than our average nun. Paradoxically because of her background. She picked up her vocabulary wrapped in refined accents. From the streets and her deviant establishment.

More than articulation and fluency with language, her gift of the surprising and evocative phrase, flavoured with metaphors from her past experiences.

Her performance at the police station calls for applause. Was like a play reading. Masterful.

Yesterday she put me to the test.

Sister, I have read the physiology and nursing books you gave me.

Yes.

I now know most body parts.

Good.

I was wondering. Which of these parts is the most important?

And your conclusion? I asked her.

At first I thought it would be the brain?

Why the brain?

We think with the brain. But then...

Yes.

I kept thinking of my own body.

Yes. Go on.

I believe my whole body is a brain.

Interesting. Go on.

Every part of my body can "think" and that ....

Go on.

I believe that my fingertips think. And my nose, eyes, my genitals. They think. Down to the cells in my blood and my skin. They not only think. They are extremely smart.

Yes. Yes. Go on Lachmi.

Very often I hear my body thinking. Even speaking to me. Telling me to do things without talking to my brain. I feel it in my bones. In my skin. In my stomach. Yes, my body has a mind of its own.

Can you remember when that happened?

When I was with Parvati. Scratching her back. When I was being carried by the chachas. When I was doing those things with those men. My body, not my mind understood their bodies. My body, not my brain was thinking. I have a clever body Sister.

Yes, Lachmi. I am beginning to believe that. You have an unusually clever body.

***

At the office of the Police Inspector

Inspector Lata Narain at our next meeting. A Stunner. Not just her appearance. Her greeting, rather jovial, designed for surprise.

> *Dominus Vobiscum. Sorry to drag you away from your Lauds. Or is it Terce – at this time of day, Sister?*

This session is as much of a Lauds as the one we do on our knees, Ma'am.

> *Call me Lata, Sister, she interrupted.*

By the way, how do you know Latin ... about Lauds and Terce ....?

> *And the Office of the Blessed Virgin and Benedictions and all that. I'll tell you some other time, Sister.*
> *Right now I am looking forward to Lachmi's story.*

Lachmi held centre stage again.
Raconteur-heroine, she had us hanging on her every word.
Inspector Narain began her interrogation.

> *Your trip to Delhi. What happened then?*

Delhi is where it all happened
We had to almost strain our ears to listen to her. I couldn't help feeling that she had it all rehearsed.

Did you like Delhi?

Delhi scared me. I would die in Delhi. Too cold. Death for street children.

Paused to see the inspector's reaction.

Go on. I want to hear your story.

I was taken to the studio.

Film Studio?

My question too, to Mrs. Kumar. "'No.'" she said. "'You will see.'" I saw. Houses all in a row. Not big buildings like in Bombay. Not chawls. Nice looking houses. All stuck to each other. Like a long brick and cement train.

Yes. Greater Kailash One. We've seen the place. Go on.

We stopped in front of a beautiful house with a garden. Looked like it had popped out of a picture book. White, with the front done in stone. It had a ground floor, another floor above it.

"This is our house. We stay here when we are in Delhi," said Mrs. Kumar.

We know the place. Go on, Lachmi.

She pointed to the house to the right of it. Different

design: a ground floor, another floor and a terrace on top.
"That is the studio", said Mrs. Kumar.

Studio. What was that?

All our ... what should I say? .... Work?

I know what you mean

It was all done in the studio.

Why was it called a studio? Do you know?

Mr. Kumar said we were doing art there.

He called ... that work .... Art?

Yes. He did. And he believed it.
I will tell you more about it.
Lachmi paused.
First, may I take you into the studio, Inspector? You may
find it interesting.

Please do. I am all ears.

Inside the studio. A tall lady met us at the door. Wearing an
ankle-length black dress. Pearls hanging like chandeliers
from her ears More pearls choking her neck. She must have
been in her sixties. Looked very beautiful. And rich. And
important. When not smiling, she looked stern.

Mr. Kumar said to her: 'Meet your new apsara.' To me he said: 'This is Noor Jehan'".

What did he call you?

Apsara. Lachmi replied.

Did you know what that meant?

No. I did not.

Right, Lachmi. You can get on with your story. By the way, you are a very good storyteller. Mother Superior has done a good job.

The Inspector looked at me and smiled.
Then turning to Lachmi,
what happened next?

What happened next was ... how shall I say it? A movie projected all around me.

Tell me. Did you write all this down in an essay before coming here? Or did Mother Superior write it for you.

Pause. Lachmi looks confused. I interrupt:

This is as new to me, as it is to you. Not the story, but her narration. For Lachmi metaphors are mere slips-of-the tongue. The way she spoke even before she could write.

I take your word for it, Sister. Ok Lachmi. Tell me more.

I felt gentle hands around me but firm. Noor Jehan.
Pushed me like a toy on wheels inside a big room.
'Nice,' she said. 'Beautiful. She's beautiful.'
Mr. and Mrs. Kumar followed behind us.

Pause.

Inside. I saw ladies sitting still on big, plush sofas. As if
to be sketched by an artist.... and then, it was ... like a
painting come alive.
One of them started playing a musical instrument. A
bulbul tarang, I was told. She was dressed in colourful
patchwork with big round mirrors. I have seen ladies on the
streets wearing them. Parvati called them banjaran.
Gypsies. Always very dirty. But this lady was clean. Very
clean. Like a new doll. Big silver earrings. Bangles right up
to her elbows. Heavy silver in her jet black hair. Young,
beautiful with eyelashes flirting with ceiling and floor. She
looked like she was about to do some magic.
Noor Jehan told me her name: Tamarra.

You are an artist, Lachmi. This was fine art. The picture you
painted.

Another tall lady. Mystery and enchantment... wearing
a blood-red long burkha. Stitched tight to the shape of her
body. A red veil covered her nose and her mouth. Showing
only eyes. Deep, shining pools that made you want to keep

looking at her. Look long enough and you see eyes laughing at you. although you did not see her lips or her face.

Then she uncovered her face to greet us. It felt as if I had bitten into a hard shell to find the sweetest juice filling my senses. Facial striptease, Mr. Kumar would say.

Her name was Fatima.

There were some more ladies, I am sure.

There was this English lady, not very young. Fifty years old I think. Maybe more. Looking at her I thought she would suddenly float up in the air.

Why do you say that?

She had a balloon for a face. A sweet looking balloon for a face. A nice soft roundness all over. She wore a low cut neckline. When she laughed it looked as if someone was still blowing on those balloons.

They called her Aunty.

Were you being a little naughty in the telling, Lachmi?

No Inspector. I like balloons. They are bubbles that last longer. I like bubbles. I liked Aunty.

Alright. I will let it go at that. But I see a twinkle in your eye.

There was a Russian lady, with yellow hair. Not as beautiful as the others, I thought. As if her calf muscles had been stitched on to her face. Square jaw. Green eyes. Long

legs. Like shapely stilts on high heeled shoes. She wore a very tight, short dress that held her big thighs together.
Her name was Sasha.

Pause.

And a black-as-night lady with spring-tight curly hair. Lips like the pumelo slices. Always n a pout. Black shoe-shined forehead. Fluorescent white teeth, whiter than any I had ever seen. Her dress, tighter and shorter than the Russian lady's. Not nice, I thought then. It showed her big behind.
Her name was Miriam.

Sister. This not an interrogation. It's entertainment, don't you think?

I am used to it, Inspector. She can be hilariously enlightening. But we are making her self-conscious now. There is more to come. Surprises. If not shocks.

Sorry Lachmi. Go on.

Then there was Gina. Italian. The most attractive lady you've seen. Oval face. Lips as if drawn by a giddy headed teenager. Sleepy black eyes that made you want to look at her. Jet-black hair cut short. I have heard talk of hour-glass figures. Gina had one.

You speak innocence and think naughty, Lachmi.

Mr. Kumar made a sign to everyone to follow him. He entered another room. "This is the classroom,'" Mrs. Kumar said softly to me.

Classroom, did you say? **the inspector asked.**

"Yes. Classroom. Blackboard, whiteboard and all. It had black curtains for the windows. Only one light was switched on. There were desks and benches. A few mattresses. We sat on the benches.
Mr. Kumar called me to the front of the class.
"'This', he said 'is Guddi.'
"'Lachmi,' I said, to correct him.
"He looked at me sternly.
"'From today onwards, your name is Guddi,'" He said
"All the other girls clapped their hands."

Inspector Narain looked at her watch and ended the interrogation abruptly.

We can stop for today. I have an urgent matter to attend to. I think this was very good, Lachmi. Both your memory and your narration."

She led us to the door. *"Let me walk you out Sister."* She said.

As we walked slowly across the passage to the exit, I said,
Inspector. You were going to tell me: how do you know Latin? Our liturgical hours and services.
May I ask..."

I am a convent girl, Sister. I can recite all your prayers, some even in Latin. I almost became a Catholic." She laughed softly. *But I didn't.*

"You studied in a convent school; not uncommon. But familiarity with our rubrics; that's not."

Not just a convent school, Sister.

The Inspector held my arm while Lachmi followed behind us.

I lived in a convent.

"Where? Which order?"

Daughters of the Cross. Jullundar. I was taken there as an orphan at the age of four. The nuns saw to my education right up to graduation. I did my higher studies after I married Dr. Prem Narain. So now you know why I wanted to do the interrogation myself.

As we were leaving, she said, *And Sister. Please call me Lata. I relate to my name better than to my position in the Force.*

Police Interrogation Tape No. 3

INSPECTOR NARAIN'S VOICE: So now. Where were we? You were saying that Mr. Kumar changed your name.

Lachmi's voice: Yes. To Guddi.

Inspector Narain's voice: Did you like that name?

Lachmi's voice: I never thought of myself as Guddi. Always Lachmi. An actress taking on another name for a movie.

Inspector Narain's voice: Please continue.

Lachmi's voice: I had come there in my everyday clothes. I had the three school uniforms in my hands. Noor Jehan told me to strip and put on the red school uniform. This I did.

She said, "Nice. Very nice." And everyone echoed, "Nice, Very nice."

"No!" Mr. Kumar said loudly, almost shouting. He came slowly over to me. He put his hand behind me. With his fingers he twisted the buckle of my bra through my uniform and the buckle came off. Then He put his hand inside both my sleeves and without taking off my dress, he pulled off my bra. Then he looked at me with his head bent to one side. He nodded and said.

"That is better. No bra for Guddi. Remember."

And everyone said, "Nice. Very nice." And they clapped their hands. Noor Jehan and Mrs. Kumar came and kissed me on the cheek.

Inspector Narain's voice: Sister. Did you know all this?

Sister Mary Angelina's voce: Yes. She has told me everything. Maybe not as well as she is doing today, but she has.

Inspector Narain's voice: What were your feelings at that

time? Did you know what was happening?

Lachmi's voice: I had no idea what was happening. My brain was ... a crumpled sheet of paper on which there were scribbles, not words. Why were we all dressed like that? What was a new bride or a lady with a burkha doing in the same place? Why was I dressed in a school uniform and why was I not to wear any bra? Though I was not frightened, I was beginning to feel uncomfortable. I wished Parvati were there with me.

Inspector Narain's voice: When did you begin to realize what was happening?

Lachmi: The very next day. Mr. Kumar gave us lessons on how to give sex.

Inspector Narain: Lessons?

Lachmi: Yes. About what we should do and especially on how we should think. He used the white board to write and draw. It was like a school. Most of them knew what he was going to say, but he was saying it again, he told us because some of us were new in the studio. Some of the things he said were not very easy to understand. He used big words. I didn't know their meaning then. I know now.

Inspector Narain: Was his wife present when he gave these lessons?

Lachmi: Yes, she was.

Inspector Narain: Did she also give any lessons?

Lachmi: No. She just sat there. Sometimes she interrupted when he got too excited.

Inspector Narain: What do you mean excited. When did he get excited, as you say?

Lachmi: We will give sex, he said, but nobody could call

us prostitutes. This was not a whorehouse. It was a temple where the gods came every day. We were apsaras, the very special friends of the gods.

Inspector Narain: (Laughing) And did you believe him?

Lachmi: He was serious. Like a teacher in a classroom. He spoke many languages. He would begin in Hindi, and then speak in English and Marathi and Punjabi and French. Even Russian and Italian to Sasha and Gina. He told us very strictly never to use the language of the streets. Because those words brought up bad pictures in the head and bad actions. We ought to use good anatomical words. He himself never used the bad words. Only the good words, the decent words. He told us that we should never say the F word because that was not what we would be doing. We also shouldn't say making love, because we were not making love. We were making sex, but in a different way. He made it clear that we had to give sex and not take it. This was not prostitution, he said. Sex work but not prostitution. There was a difference, he said. As he talked he would get angrier and angrier. Until he was red in the face. Like there was a fire burning under his skin. He waved his hand up and down as if he were fighting demons in the air. He said that prostitute work was the worst work in the world; the worst thing that men and women could do to men and women. And that both men and women should be punished for it.

Inspector Narain: (Laughing) He was not serious, surely?

Sr. Angelina: From what Lachmi tells me, he was dead serious. He seemed to believe everything he said. I think he was Satan in person. Or else he was out of his mind. He believed that he had innovated a whole new art form that he called Venereal Theatre. The girls he said were not sex workers but Venereal Artists. He attempted to brainwash his "workers" that they were artistes of a new kind; who gave their customers not vulgar sex, but a story and a stage in which the men would be heroes; anything from musicians, explorers, high priests, princes or gods. Living their fantasies. The less we talk about it, Inspector the better.

Inspector Narain: But we need to know. He was running an illegal brothel, as far as we are concerned. He has given us the slip for now. But we know where he is. And we will get him.

Inspector Narain: With all that dazzling talk in your brain you still had to do...to do... what shall I say? To do your work. Right?

(*A long uncomfortable pause in the tape.*)

Lachmi: Yes.

(Long pause. Then softly, barely audible.)

We did it.... I did ... sex work. It was as if I was trapped in a bottle. Vigorously shaken in a ~ what should I say? ~ a doctor's mixture of ... fascination .... and ....and .... madness.

Long pause.

I wanted to run away. But I could not. There was nowhere I could run. This was another city. I knew nobody. Noor Jehan's men, whom she called business executives would keep an eye on me. The other ladies were allowed to go out, because they were professionals and would come back.

(Long Pause)

Yes, I did .... sex. On the first day I had to administer it to one of the customers, I cried bitterly. Noor Jehan came into the room. "What's the matter," she asked. "Don't worry," said the customer, an old man. He must have been about 60. "I will talk to her."

"I don't want any trouble, Guddi," she said as if she was talking to a small child. She gave me something to drink. Now I know that it must have been a drug.

Inspector Narain: Our investigation around the Kumars bears out to some extent what Lachmi tells us. He is very obviously some kind of mad genius. He is a dropout of the National Institute of Design, has a Bachelor's degree in English Literature and Philosophy and a Master's in Psychology. He travels extensively, writes on a number of subjects, mainly aesthetics and has friends among the intelligentsia. It would be fascinating to meet him, but we have not been able to arrest him yet. He has given us the slip. We know he is in Australia, and we are trying to get him sent back.

Sr. Mary Angelina: Sad waste of a mind!

Inspector Narain: Lachmi. You said you did ... work... in that... studio. Were you paid at all?

Lachmi: He paid well. I was told that no other place paid as well. According to Miriam, Aunty and Gina (by the way, these were not their real names; they were names given by Mr. Kumar) this was the best they got anywhere in the world. "We're world travellers," Auntie used to say, "with a built-in ATM in our anatomy." And Gina would giggle and say, "You're vulgar even for a whore!"

Mr. Kumar paid a salary, not a commission. So they got the same pay regardless of the number of customers. He paid weekly. And then of course, there was this beautiful apartment.

Noor Jehan told me that my salary would be put aside in a separate account every month. I don't know how much the others were paid. She said she was putting by five thousand rupees every month in my account. It was a figure I could only imagine. I had never seen money like that before. I could ask for cash any time I needed it. Noor Jehan would give it to me, with an account of how much was left. I had no reason to doubt that she was putting by that five thousand every month because there always was money for anything I wanted to buy.

Inspector Narain: What about the customers? What kind of persons were they?

Lachmi: He called them our patrons, gods, high priests: he picked them. None but the very rich or powerful. Yet not just the moneyed. They had to show class or power. The top rung of government and the police department, the armed services, and of course, business. What Noor Jehan called big shots. A few godmen, gurus and priests. Movie producers and directors. Men and even schoolboys – rich schoolboys in their late teens. They had to phone and make an appointment before coming. This elite patronage was in itself his security blanket.

Inspector Narain: When the gods are on your side, who can be against you?

Lachmi: At first I was surprised by the kind of customers each of us attracted. I was the youngest of the lot. You would have thought that I would get the brats. Not so. We did get a number of rich schoolboys, but strangely they all preferred to go to Aunty.

Sr. Maria Angela: Mr. Kumar's Freudian insight at work here.

Lachmi: I usually got the old men.

Inspector Narain: did you know all this, Sister?

Sr. Maria Angelina: She has told me everything.

Inspector Narain: Shouldn't you have informed the police? This could be viewed as shielding and abetting paedophilia.

Sr. Maria Angelina: We were just trying to protect Lachmi from further trouble. We knew she would be safe in our convent.

Inspector Narain: I'm not sure that was the right thing to do, Sister. Anyway, carry on, Lachmi. You say that you were picked by older men?

Lachmi: There were exceptions of course. There was this one rich schoolboy who used to come to me and to me only.

Inspector Narain: A schoolboy?

Lachmi: Yes. A very rich schoolboy. The first time this boy visited, he sat down on a chair opposite the bed. He kept looking down at his shoes. According to my stage directions, I was supposed to do nothing; just stand in front of the little god. This I did. I stood in front of him as he sat on the chair. After some time, he very slowly looked up from his shoes. His eyes travelled from my feet to my legs and up my body. Very shyly he looked at my face and then looked down again. I kept standing there, waiting for him to do something. He just sat there. He looked up at my face again and in a very quiet voice, asked me my name.

"Guddi", I told him.

"That does not sound like a name," he said, "but I like it. Guddi means doll, doesn't it?" I did not reply. I just stood there in front of him. After a long silence, he said,

"My name is Prashant ~ Prashant Lobo." And then he said very shyly, "Guddi, you have a beautiful face."

I should have thanked him for the compliment, but I didn't say anything. I just stood there. He was spoiling my script. I wanted to fling a few of our customary abuses at him and tell him to get on with the job, but there was something in his manner that stopped me.

He said softly, "Why don't you sit."

"Aren't you going to do something?" I asked, still standing in front of him, inching a little closer.

Very softly he said, "I like your face," he said. "May I touch it?"

"If you want to," I said.

Gently he caressed my face. He put his palms on both my cheeks, and then he felt my eyes, my nose, my ears, my lips, and my chin like a sculptor. He stopped at my neck. "Nice," he said.

"You are supposed to take off your clothes?" I said. He waited for some time before he began to unzip his trousers. He got out of them and I could see that he wanted me.

"Don't you want to ...?" I asked.

"Very much," he said. He stopped. Put his hands over face. "No." he said. "I will not." He began putting on his trousers. "It's a sin. I will have to go to confession."

We were speaking in Hindi, but he used the English word.

"Confession?" I asked, "What's that?"

He told me what it was; that he was a Catholic and that he had to tell all his sins to the priest, the big ones and the small ones, and how the priest would listen to the sins and then bless him. He told me he did not like telling the priest all the big sins. He said that telling lies and disobeying parents and teachers and copying in the exams and cheating at games were all small sins. Venial, he called them. These were not difficult to tell the priest because everybody does those things. But he did not do those things much. Doing sex with a girl was a big sin. Mortal, he said. Like stealing or murder. People who do big sins like that go and burn in hell after they die.

I laughed and said. "Then will I go to hell? I am doing sin every day."

"It's alright for you," he said. "You're not a Catholic. It's not a sin for you. Then he looked at me and asked, "Do you feel that you are doing a wrong thing?"

I laughed again and said, "This is my job."

"Do you feel good doing what you are doing?"

"That's none of your business," I said, punctuating it with the Hindi abuses that I am now trying not to use. I felt bad after saying that. He was a gentle young fellow and when I spoke to him like that, I could see an expression of pain cross his face.

"I'm sorry," he said. "I want it very badly and I am very angry with myself for wanting it. I don't want to go to hell. And I don't want to have to confess a sin like this."

I didn't know what to say.

"You must be laughing at me," he said.

"No." I said, out of kindness. I sensed an imperceptible wipe inside me. Of the usual reaction to our customers and the words we used with them.

We just sat there. He looked at my face furtively. The rest of the time it was his shoes that got his attention.

Mr. Kumar had advised us against using ugly words. We did so nevertheless. I might have used them on this strange boy but I didn't. My pavement tongue was still at its vicious best. Those words were part of our staple vocabulary. Swear words were our chewing gum: our oral gratification and our verbal substitute. They would nicely take the place of the perfect word and even add a certain kind of force to what we wanted to say. The swear words we used were not many. Each one of us had just four or five of these versatile stunt words – all around genitalia and fornication – that we used all the time and we used those words to add force and even meaning to what we wanted to say. Today I see how those four or five words were used as nouns, pronouns, adjectives, prepositions, verbs or adverbs at different times. Our entire dictionary and grammar book could be written down on one page of a notebook and yet we were never at a loss for words. Today, with a vocabulary that is perhaps a hundred times bigger than it was, I find myself searching for the right word. I find that search exciting. When Mr. Kumar told us to stop using 'bad words', he expected us to use the right words for genitalia and other parts of the body. He could not possibly have expected us to stop using swear words as our form of common expression. Somewhere inside me, however, he succeeded in resurrecting that urchin who picked up language from strangers. I found the 'good words' attractive. And so, with this strange schoolboy customer, I spoke gently.

"What do you want me to do?"

"Nothing," he said. "I'm happy just looking at you."

After a while, he stood up, tucked his shirt neatly into his trouser and walked to the door. He stopped, turned around and came back. He took my hand in his and kissed it.

"Bye Guddi," he said. "I don't know why, but I like you."

I like you too, I almost said but didn't.

He left the room. I remembered what Mr. Kumar had said about emotional detachment. Until then, I did not feel a thing towards any one of the customers. Many of them were nice to me and laid on the butter. I learnt to take in all of that as part of the tip. This boy was different and I hoped that he would not return.

Inspector Narain: I can bet he did.

Lachmi: He did. He visited me a number of times. He did not go to anybody else. Just me. His second visit was almost a repeat of his first. He went through the usual caresses, paying me compliments all the time, but he stopped short of stripping himself. After the caresses, he dropped down on the bed, sat with his head bowed for a while and then told me that he would not have what he paid for. Spoke Hindi well though I was sure that he spoke English at home.

On the third visit, he just looked at me. He didn't touch or caress. Just looked at me for a long time. Then he covered his eyes with the palms of his hands and sat for a while before leaving. On subsequent visits, he would enter the room, take both my hands in his, kiss them and sit down. He would talk about his teachers and his school subjects and his examinations and then he would shake my hand and go away. He certainly had to pay for each time he came to me, but he did not ask for the paid for favour.

After one of these occasions I was summoned by Noor
Jehan. She said that I was on dangerous ground. Sinking sand,
she said. It looked like he was beginning to feel something for
me and there was a danger that I too would start feeling for
him. She asked me how I felt about him. I told her that I
didn't know. I said that I liked him.

"Danger," she said. "Send him to someone else."

Then it struck me that Noor Jehan knew everything that
happened in my closed room with this Prashant Lobo.

"How do you know everything that happened inside our
room?" I asked her.

"I know," she said and walked away.

Aunty told me: hidden cameras. Mr. Kumar has had
them set up in a number of places in each room. So they know
what's happening. Some months ago, a new customer was
refusing to put on the condom; being very difficult. It was all
visible to Noor Jehan on the screens. Their business
executives went in and spoke to the gentleman, who of course
was okay after that. He is still a customer. He knows. They
have some pictures of him that he would not like his wife to
see.

It dawned on me that Mr. Kumar was not just a mad and
learned artist. He was a very shrewd person, a businessman
who knew the ways of the world. He was like two or three
persons in one. He knew people in high places and he knew
how to use them. He took great care not to make himself
visible. He talked to us and instructed us. Was never in touch
with the customers. That was left to the business executives
and to Noor Jehan.

Sr. Maria Angelina: Mr. Kumar was clearly a mad genius.

In him creativity, cunning and perversion lost their defining boundaries."

Inspector Narain: He may be a devil. But he is a fascinating devil.

Sr. Maria Angelina: Devils are fascinating. Or there would be no such thing as temptation.

End of Tape 3.

Interrogation Tape No. 4

INSPECTOR NARAIN: Well. Here we are again. This case is turning out to be more interesting than I had imagined. Lachmi, I think we have heard enough of Mr. Kumar and his establishment. Can you tell me how you got away from it?

A long pause. Lachmi's story that followed was narrated slowly, with stops in between.

Lachmi: It was a night in January. Delhi was freezing. Some of us girls at Mr. Kumar's studio had worn warm underwear and were sitting around the heater. Gina, Miriam and Tamarra were with the gods in their rooms.

Noor Jehan's phone rang and she picked it up. From her face, which had turned the colour of ash, we could see that something was wrong. She put the phone down and said, "That was Punkaj. He says the police are here"

"Hell," said Aunty. "My things!" Within seconds, she had rushed into her room, as did everyone else to collect their belongings before leaving.

I hesitated. Instinctively, I did the unexpected. I did not go to my room or leave the house from the front door or any of the other doors on the ground floor. My street instincts came back to me. We were experts in running away from the police. I ran upstairs to the first floor and then to the terrace. It was dark in spite of the half moon and the clear starry sky above. It was cold, and I shivered at the first shock of the outside air. I locked the door from outside and looked over the parapet. I peeped down at the entrance to our house. There were policemen surrounding it. I saw Gina trying to escape, but she was stopped by one of the policemen. I moved away from that side of the house and moved to the parapet that joined our house to Mr. Kumar's. I looked over the terrace onto Mr. Kumar's house. It was at a slightly lower level. Quite a drop. But I knew I could handle that. I jumped.

I was now on Mr. Kumar's terrace. He was away on one of his trips outside Delhi. His house was dark. I looked over his parapet into the next terrace, which was even lower. It was just a ground floor house with a terrace. I jumped. There seemed to be a party on in the house below. Loud music and jovial screams could be heard. I went around the terrace to find the drainage pipes. I slid down one of them. I scraped my knees and dirtied the school uniform I was wearing. I landed as noiselessly as I could at the rear of the house. The party sounds continued inside. I found and opened the gate that led to the service lane outside the walled compound.

Once there, I ran - over all the dirt and garbage in that lane. I found a dark spot and I thought that I would hide there, but it was too cold and I shivered uncontrollably. I ran again till the end of the block. I crossed the lane and entered the service lane of the next block. I cannot remember how many blocks I ran past. I came to the end of the service lanes. I had to turn left or right. I think I turned left. I came to a long block of houses. There were lights in most of them except the third house in that row.

It was dark. They must either be asleep or the family must be away on holiday, I reasoned. It had a covered porch with metal gates. There were two rows of benches in the porch, which, I thought was quite unusual. I opened the gate as noiselessly as I could and went in. I sat down on a bench in the second row. I looked around to see if there was anyone around. There was nobody. I sat for a while longer. Then I curled up and lay down on the bench. I thank my pavement days for my ability to sleep anywhere, however uncomfortable. It was not easy. The streets of Bombay did not prepare me for Delhi's January cold. Our pavement community could never have survived on Delhi's cold streets. Bombay's weather is kinder. At least it will not kill you.

I slept. My last thought as I dozed off was how to get back to my friends in Bombay. To Parvati and Damodar Chacha. To those chachis with babies perennially at their breast.

I slept through the night and woke up while it was still dark.

Someone was opening the door to the house. They were large folding doors that folded three times to open completely. A middle-aged man heavily clothed in sweaters and a jacket opened the doors and went back inside. He did not see me because it was still dark and I was hidden behind the benches in front of me. Inside, a small lamp was burning on a table. The man switched on a light. I could see the room clearly now. The room was covered with mats. No furniture. Against the walls were pillows. Some pillows were scattered over the mats. I wondered what kind of place this was.

It was time to start running, I told myself. It was still dark. I could do so under cover of darkness. I could run to a safe place and then decide on my next course of action. What could be a safe place now? And what would I do next?

My mind, sharpened on the pavements of Bombay did

some quick thinking. Any place is safe now, I told myself. The police are not really looking for me in particular. They won't waste their time coming after me. They are going after Mr. Kumar. As to what I was going to do next, my clever feet would dictate that. I did not know anybody in this city. Living on the pavements here was not an option. The climate was too cruel. I would not be able to take it. My clever feet told me: one step at a time. One moment to the next. So, this could be as safe a place as any other.

I sat down on my bench. The man went inside another room and came back with some more pillows. He switched on two heaters that I had not noticed earlier. As they glowed, I could feel the heat spreading in the room. Just then he spied me. He was surprised to see a girl in a school uniform.

"Oh dear!" He exclaimed in Hindi. "You're much too early! Is this your first time It will be another hour or so before we begin. Come in." he invited me in.

I put on one of my Mr. Kumar studio smiles, stood up and entered the room. It was warmer inside, more comfortable. I sat on one of the mats.

In time, a few people entered and sat down on the mats. They were mostly young men and women. But there were older people as well. They came and sat cross-legged.

I smoothed out my slightly crumpled dress and combed my hair with my fingers, tightening my plaits as unobtrusively as I could.

Winter is a well-dressed season in Delhi. Even the street sweeper wears a jacket. I didn't want to draw attention to myself because of my looks. I only had my uniform on because, when the raid happened we were seated round the heater and some of us had shed our warm clothing. I was wearing warm underwear, but that was all. I had run without thinking of putting on a warm cardigan or a sweater.

A bell rang in an inside room. A man entered from the door in front. He was dressed in a saffron dhoti and a long saffron shawl, which he removed and kept aside. He began to speak. He said something to the people and they all lay down on the mats. I did the same. I did not understand anything of what was happening, I tried to follow the gestures of the people around me. Most of the time, they had their eyes shut. I kept mine half open so I could see what they were doing. I am sure that the people who were next to me knew that I was a newcomer.

I know now that it was a yoga class in session.

After the class, I got up. I was trying to move out with the crowd. The yoga teacher gently stopped me and took me aside. He was a pleasant, middle-aged person whose lips seemed naturally curved in the shape of a smile. Even when he was doing his thing in front of the room and when he gave his talk, the smile never left his face.

The smile spoke to me in Hindi. Asked me my name and where I lived, where my parents were. I thought that I should lie to him and just slip away. I was afraid that he would report me to the police. But he spoke kindly and he looked like he wanted to help.

I told him my name was Lachmi; that I had no parents and that I had no home to go to. That seemed to surprise him. He looked at my school uniform and asked me which school I went to. I told him that I had never been to school. He was visibly puzzled.

"Breakfast?" He asked. "Have you eaten anything yet?" I shook my head.

He took me up to a room where there were more mats. No furniture. There was a younger man dressed in a kurta pyjama. The older teacher said, "This is Lachmi. Let's have some breakfast, shall we?" We sat cross-legged on the mats and had *upma* for breakfast. In shining stainless steel saucers. Followed by tea served in stainless steel mugs.

The curved lips spoke again. He asked me how I happened to come to this place.

I decided that I had nothing to lose if I told him the whole story. I told him that I had run away from a very bad place. I did not tell him Mr. Kumar's name or the names of the other girls. I just told him that I wanted to get away from this place where we had to give sex to men.

He was shocked. The smile had gone. "How old are you?" he asked in Hindi.

"I don't know," I told him.

"You must be hardly twelve," he said. "How long have you been doing this?"

I told him that I didn't know for sure. From the time I came to Delhi, there was one cold season and two hot seasons.

"That would be a year and a half. So you must have been just about eleven." He shook his head in sad disbelief. And where were you before you came to Delhi"

I let the story spill: my life on the streets, my fantastic begging skills, the naked run in the rain through Bombay's streets; the appearance of Mr. and Mrs. Kumar (I still did not give away their names) and finally, the flight to Delhi and my life as a sex worker in Mr. Kumar's "studio".

The younger yoga teacher was listening in on my story. The older man, who I came to know later, was Swami Ram Kumar Mudaliar turned to the younger and said, "What do you think we should do"

"Report it to the police." He said

"No!" I almost screamed.

The two were taken aback. An uncomfortable silence.

"There's no point," said Swami Mudaliar finally. "The police have already been there. Must have made some arrests. They will question them and get the entire story. Why put this poor girl in the hands of the police? They may not be kind to her."

"All that means nothing," said the younger swami. "Money will change hands, people will talk to other people in high places and the brains behind it all will go free. They will move out of the present place to somewhere else. And life will go on as usual."

"That is also true," said Swami Mudaliar. Then turning to me, he said, "Who were these people? Can you give us their names?"

I thought about it. If I revealed Mr. and Mrs. Kumar's names, they would go to prison. But then, the police would get me too. I did not want to get involved with the police. I would rather go back on the streets.

"I don't want to give you their names," I said.

"But you must," the younger man insisted. "We have to go to the police."

"I cannot tell you," I said. "And if you insist, I will just walk out into the streets and find something for myself."

The younger man shook his head and went about doing

other things, as if he was not interested in me anymore. The gentle swami continued being concerned. He said, "What do you want to do now? Do you know?"

"I don't know anyone in Delhi. I think I should go back to Bombay," I said.

"But how will you go?" He asked me. "By train," I said, without thinking.

"Do you have money for the ticket?" He asked me.

"I know how to travel without a ticket," I told him.

He smiled. "I could give you the money for your ticket," he said. "But do you really want to go back to the streets and beg for a living?"

I didn't say anything for some time. Swami was making me think. Sitting there I could picture myself on Bombay's streets. I was free. The dadas and the mukadams made us do things. But life was otherwise free. I saw the hurried, strenuous lives of the people going to work every day, the men and the women, young and old, the ordinary working people. They had frowns on their faces. Our faces were happier. We had more freedom than they. More freedom than all those rich and important looking people in motorcars. Life in the studio, doing "venereal theatre" was extremely comfortable. It was not as free as the streets, but it was comfortable. We ate well, dressed well and visited the stores. We had as much money to spend on ourselves as we wanted. I had no qualms of conscience doing the work I was doing then. Would I do it again if I had to? Yes, I thought at that time. I would, because it was easy.

"What else can I do?" I said. I was not asking him for his advice. I was making a statement of the position in which I found myself. But the good swami creased his forehead in thought. The lips regained their smiling shape. Then he looked at me and said, "I will speak to someone. She is the Superior of a convent here that runs a school. They also keep boarders and orphans and girls without families. They could keep you there for the time being; give you a place to stay and simple food to eat. They will also send you to school. Would you like to go there if they accept you?"

I did not reply. I was not sure that I would be comfortable with that kind of life. I felt that I would be imprisoned behind walls with people I did not know. People quite different from me. Of course, in Mr. Kumar's studio, I had spent time with people from all parts of the world and I was comfortable, but then I was earning money for myself in that way. I did not like the thought of living in what this swami called a convent. I thought of telling him what I thought. The idea of going to school attracted me, but I was not sure how I would cope.

Without waiting for my response, Swami Mudaliar picked up a phone that was at the far end of the room and dialled a number. He spoke to someone whom he called "Sister". He told her all about me. When he had finished speaking, he put the phone down smiling. He said, "Mother Superior of the Marys of Magdala says that she will be happy to have you. I'll take you to her."

Inspector Narain: Not you, Sister. It is Swami Mudaliar who should be booked for aiding and abetting the crime. After his younger colleague had suggested going to the police, he goes and dodges the law.

Sr. Maria Angelina: The Swami is a good man. He did what he thought was best.

Inspector Narain: What happened next, Lachmi?

Lachmi: The good swami took it for granted that I would like to go. It was so quick and he was so excited about it that I no time to think. I just went along with him. He picked up a cloth bag, a set of keys that were lying on the table and said, "Come, Lachmi, let's go." He led me downstairs to his scooter, saw that I was securely seated and took off.

The convent was quite far from the yoga centre, he said. It was in Karol Bagh, while the centre was in Greater Kailash. We rode for more than forty-five minutes before we reached the convent.

I took one look at Mother Superior and I knew that I would like her. It was the beginning of a new life for me. I am happy now. Do you think, Inspector Ma'am, that if they had gone to the police, things would have turned out so good?

Inspector Narain: Let's not think about that now. You have given me a lot of other, more urgent things to consider. I thank you both for your help.

Sr. Maria Angelina's Diary

On Vanity. On Success. We decide Lachmi's future.

OUR EGOS dip into our protégés' triumphs. Mine, right now, soaked in Lachmi's brilliance at the police station.

There are other hurrahs. Lachmi, Christina and the others' success in the Open School system. Find me glorying in it as if it were mine.

Under the modesty of cloth and demeanour we, the Marys of Magdalene hide our vanities. To be seen only through the trellised window of the confessional.

Now. Future planning for our girls.

Second thoughts with regard to Lachmi. Her incandescent certificate gives us pause. High marks in all subjects, particularly English. Should she take nursing or get an English Honours degree? It will cost us a bit. But we never have a problem with money. The pious among us say, "God gives when we need." But my ear picks up less sanctimonious sentiments: Whispers about the nunnery's holy face of extortion everywhere. I am prepared to live with that quite shamelessly.

We will find the means to give Lachmi a graduate degree.

I put the idea to Lachmi. Whatever you think is right for me," says she.

"You will make a good nurse," I say to her. "but then you have a good head for other subjects as well. You love reading and writing and new ideas. You tell me, my girl, what would you enjoy doing?"

She spoke her thoughts as they came into her head. I like when she does that. Of late I have sensed in her a caution that does not become her. Is that a function of the language she is picking up? I wonder.

Vocabulary and grammar replacing spontaneity?

"I read the nursing book you gave. Fascinating. Am waiting to actually work as a nurse; To see and do all the things I read about in the book."

Pause.

"The Prince of Wales Museum in Bombay," she said. "Often I wanted to go in to see what was inside. I think that the body is like the Prince of Wales Museum. I have seen it only from the outside. The nursing book took me inside that museum. I feel that there are many things that I can do there."

"Well, then, it's the museum for you." I said.

"I would like to be a nurse," she continued.

"I love reading. I know that whatever else I do, I will continue to read.

"Good. So, that's decided," I said.

"A nurse you will be. And a good one, I think.

But before that: two years of junior college before you start the nursing course. A diploma course. Stay in a hospital, work there and study there. Most of your learning will be through the work you do.

Yes, she said. Yes.

She would be a resident student-nurse.

Lachmi's Notebook

Big trouble last week. I have to talk about it.

I, a non-paying boarder, had work to do. Clean the room. Laundry. Decoration. Needlework. Not very good at it but had to do it.

Six months ago, an added responsibility: Given charge of a three-year-old girl. Her mother had died by her own hand. Father, a jobless drunk. Inflicted his stupor and muscle on the child. Beat her mercilessly. Bruises on her skeletal frame.

From day one I felt it. Invisible sinews binding us together. I spent all my free time with the little girl. The doll I never had. Preeti.

My heart did a little dance when she was with me. Reminded me of how Parvati mothered me. Parvati's love I transferred on to Preeti. Like a garment that was mine and now hers.

I had looked after little children before this. On the streets. Preeti was different. She was special. She was mine. The cutest child I had ever seen. Hardly ever cried. I sensed every little thing that was happening inside her. I felt her hunger pangs. My eyes drooped when she felt sleepy. My tummy rumbled when she wanted to go to the bathroom.

Last week.
Playing with Preeti in the garden.
Saw Preeti's father stumble to the garden gate.
He spit-bubbled a drunken *I want my child back.* Lunged toward the child, unsteady on his feet.

I rushed and grabbed her away; Held her tight in my arms.

He came towards me and pulled Preeti away. *This child is mine. You thief!* The spit-bubble sputtered. Preeti crying and trembling with fear. Struggling in his drunken arms.

He hit her hard a number of times, saying, *this will teach you to run away from your own father."*

He kept beating her.

I felt within me the sharp pain of those rough hands.

I picked up a rock and went towards him.

He laughed in his drunkenness, spit spraying out of his discoloured mouth.

He dropped the child like a stone. Picked up a rock himself.

Come on! he challenged. *Come on, you little pig.* He flung the stone, but it was a drunken man's aim and it went way past me.

Mute collection of boarders and nuns. Like spectators at a pavement tamasha. Too scared to come close to where the action was.

I approached the drunkard with the rock in my hand. Screaming out the words of the streets, Words coated with its slime and muck. Challenging him to come closer.

.

With the rock still part of my fist I hit him with all the fury that was raging inside me. I got him on his hand. Brought up in front to defend himself. He fell to the ground. In my rage-fed madness I kicked him hard a number of times, With verbal abuse as my energisers.

I was going to fling the stone at him, when I heard the sisters scream, *"Don't!"*

I stood there trembling; looking down at him.

Hoarsely I shouted *Get out!*

Unconsciously, I spewed out with relish, the words I promised Mother Superior I would never use. The sense-rewarding, robust vocabulary of the street now surfaced like bubbles in a sewer.

The man got up and staggered out of the gate. He looked back and raised his fist, brought it down to his genitals and made a gesture, cursing. I let the stone fall from my hand.

I heard more than one sister say, *"Shame on you!"* The boarding mistress looked with disgust at me and said, *"Go back to the streets where you belong."*

Mother Superior was not there.

Christina put her hand on my shoulder and whispered: *"You're so brave!"*

Sister-in-Charge called me into her office. Looked at me as if I was something fished out of the drain.

"I'm disappointed in you," she said. *"I had hoped you would have changed. From your days of prostitution and the pavement. With all our training, I thought you would be a lady. You're a disgrace to this place. The convent cannot keep people like you. You will have to go."*

Head bowed down I walked into my room. Christina was there with Preeti, still crying. A sister came in and took Preeti away.

I had been given a steel trunk for my things. Slowly, I folded the few clothes that I had and I placed them in the trunk. There were books too and I was putting them in. Remembered that they were not mine. The convent paid for them. Sadly, I kept them on the table. It then occurred to me that even the trunk did not belong to me. I took the clothes out of it and kept them aside.

Sister in charge entered the room and said, *"Mother Superior wants to see you; you child of the devil. I hope she gives you a good whipping before sending you away.*

I picked up my bundle of clothes and followed her to Mother Superior's room.

"Sit down, my child," Mother Superior said.

I was still holding the bundle of clothes close to my chest.

"What's that?" she asked.

I looked down at the bundle. Realized that all those clothes too were not truly mine. They belonged to the convent. Hand-me-downs from girls who had outgrown them. After me, they would be given to girls who came later. Even the dress I was wearing belonged to the convent. In the bundle of clothes, there was only one dress that belonged to me – the school uniform in which I came to the convent. It would not fit now in any case. I picked that dress out from the bundle. Handed the rest of the dresses to Mother Superior.

She looked at them one by one. Then she spoke to Sister-in-Charge.

"These dresses need to be replaced. Look at these two. They are old and faded. This one could do with some mending. Get Lachmi to do it. Oh, but I know, she is terrible at needlework. Get someone to do it. And please replace these two dresses, Sister." Turning to me she said, *"You'll get your new dresses in a few days, my girl. Till*

then, you can manage with what you have."

"But Mother..." said Sister-in-Charge in a tone of surprise and some anger.

"Yes, sister?"

"Aren't you asking her to leave?"

"She used foul language, I hear" said Mother Superior.

"Of the worst kind," said Sister.

"And she was violent. Wasn't she?"

"She was. Like the filthy people of the street."

"Ah! Then we cannot let her go. You and I have still a lot of work to do with her, Sister, don't you think?"

she said with a smile.

"But... I'm sorry, Mother. I think you are doing something terribly wrong. What kind of an example are we setting our other girls?"

"Sister, we are here to do a job in perfect imitation of the Christ, who is your bridegroom. Remember? Tomorrow I will speak to everyone – the Sisters and the girls. And I will talk to them about what happened today. And I will talk to them about what happened two thousand years ago And then all of us, you and I and all the girls will make a silent examination of conscience. We will ask ourselves if we are truly following in His footsteps. Are we truly Marys of Magdalene? It will be a prayer meeting that you will love, Sister. I promise you. You can leave now Sister. I want to talk to Lachmi."

I could see the ire trailing behind Sister as she left the room. Tears, hot and shameless trickled down my cheek. I did not try to hold them back. I could not say a word. Inside me there was a feeling for Mother Superior so strong it was violent. I wanted to crush her to my bosom. But I did not move.

She who stood up, came up to me, lifted me up to my feet

and held me in her arms. She held me long and tight. So did I, weeping on her breast.

As I held her, I felt love. A waterfall rushing from a great height on to my heart. So strong, I thought I would burst. I wanted to tell her I loved her, but all I could say, with my face buried on her breast was a litany of my streetside abuses in hoarse, hard whispers. I continued saying those words till they became weaker finally melting into words of which I myself was not aware.

She kissed me gently on the top of my forehead and held me tighter. I sobbed without control. I could feel a warmth coming in waves from her heart and touching mine.

Very softly, in a voice that I could only just hear, she said, *"You're precious, my child. You are very, very special."*

I kept holding on to her and I did not want to let go. I wanted to tell her that I loved her very much, but I couldn't find the words to do so.

Slowly she led me to the door and as I left the room, she said, *"God loves you, Lachmi. He loves you very much. Don't you ever forget that."*

***

I take a very big decision. One of the biggest in my life

It happens, I know now.
Sense and consciousness slip into a mist
And I walk in a dream.
I leave Mother Superior's embrace and the room.
Involuntary feet sleepwalk into the chapel.
No thought of prayer.
Been here before but never alone.
Always with others. A white curiosity.
Mouthing common prayers heard so often.
Office of the Blessed Virgin Mary
Savouring the sound of the words, their feel on my tongue.
Lollipop phrases for oral gratification.
Little more than a tape recorder playing back.

Today. Empty chapel. A lonely pavement.
A translucent solitude, sensing other presences.
A coming alive of the chapel's aesthetics?
The tall wrought iron cross.
The stylized depiction of Jesus and Mary Magdalene in acrylic
The oil lamp, winking at the end of a long chain.

Today. Now.
I notice nothing. I see nothing. I utter no prayers.
I kneel on the first pew, head between my hands.
I weep.
I do not know how long.
The tears had to stop some time. I get up from my knees,
but do not leave the chapel. Sit there and stare at blankness

as if it were a thing.

The bell rings for Vespers and the Sisters come in one by one. I do not know whether I should stay or leave. I sit through the Vespers.

The next morning. I go to Mother Superior's office. She looks up from her papers.

Yes, my girl, what is it?

I want to be baptized. I tell her, just like that. As if the words were not mine. Spilling out of an overflowing begging bowl. I hear them as in an echo.

The tick-tock of the timepiece on her table measures the eternity of a few seconds.

Why Lakshmi? You are fine the way you are. I don't want you to change as a person. Put away all these thoughts for now."

But I want to, Sister.

As if the words had made up my mind for me.

Give it time. Baptism is a big step.

Do you think I am not ready, sister?

Not that. It has to be a long journey of the soul.

A change of heart. A change of spirit.

That long journey has happened in an instant.

You will know when it is time.

It is time, sister. I know it?

Why do you say that?

Something happened inside me yesterday. When I was in the room with you.

What happened?

I cannot explain it. It was... an earthquake.

You were angry, were you not?

Violence, yes. But not anger. It was love. Violent love. I wanted to crush you to my bosom to stop my heart from bursting. I felt a mighty love for those arms that were holding me.

So did I for you, Lakshmi.

Something else, Sister.

She waited for me to continue

Those arms that were holding me. They were not yours, Sister.

She looked at me, waiting for what I would say next.

I do not know, Sister... Could it be... His? You have talked about your Jesus. I have found the stories fascinating.

Nothing more than that. Yesterday, when you held me to yourself, I had the feeling that it was He.

And all that time I was using those terrible words!

After a time, it was not those terrible words but gibberish. It was as if you were speaking in tongues.

She came and hugged me close to her again.

I'm happy, Lakshmi, my child. I am still not sure about your baptism. Today, I know that it is not you, but someone else who has made this decision for you. But you will have to wait. I will speak to Fr. Mathoor. He will insist on a period of preparation before baptism.

I will wait. I told her.

Lachmi's Notebook

Preeti teaches me ... that I am a bad teacher

PREETI HAS been returned to me.
A part of my body, stolen, now given back.
The hollow in my bosom, now filled.
I feel whole again.
Eyes squeezed tightly shut at night,
I see a dazzling blankness and embrace the pain of labour
       as in heroic silence I give birth
           to this full-grown three-year-old.
I hold her in my arms.
Preeti is mine again. Mine.
From this moment on to an endless tomorrow.
I hug her to my bosom as I fall asleep.

Preeti. Love. Wrapped in joy
Rushes into my arms every morning.
I hold her close to my heart.

    I relish the time spent with her. Skip study in order to be with this, my baby. Play mother; play Parvati; tell her stories: fairy tales, fables, tales from the Panchatantra; read to her from scraps of newspaper. Tell her tales of my own making. I try teaching her to read, but she just cannot form words with the alphabets. She looks at the different letters as living things. Alphabets as live forms. Sees people in them; animals and birds and insects. Running, flying, crawling. She hears a roar in the letter "O" and puts her hands to her ear when she sees it. She shrinks from "S" and gently caresses "Q". She shrieks with delight at "M" and "W". The alphabets are beings and things in themselves. She will just not put the alphabets together to form words. Try as I might, I cannot get her to understand alphabets as symbols of sounds and language.

Preeti is a bright child, I tell myself. It is I who have failed. I am disappointed in myself. It dawns on me that I am a terrible teacher.

Christina tries to console me.

It's not your fault. It is the way Preeti is made.
What do you mean? I ask, bristling a little.
Preeti is a bright child.

I'm not saying she isn't. It may be that her interests lie elsewhere.

But I want her to study and be a great lady. And I don't know how to teach her.

The problem with you Lachmi is that you're such a good learner. So good that you don't know the learning process.

What should I do?

Give her to a duffer like me, she says laughing. *I would love teaching her.*

And that's what I do.
I hand Preeti over to Christina for her early education.

Just a few months left for my 12th standard examinations. I am not too worried about them. In fact, my subjects take much less time than the hours I steal snacking on more appetizing reading. I am a glutton for literature. Fiction. Short stories. Drama. Poetry. Not just the poems but their design and structure. I read about prosody. About iambs and dactyls and sprung rhythm. Not all of it seeps into my understanding. But I sense an excitement in just reading about it. Recently it's been, of all subjects, classical mythology. I got interested in it through the books I picked up on art. Reading is heaven. I mouth Parvati's hymn. *Yeh swarg hai. Suchmuch swarg hai. This is heaven.*

***

I was baptized today. I took the name, Vimla.

Before the baptism.
Mother Superior and Fr. Mathoor. Both Catholic. Both religious. With different points of view.

Fr. Mathoor: *Lakshmi has to change her name.*
Mother Superior: *I don't see why.*
Fr. M: *Lakshmi is the Hindu goddess of wealth.*
Mother S: *So what?*
Fr. M: *Can't baptise with that name.*
Mother S: *I don't see why not.*
　　　　To me: Lachmi. What would you like to be called?
Me: *I've always been called Lachmi, I'm comfortable with it.*
Mother S: *Lachmi is really Lakshmi. We can christen you Lakshmi.*
After a pause;

Me: But *I think I would like to take another name, Sister.*
Mother S: *Any reason?*
Me: *To remind me of a change in my life.*

A long pause.

Sister looks at me.
Fr. Mathoor looks at Sister.
Sister looks at me again

Me: *Can I have a name with a meaning?*

I look at Fr. Mathoor.
Fr. Mathoor looks at Sister.
Sister looks at me and then at Fr. Mathoor.

Fr. Mathoor: *But of course you can.*

For the next couple of days, the convent is abuzz. A treasure hunt for names. Monica, Christina, Versha and all the others are making lists. Of friends, relatives, movie stars, playback singers Monica the Catlick came up with Beatrice, Leonora, Venus and of course Monica. All of which got the padre's nod. Sister said that they were not Christian but pagan names. Anglo-Saxon pagan names.

I preferred the sound of the Indian names. They had meaning. I narrowed down to two: Samhita and Vimla.

I picked the latter.

At the font:

As the water was poured over my head, I had expectations of

a Jordan experience –
The heavens opening up inside me.
And a voice saying He was pleased with this daughter.
Unrealistic, I know now. But.
I expected the unrealistic, the supernatural.
A sacramental miracle. The magic of ritual.

After the ritual, the deflation.
Nothing happened. Inside or outside of me.
Nothing.
On my knees after the ceremony.
Eyes shut, waiting to feel those soul-filling graces.
Nothing.
Placidness. Blankness. A clean nothingness.
Spirit laundered by the waters of the Font?

The wetness of Baptism still in my hair.
Would that seep down as grace to my heart?
Help me be a good Christian?
Whatever that means.

Before that wetness on my head, religion was a painted
canvas for me; a collage of bright colours. A kaleidoscope of
gods and goddesses. I met them on pavements and pavement
temples, Fantastic in their strange shapes. Melding man and
beast into anatomical surprises. The physiology of divinity as
I saw it then. My baptismal water had smudged the many
coloured images into one indistinct unity. A faceless blotch.
An abstract painting to my mind and spirit.

I'm a body person I told the Lord.

I need to see.

If not with my eyes, with my other senses.

Can I, smell your body odour?

Like I did with the dadas who carried me around the streets?

Feel the hair on your chest?

Can I chase the *kujli* on your back with my nails?

Like I did with Parvati?

To give you relief from the itch?

Feel your fever or the gripe in your stomach?

Can I feel the slap of your hand on my face?

Can I, Lord?

I want to see. I want to smell, feel, hear and touch you.

Later, I spoke to my other self about this. Mother Superior, the older me who speaks to me from the outside, calming the storms within my mind and breast.

She smiled and said, *I'm very happy that you feel that way, Vimla.* The first time after the naming that I was so addressed. *Continue to expect the unrealistic. It may never happen, but that expectation is, I believe, one of the marks of a being a Christian.*

Why do you say that, Sister?

Sister in an unusually bubbly mood.

Laughed and said,

Everyone expects the realistic, the possible and the probable. The fine, finite assurance of logic. Bounded on all sides by the possible. Or even the probable. There's nothing extraordinary about it. Expecting the impossible, on the other hand, is a mark of the mystic; of madness, creativity and faith. It is this unrealistic wonder called Grace knocking at your door. It requires faith to expect the unrealistic. An exquisite madness.

But I am a realist, Sister. At least that's what I think I am.

I know. You've had to be one. To live by your wits. A forced realist.

A realist who bowed down before technicolour gods.
It mattered not if they were Hindu, Parsi or Christian.
We begged for favours at those intrusive roadside altars.
The borders of superstition. Sister said, shaking her head.
Such as you may find even among our Catholic piety.

I myself did not believe in anything particular.

Did you ever daydream? she asked.

Yes, I said. Days when I had to beg. Meeting those foreigners in the park, I dreamed of speaking English the way they did. Imagined giving speeches in perfect English.

You expected the unrealistic. And look! It has happened. In the few years that you have been here, you can speak English better than most today! Your daydreams have brought you to where you are today. Your unrealism was in fact prophesy.

I don't know how much of it is my vanity. After coming here and listening to the lives of the saints, I dreamed of being like them; a *saint who could work miracles. Looked upon with wonder by people around me. Not any desire to be holy or spiritual or even plain good.*

Not an uncommon daydream among young Catholic girls. They all want to be saints. It is another form of glamour, a different kind of vanity. Not quite the same as faith, but it could lead to it. Faith, Hope, Charity – They are forms of a holy madness.

***

Have neglected this little note book. A few jottings now. Board exams done. Did well. Waiting for results. So did Christina, Monica and the others.

Plans for later.

Monica has decided to join the convent and become a nun. Prays a lot. Prayer is her brain food and study guide. Monica, the holy one. Sits down with me for a chat.

You will do first class, Lachmi. She says.

So now what?

Nursing I tell her

That's good, and all, she says. *But you are thinking of God, aren't you? He has done good things for you. Picked you up from the roadside and all. Don't you want to work for Him? No?*

I noticed that her English had improved. I did not know what to say. My honesty would shock her.

I was not conscious of any gratitude to God. To Mother Superior, yes. but God was still this smudged picture that mystified me. Mother Superior could take it; not Monica.

I read the Bible and I am in awe of Yahweh of the Old Testament. His wonderful works in Exodus and Kings. I love the stories of the Old and New Testaments. I have been taken in by Jesus, his clever parables and crazy teachings. I read commentaries on the Bible. Even a few books on theology. I wish I had not read them. The physics and mathematics of God. *Studying* about God does not help me.

I want to feel this God myself. That feeling is not there and it disappoints me.

I spoke to Mother Superior about it. She laughed as if I had cracked a joke.

> *You have started taking yourself too seriously.*
> *It is unlike you, she said.*
> *Be yourself before being a Catholic.*
> *Baptism should lift your spirits up; not allow it to sink.*

It's you who lift up my spirits, Sister. I said.

Smile, she commanded me. Do the four hands clap like you used to. Hold fast to the freedom that the pavement gave you. That's a precious gift. You have had two baptisms. The Baptism of the Pavement. And the Baptism of the Trinity. You have much to offer God. Being a nurse is as much a calling as being a nun. she said.

Arms around my shoulder, she skipped me to her room.

Come. I have something else to discuss with you.

She showed me a leaflet. Details of a course on holistic

healing. Conducted by an ashram run by another order of nuns. A ten-day residential course. As a special case, the ashram was offering it free to one person from our convent.

I think you are the right person for this course.
I think you should consider it.

Of course, I will if you think I should, Sister.

It was decided. I would do the course.

***

I do the course on holistic healing

The course, a magical mirror. Made me see myself in a way I had never done before. The mirror: Ten days of intensity. Yoga. Pranayama. Meditation. Acupressure. Water therapy. Reiki. Pranic healing. Testing the elasticity of muscle and mind. The yogic asanas and the pranayama, I found easy. My rubber body twisted and stretched like a doll's. A live book of asanas: *hala, paschimhothan, matsya* ...

I got a little bored with them. Distracted. My mind a butterfly during pranayama and meditation. I could do almost any asana naturally. I knew I had the body, But not the attitude for it. I went through the motions with not much interest.

I related more to the other courses. Reiki, Pranic Healing and acupressure. They seemed to come naturally to me. My fingers and my hands became eyes. Looking beneath skin and bone.

Found myself applying Reiki and Pranic healing to the other participants. They all queued up for 'Vimla Treatment'.

I was discovering a new me. Related to an older me. Memories of my back-scratching days with Parvati. When my fingers would 'see' the itching *kujli* and chase it across her back. Causing much grateful wonder in Parvati. It was like looking at my hand one morning and finding a sixth finger or overgrown eyelashes.

Ten days. Serious introspection. A looking inside. I saw or I thought I saw: My mind and body shaped for excitement. Hills and valleys: ideas, sensation, desire.

What about feelings? Tried running my fingers over them like braille. Flat? Did I have none? No peaks of feeling – either of love, or fear or sadness or even hatred. Am I just a body person and a mind person. Sensations and thoughts flattening emotions. Was my heart more flesh than feeling. Was that good or bad? How did this place me in Mother's Superior's scale of values? I wondered. Did this make me less of a person?

I looked back. At those few dark moments when I did display emotion. Those robust, fleshy verbal abuses of the roadside. My strongest triggers to at least some passion. Now I had put them out of reach.

I remembered. That naked run in the rain. There was feeling there.

My encounter with Preeti's drunken father.

That emotional cataract in Mother Superior's embrace. Yes, this flesh had some droplets of emotion left. They had to be squeezed out of me as out of an old tube of toothpaste. Or, should I say, squeezed into it by timely provocation?

This emotionally empty tube of flesh and blood!

Back in the convent. An ecstatic report on the course. And then an about-turn to the future.

Next steps. My admission to the nursing course. All arranged by Mother Superior. Four years training on the job. In one of the finest training hospitals. The BB General Hospital.

Bombay! My pavement home. Will I meet my Parvati? Will she want a back scratch?

I have been registered in the name of Vimla Lachmi.

Part III

THE BODY. HEALING.

Lachmi's diary

Back to Bombay. Now Mumbai.

Arrived by train, just my suitcase and me. A feeling of coming home. The buzz and the very smells I knew came back to me. Like a stubborn dream that refused to go away even after you were awake.

Bombay on that day was a pet dog wagging his tail at my return.

But Bombay was no longer Bombay. It was Mumbai. I liked the change. It wasn't even very new to me. On the pavement Bombay was always Mumbai. Bombay had changed to Mumbai while Lachmi had changed to Vimla.

Hello Mumbai. Here I come again. Not the Lachmi you knew, but Ms. Vimla Lachmi now.

Now this is Vimla Lachmi bragging about her hospital. The Sir Byramjee Batliwala Hospital – BB for short. Counted as one of the finest teaching hospitals in the country.

Arrival day. Booklets handed out like bread: Rule book and history of the hospital. Gobble up the rules, we are told. Digest them.

The senior nurses speak to the new batch. BB is a public hospital. A conveyor belt of patients.
From the pavements and slums to South Mumbai's rich: beggars, prostitutes, criminals, police under-trials, accident cases, A lavish buffet of medical cases. Attracting the best-known doctors in every field. They can never hope to get a wider experience in another hospital in the city. They may be consultants in elite hospitals and have their own private

practices, but they clamour to be attached to the BB. Bank of medical experience and visibility. The shining currency of a medical reputation.

The best doctors, yes, say the nurses. But finally, it is we who save your lives. Not the doctors.

Sr. Superintendent's address to the new batch of nurses

I see in front of me fifty of the world's luckiest girls today. Heard that? World's luckiest girls.

For each one of you there were at least fifty others who would have liked to be in your place. Heard that? Fifty others.

You ought to know that this is the best nurses' training hospital in the country and you are very lucky to be here.

I want you to clap for that.

(Obedient applause)

Proud you must feel. Heard that? Proud.

Not proud of yourselves (what have you to be proud of? Nothing yet, nothing.) but proud of this institution, the great BB Hospital and Research Centre.

On my part, I would like to be proud of each one of you, but looking at you today, I am very far from that feeling.

More than half of you look like something hanging on a slum clothesline. Heard that? More than half of you. Now which half, I will let you decide.

Your uniforms though new are not pressed perfectly and not even worn correctly. Your sleeves and collars still have wrinkles and they show on your faces. I see expressions of frightened rats in some of your eyes. You look sad and do you know why? Very simply because of the way you are dressed. A well-laundered and pressed uniform is your best makeup.

Take pride in your uniform. Take pride in your hospital. Take pride in your great profession. Nursing. You are the Florence Nightingales of the 20th century. But not yet. You have a long way to go before you can feel the slightest pride in yourselves.

There is much to learn. Heard that? Much to learn.

The first and most important thing you learn is the rulebook. All of you have been given one. Look on it as your prayer book. Learn it by heart. And follow it like a religion. You may be Hindu, Christian, Muslim or Parsi. That's your first religion. The rulebook is your second religion. You break any one of the rules and you will have hell to pay. Heard that? Hell. I will not hesitate in sending you back to where you came from. I have done it in the past and I will do it again.

On my part, I have promises that I make to you.

The first thing I promise you is a hard time, a very hard time. Life will not be easy here. So if you do not like hard work, today is the time to decide your future. Think about it. If you don't see yourself working hard, just fall out of line right now; take your bags and leave. I give you two minutes to make that decision.

(She stopped speaking and stepped away from the microphone. She walked up and down, looking at her watch. Exactly two minutes later, she started speaking again.)

But hard work alone does not make a great nurse. There is this thing called dedication. It comes from the belief that what you are doing is important and good work; work that few others can do.

I promise that I will be fair. I promise to look after you because you are now in my care. And I promise that you will all be the world's best nurses at the end of the course if you live up to the programme that we have designed for you.

.... And on and on.
Harangue for an hour or more.
On the reputation of a hospital.
Built on good nursing.
The importance of study.
The best nurses are the ones who know most.
Head on shoulders, heart under lock and key.
Limbs always wound up for work.
Use head with your patients not heart.
Or be ready for trouble.

A paler shade of Mr. Kumar?

I begin life as a trainee nurse.

My dorm days are over. Am I happy? I don't know. We are housed in a hostel, four to a room.

Meet Mehnaz, a lively Parsi girl who loves to eat. In her drawer, snacks (tongue tingle, she calls it) keep company with love letters to herself. And pictures of film stars, mainly male. *"Ketlo sweet che dikra! Cho Chweet, this boy!"* Kisses one or two of them before going to bed. Entertains us every night with Hindi, English and Gujerati songs, Sung out of three separate songbooks.

Two Keralites. Padmini and a girl with my original name, Lakshmi. Both from the same village in Kerala. *"Don't call us Keralites,"* they instruct us with finger raised. *"We are Malayalees and we speak Malayalam."* Their skin is darker than even mine, Both attractive, with long black hair and big black, almond shaped eyes. Kathakali eyes, they say with the neck shake. Padmini, has a round face and fleshier lips. Giggles every sentence. Even if it is something very serious. The giggle is part of her voice. A crazy yodel into which she injects her words.

Lakshmi. Intense, very religious. Bedside table as altar, Images of goddess Lakshmi and Lord Siva.

Morning and evening puja before the images.

In the room next door there are only three. One of them, Petula wants me for a friend.

"I am scared baba. Dis is de first time I am leaving home. My mummy told me not to trust to anyone."

This does not ring true to me. Petula is very outgoing and garrulous. Makes excessive gestures when she speaks. Hand and eye movements, borrowed from the movie screen. Pouts her lips and flaps her eyelashes as articulation. She would like to have me in her room, she says. *"Aks dem to move you to our room. We are only tree."*

She speaks English without all those nice, dental "th"s. Lips curled, head bent, she says: *"How you be in de same room as Padmini and Lakshmi?"*

"They are alright," I say.

"Look at de way dey speak Inglish Jus like de unda-gundu language, no? And then: *"I like de way you speak Inglish. Did you grow up in foreign?"* she asks.

"My last home was the convent in Delhi."

"*And where were you before dat?*"

I have decided to screen my past from my colleagues. It would unnecessarily bias people's opinions.

Mother Superior advised me not to talk about my past. "Don't be ashamed of it; don't lie about it, "she had said. "But don't talk about it."

"The past is not important," I tell Petula with a smile. "We have to look to the future."

"*Sad story, no?*" she asks with feigned concern. "*Where are your mudder and fadder?*"

"Guess where?" I say and turn to walk away.

"*Ah!*" She says. "*I know it is a sad story. Dat's why you don't want to talk about it.*"

The next day, Padmini and Lakshmi come to me.

We are sorry about your sad past, they say.

You should talk about it, they say. *You'll feel better.*

In a few days my "sad story" is all over the place: My parents died of cholera. They committed suicide. Run over by a bus; they were in jail. The stories make their rounds.

***

This is terrible. Unconsciously I get into trouble.
And then, a small perverse thrill.

My training did not start on a happy note. My class work was excellent. My ward work was terrible.

That was Sister Matron's word. Terrible. *Chheee! She said, Terrible, terrible. This just won't do, Sister Vimla, Terrible.*

My bed making left much to be desired. Could never do

it perfectly. Loose ends and creases were my bed making signature. Not easy. Try making a bed with a patient on it. Roll tons of inanimate flesh to one side while you make the other.

The others were better bed makers. *Watch Padmini, Sister Matron* told me. I watched Padmini. She did it with ease. Finished the job in half the time I took to do it. Strangely, I feel no shame.

I am better with the TPRs – the recording of temperature-pulse-respiration. We had to do it twice a day with all our patients. I liked doing TPR. It brought me in contact with my patients. It energized me.

I did not take just their temperature, pulse and respiration. I smelt their fear. Felt their pain. Sensed their impatience, their boredom and their listlessness.

I thought that I was doing well with this part of the job.

This morning however, as I put down the TPR of a patient on her chart, I felt a hand on my shoulder. It was Sister Matron again.

"*Come with me,*" she ordered sternly.

I followed her not knowing what wrong I had done. She took me to the nurses' station. She glared at me with a dreadful anger. Those were glowing coals, not eyeballs.

"*Besharam! Shameless girl! How dare you do that?*" she asked in Hindi.

"Do what?" I asked.

"*Don't fool with me,*" she said. "*You really think I didn't see? I watched you do all the four patients in the room. I saw how you did it.*"

I lost all speech because I honestly did not know what

she was talking about. She waited for me to say something and when no response was forthcoming, she said: "You wrote down those TPRs without actually taking them. Do you know what a terrible thing that is?"

I tried to think back and visualize what I had done. We were given a detailed process for recording TPR. We had to take our tray with the glass containing antiseptic solution in which we kept the thermometer. With most patients the temperature had to be taken orally after making sure that the patient had not had anything to eat or drink at least fifteen minutes before the TPR. The thermometer had to stay in the mouth for two whole minutes, though some of the newer meters needed less time. While the temperature was being recorded, we had to note the bpm, the beats per minute. It was recommended that we observe the beats for a minute and spend the next minute counting the respiration of the patient, the times the stomach went up and down in a minute.

I shut my eyes slightly to remember what I actually did in that ward.

It was like a cold water slap in my face. I 'saw' that I had indeed not followed the procedure. I had just put my hand on the forehead of the patients, felt their pulse for only a few seconds and had written down the TPR. That was terrible.

I hung my head down in remorse and said, "I'm sorry."

"Sorry will not do," she said. "I have to report this to Sister Superintendent."

Then she looked down at the TPR recordings just made.

"This won't do. It will certainly be all wrong. We'll have to do this again. Come with me." She took the tray and the charts with her and we went to the ward again. She went to the first of the four patients and recorded her TPR. To make her point, she took longer than was needed. She kept the thermometer in the mouth for two minutes and felt the pulse for two minutes. As she took her pen to the chart, she stopped. I saw her jaw drop a little. Her recording was the same as mine to an exactness that surprised her. She looked up at me and said, "This is a fluke."

Then she went to the next patient, went through the same procedure and found the same thing. The recording was exact.

All four patients showed the same TPR as the one I had recorded.

"I cannot understand what's happening."

"I think I can tell the temperature by just feeling the body, Sister. And I can tell TPR and pulse rate by feeling for only a few seconds. I did not mean to take a short cut. I think I was absent-minded when I took their TPR." I said.

"Come," she said. She took me to another ward and asked me to tell the temperature of a few patients there by just feeling them. I was exact to a margin of a few decimal points.

"Okay." She said. "You can tell temperature by just feel. *Woh kohi badi baat nahin*, not a big thing, you know. Many people can do that. But this is a hospital. We do things here properly, scientifically. We have thermometers here and we have to use them. Do you hear that?"

"Yes," I said meekly.

"I will let you go now, but the next time I catch you doing anything like this, you're finished." She said.

I went back to my work in a daze. I was appalled at my transgression. Yet underneath the contrition, there was this faint streak of excitement. Immodest whisperings in my brain about being specially gifted. A pagan ringing of bells and a *bhajan* to the memory of that little pavement devi. I can actually look inside a patient with only my intuition. I am gifted. I quickly dispelled the thought and resolved that I would never again do what I had done in the ward today.

Theatre of Horror and the Devil's jigsaw puzzle

Nursing has become my new scholarship.
A literature of the senses.
A thesaurus of the flesh.
The Body engages me in a compelling way.
Anatomy for me is palpable poetry.
The prosody of pulse, peristalsis and pulmonary motion:
 Sprung rhythm to my senses.
I feel the drumbeats of health against those of sickness:
The rapid stomp of a 105°F fever
Against the funeral march of the dying breath.
The burning brow, the clammy palm, and the bloodshot eye.
They speak a language to which I respond.

***

My real everyday interactions with the patients fill me with a feeling of fulfilment. It is the related work ~ the bed making, the filling up of charts and forms, the preparation of dressings and instruments in the autoclave and then arranging them in order for use in the wards ~ that I find a chore. I have realized that I am not a hard worker. I have little stamina and cannot do physical labour for long hours. I have to consciously push myself to do it. I think I have managed satisfactorily, or just about. The specialist doctors who sometimes take classes are impressed with my study and my work in class and with my understanding of individual cases in the wards.

I sense a change in Sister Matron. With the effort that I have put in over the past few weeks, she too is beginning to warm up towards me, but I can see that she still keeps an eye on what I do.

It has not been easy. From the first week of my being here, I had glimpses of hell. In this theatre that I wanted to see from the inside I have been audience and actor in scenes of horror. Even my life on the pavements did not prepare me for the ugliness of human pain.

We saw accident cases every day. Disfigured and dismembered bodies were brought in as a matter of routine; like fresh supplies to the local market; corpses of gangsters who were either shot by other gangsters or by the police.

One heard the deafening screams and hopeless wailings of mothers and even grown men at the sight of the mangled flesh that was once their son.

We saw the callousness of spectators, ward boys and policemen for whom that piece of bleeding flesh was no more than raw meat.

I have witnessed a man brought in on a bicycle, trying to hold in place the entrails that were spilling out of a stab wound.

I have seen a woman attempting to do the same with the severed hand of her husband that was chopped off during a chawl fight.

Among the most distressing and difficult sights were burn cases, mostly suicide attempts by women. They came in screaming with pain, their faces and bodies disfigured and discoloured, looking like those monsters designed for some unlikely third-rate horror movie.

At times like these my mind made a fleeting, unholy trip to those seductive lectures of Mr. Kumar on the beauty of the human body, the aesthetics of parabola, symmetry, hue and texture; their power to evoke passion and to drive men and women to madness.

Then my eyes swerved back to the visual offering of the casualty ward and the morgue. I shudder at this reality that hits me every day – those flesh and bone pieces of the devil's own jigsaw puzzle.

Though the sights in the ward were not always so gruesome, we were in touch from moment to moment with the vulnerability of the human condition.

We stood in awe at the stubborn resilience of the body in the face of near-hopelessness. Every day we saw patients on the brink of death, recover and go home with smiles on their faces. Every time that happened there was a minor wave of quiet joy in all of us, privately glorying perhaps in the feeling that we had a hand in that small miracle.

There were of course degrees of personal involvement among us nurses and trainees. Many of them, even the experienced ones went about their duties with efficiency more than concern, but there were others who would think and talk about their patients even after duty hours in the hostel.

For me, the interaction with patients was sustenance, though it was draining. Evenings I would go back to my room and flop on to the bed without the energy for my other passion - reading. I would take a book to bed but drop off before I could flip a couple of pages. Hopeful of finding the time and energy to read, I would still buy these books, often from the pavements, with the small stipend that we received. I did not have to spend for much except my toiletries and knickknacks. We didn't have to pay for our boarding and lodging. It was part of the training program.

The stipend was insignificant. The real reward was in my work. It was fulfilling for me. In a bigger way than I had imagined. Every moment spent with the patients did something to me, mentally and physically; bordering on the strange; setting off within me a parallel existence with that of the patients.

Often I found myself hurting in the very spot that was hurting the one in my care. My own pain would diminish in direct proportion to the relief I could give my patient.

Very often he or she would suffer extreme discomfort without knowing what was wrong or from where the pain emanated. From the outside I knew and I did what I could to alleviate the suffering.

I am not sure that it was the holistic healing course that helped me give this invisible succour. I did not consciously use any of the techniques that were taught us. Besides, as nurses we could not start any form of treatment on our own.

***

Another perverse thrill: my body plays tricks on me

Strange occurrences.

Just yesterday morning Sister Matron asked me to do a couple of sponges and a digital evacuation. I started with the sponges. The first was a young man who was admitted a couple of weeks, ago delirious with fever. The high fevers, often touching 106 F had continued for two weeks before that. He was treated with antipyretics and antibiotics for the usual PUO, malaria and typhoid. The fever just refused to come down. They admitted him to get tests done - blood tests, lumbar punctures and a battery of other checks. In the meantime, he is given antipyretics. They bring the fever down to around 102F but in a couple of hours it rises again to the highs of 105F and 106F. This has been the pattern on his chart for the past two weeks.

Yesterday at 7 a.m. I had a look at his temperature chart. At 6.45 a.m., just 15 minutes earlier, it was 104.8° F. I went into his room with my bowl of water and the swabs. I drew the curtain and looked down at his face. I could see the fever in his face. I touched his forehead. According to my intuitive reading, which I was forbidden to do, I knew that the fever was even higher than what was recorded.

I kept my palm on his forehead. I could feel a heat enter into my body. Within seconds, I felt myself burning all over.

I burned with a rigor as I started the sponging - the usual face, neck hands, back, abdomen and legs. I did it slowly, slower than usual, often letting the palm of my left hand slide over his skin after the swab had run over it.

Slowly, as if applying a poultice, I swabbed his body. At

that point of time, I remembered my experience with Parvati. The back-scratching. My hand "seeing," chasing and 'killing' the itch.

By the time I came down to my patient's shoulder blades, I seemed to feel the burning in my face subside, and as I swabbed lower, over his abdomen and his back, I felt much better inside me. I saw him open his eyes as I completed his thighs, calves and feet. I was feeling completely normal now.

The whole procedure took about 25 minutes. I dried him thoroughly and I touched his forehead again. 101° F to my touch. This was impossible, I said to myself. He smiled faintly and said, "I feel better today. What did the doctor give me?"

Just then, one of the senior nurses came in with his medication. He smiled at her and said, "I'm feeling better, Sister, what did you give me?" A little surprised, she said, "I have to give you something now. You have a very high fever."

"Very funny," he said, "but I'm feeling quite well."

She smiled and said, "That's good news." Then she felt his forehead. "It doesn't feel too hot," she said. "Wait. Let me make sure." She said and left the room. She came back with a thermometer and took his temperature: 100° F.

"That's funny," she said. "Just a while ago it was nearly 105° F." She stood for a while at his bed. "I will have to check with the resident doctor if I should give you the fever tablets."

We left the room together as he said, "Thank you, Sisters."

The second sponge was without any unusual incident, but I could not fathom what happened during the first. Was I imagining things? Was I myself unwell?

I had no time to think about it because I had to attend

to the digital evacuation. That's when I experienced my second shock of the day.

The patient was a delicate looking, middle-aged lady. She was brought in for haemorrhoid treatment and was having trouble with her bowel movement from the time she was admitted. Any amount of oral laxatives would not help. Suppositories and enemas seemed ineffective.

The poor lady was in misery. Every four days she had to have assistance with the evacuation of her stools because she couldn't do it herself. This, the nurse had to do with her gloved finger – not a very easy or pleasant procedure for both nurse and patient. Every time it had to be done, she would weep and beg of them not to do it. It made her feel like a soiled rag, she said. She seemed a very shy and sensitive sort of person, gentle and refined in her manner. She said it made her feel less than a human being and she hated the procedure. But of course it had to be done.

Yesterday I was asked to do the digital evacuation. I drew the curtains around the bed. Before I wore the gloves to do the job, I looked at her face and saw her expression of pained pleading. She did not want it and yet there was this extreme discomfort that she was feeling.

At that moment, I felt (was I imagining it?) as if I was suffering the same symptoms as she. There was a fullness in my stomach and a feeling as if I was badly constipated myself. This was imagination, I thought to myself, I must push this feeling away. But it persisted, like a mischievous leprechaun inside my intestines. I looked again at the unfortunate lady and her pleading eyes.

I put my hand on her abdomen and kept it there for a

while, feeling that same discomfort in me all the time.

I suddenly felt a strong urge to swallow a lot of water. I wasn't thirsty but there was this cry from within for water. I left the lady there, went into the pantry and poured two glasses of warm water. I gulped down one of the glasses and took the other to my patient. I made her sit up and drink the water, which she did very slowly.

She handed me the glass and said, "How did you know I was feeling like it?"

I smiled and laid my palm on her abdomen again. I put my hand inside where the hospital garment separated in the middle. Her skin was cold to the touch. I rubbed her belly making larger and larger circular motions around her navel without applying any pressure.

I stopped for a while and closed my eyes. I could feel an involuntary movement inside her, under my palm. Peristalsis, I told myself; it is happening. I continued the circular rubbing as I felt the skin get warmer. I felt more movement inside as I moved my hand lower, gently, hardly touching her skin. I did this for some time, all the while sensing (or was I imagining it?) a warm sensation in my palm and definite internal contractions of her muscles.

She moved her hand towards me to draw my attention. "Now!" she said. "Now!" Quickly I reached for the bedpan. "No." she said. "Not that. I'll go to the toilet." She didn't need my assistance. She walked to the bathroom.

When she emerged a while later, you could see the relief on her face, but there were tears streaming down her face. She went back to her bed, took my hand in hers and kissed it. "You're an angel," she said. I had about enough time to smile and thank her because at that moment I myself had to do a little run – to the nurses' bathroom.

A mixture of dread and excitement. Have I been burdened with a gift? An abnormality that will cause me more pain than reward?

***

Mumbai, my pet dog is wagging his tail.

I want to look closely at those eyes again. Stroke his back. Pick his fleas. Hear that growl.

The pavement calls.

My friends are where they were. I am where I am. Lifted as if by claws of some powerful eagle and dropped here. Same city, another station.

My life has changed. I find facets of myself for the first time. Like broken coloured bangle pieces in a kaleidoscope called Vimla Lachmi.

From the time I touched Bombay Central Station, (is it Mumbai Central now?) the pavement called. To meet my friends. Particularly Parvati. I have already started moving out of the hospital on off days, to Bhendi Bazaar. Even farther, to Crawford market. I note the bus routes that will take me to Hutatma Chowk and Churchgate and Cuffe Parade. These were the areas in which we roamed. The dadas and the mukadams would not allow us to go beyond these boundaries. We could go along the waterfront up to the gymkhanas, but were not allowed to go beyond. The localities beyond these boundaries belonged to other pavement groups and were guarded by other dadas and mukadams.

I think about it for days. Should I or should I not? I visualize reactions. Parvati's whoops of joy. Damodar Chacha lifting me off the ground. And the others. Would they still be there? Would it be safe? Would they hold me back by force? What should I wear? My nurse's uniform? It would startle Parvati and deter the others from doing anything brash.

Yesterday morning, a Sunday. I decide to make the trip. I attend early morning Mass at the Gloria Church and directly leave for my old "home." I dress up in a simple *salwar khameez*. I take with me a small pouch with just enough bus money back and forth. I take the A4 bus and alight at Hutatma Chowk. Familiar territory.

I stroll across the maidan and across the pavements from Churchgate Station to the waterfront. Nothing has changed. The maidan is exactly the same as I had last seen it. It looks as if not a new leaf has sprung since then. Nothing changes here, not in the general appearance of the place - no new structures, no new stores, nothing. The same photograph, not even turned sepia.

When we lived on the pavement, we saw the same people every day. Mechanized marionettes hurrying along. From the station to their places of work. Passing by the same landmarks at precisely the same time daily. What changed, but slowly were the hawkers, the beggars and the pavement dwellers like us. They would drift away or be evicted by the police or by other pavement dwellers.

Nothing has changed except for a patch of pavement from the railway station to the petrol pump. It has been cleared of all hawkers. It looks cleaner and less busy.

But turn the corner towards the waterfront, and it is like

turning the pages of my best loved classic. The same familiar pages. It feels as if I were here just yesterday. I look around at the same old restaurants and offices, whose colours and signboards are all etched in my memory. I didn't know their names or what they stood for then. Today I read them for the first time. Gaylords, Kamling, WIAA, Satkar, Asiatic, Rustom's Ice-cream and so many others. It is as if I am being introduced to celebrities with whose faces I was familiar but whose names I didn't know.

I amble slowly past these signboards with an unspoken "Pleased to meet you" in my mind. I look for the old familiar faces. At the shoeshine stands. At the corners where some of us congregated. There is nobody there I know. As I approach the entrance to the Brabourne Stadium, a few faces turn to look at me. I recognize the man who sold shoes and another who sold old books. I stop to browse. The man looks up at me and says, "I've seen you before." Of course, he has, but he does not know my name or who I am. The hawkers just saw us as so much trash, people of the street with whom they had no business.

"Lachmi!" I hear a voice call.

I look in the direction from which it came. I spot Thambi in between the hurrying crowds. He has a portable shoeshine kit on his shoulders. He comes towards me with a look of amused puzzlement.

"Baap re baap! Dear O dear! Look who's here. Lady Lachmi or what!"

I ask him where the others are. He tells me I should be careful. The mukadams were looking for me after I was taken away. They would catch the person who stole me and they would kill him, they had said. Luckily they are not around at that moment.

"Come with me." he says and I follow.

We turn the corner, once at the water front and then again at the Air-India building. We meet the group at the Mantralaya pavements. There is Lachman and Gopi and Radha and Bhiku chacha and a few others who I do not know. They are new members of this group. I spot a couple of little children, no more than three years old, who seemed to have the same features as Lachman and the others. The universal pavement mother is still productive; I think to myself.

I ask them about Parvati and Damodar chacha. They inform me that Damodar has become a "circus walla". He is doing his own circus acts on the pavements in Ghatkopar, Andheri, right up to Virar. He has taken Shalini Thaee and two of the little children – a boy and a girl – with him. He has trained them to perform all kinds of difficult stunts like tight rope walking, twisting their bodies through small metal hoops, jumping through fire, lifting heavy rocks with their teeth and many other dangerous acts, they tell me. He is earning a lot of money. There is nobody to do hool now, they say sadly.

Parvati had disappeared just like that one day. One morning they woke up to find Parvati missing. She had gone away during the night. This happened two months ago, they say.

They ask about me. I give them filtered truth. Leave out the sex work bit. I tell them what happened on that rainy day, when this motorcar came and took me away. I tell them that I was taken to Delhi and was there handed over to the convent, where I got an education. They nodded their heads.

They knew that their Lachmi would be an educated person someday.

I tell them that I am now a nurse. Eyes light up, reflecting pride and wonder. One of their own had done it! Shalini thaee came and patted me on the back and said," Shabash, Lachmi. "You really are a wonder" Bhiku chacha came and stood close to me with his hand on his hip. He said that if anyone gave me any trouble, I should let him know; he would teach those ... (Oh! The succulent abuses of the street! I miss them) a lesson.

I thought it best to leave then. I was not sure what the mukadams would do if they saw and recognized me. Perhaps nothing, but I did not want to take any chances. They all took turns to pat me on the back as I took leave of them. "Visit us again," said Bhiku chacha, and added as an afterthought, "but who knows if we will still be here?"

I took the bus back, thinking all the while of Parvati, projecting in my mind's screen the most unlikely sequences. Did she go away looking for me? I knew how much she cared for me. I know she was prepared to give up a lot for my sake. As the bus crawled through the traffic, I experienced a tightness in my brain. I felt pain and discomfort all over my body. I had a strong feeling that it was her pain that I was experiencing. I saw her suffering a great deal wherever she was. I felt trapped in my inability to do anything for a person who would do anything for me. She was the first person with whom I bonded and with whom I felt an almost physical connection. Everyone said that we looked like sisters. Perhaps she was my half-sister without us knowing it.

I almost missed getting off at the BB Hospital stop. As I

walked to the hostel, I wondered if I had been foolish in going to meet the street gang. They were part of a past that I ought to have left behind for good. They were by no means any family to me. The situation on our particular pavement was so fluid, it was insubstantial. At any moment of time, that ragtag group was like a full-grown tree with no roots. Their presence on that pavement was a hologram or at best a bubble; here today, gone the day after tomorrow. Except for personal relationships like that between Parvati and me, there were no lasting ties between any two persons. The trip left me with a huge sense of futility and hopelessness, particularly with regard to Parvati.

In my hostel room, my head was a lump of lead. I fished out from my drawer, for the first time, the Perpetual Succour leaflet that Monica gave me. I read the prayers, registering nothing by way of their meaning. In a strange way they helped to soothe or rather blank out my mind, the words becoming for me an effective blackboard duster, wiping out a difficult chemistry formula that I could not understand.

I strolled into the canteen. As usual on Sundays there were very few hostelites for lunch. I sat alone and had very little to eat. I went back to my room and read right up to teatime.

At around six in the evening, Mehnaz came in and flopped on to her bed.

"I'm feeling so dead," she said. "It's a wonder the vultures have not got to me yet. Dead. Dead. Dead. And my head is splitting like some devils are doing a diwali inside my skull."

Mehnaz was given to exaggeration. She had a crazy way

with words and phrases that I found amusing. The borders
between Parsi Gujerati, Mumbai Hindi and basic English
were demolished to make way for her very own colourful and
expressive language. She spoke impeccable Mehnaz. But she
truly was in pain. She held her head in her hands and
moaned. "I shouldn't have come today. But my Mummy
wouldn't listen. You have to make a good impression, she
says. You must do well. You must work hard. Don't do
anything foolish. Don't waste your time... all kinds of bosh.
Papa had bought a good wine today and I had some before
lunch. I think that was the shaitan. Aaeeeee! My head! Take
it off from my shoulders and keep it in the refrigerator till
tomorrow!"

I went over to her bed and took her right palm in mine.
Immediately I began to feel a heaviness in my head. Soon it
was a drumbeat of a headache. I began to massage at the base
of her thumb and around it. She screamed in pain. "What are
you doing, re salee? You're trying to kill me even faster, or
what?"

"Acupressure." I told her. "At least, I think it is. I have
studied it a little. Hold on. It will hurt for a while. In fact, the
more it hurts the better. Is it hurting here?"

"Like mad!" she said.

"Good." I said and continued. She closed her eyes. For
the first time, I saw a Mehnaz with her mouth shut as well.
She did not utter a word for all the while I pumped the flesh
of her thumb with my finger. I felt the drumbeat in my head
quieten down. I then did the rest of her palm for good
measure. The others in the room watched silently, sceptical,
half-amused.

Five to seven minutes later, she looked at me and said, "Sala, Vimla, this is *jadu*, I say. Magic. I'm feeling much better." I continued for another five minutes by which time her headache had gone. Mehnaz was astounded. "Bloody miracle!" she said in that excitable Parsi falsetto.

"Nothing like that." I said laughing. "This is not unusual."

"I've not seen anything like this." She insisted.

"Quite common," I told her. "At the holistic healing course, we saw acupressure work on headaches, backaches, coughs, gas problems, indigestion and other common problems."

"Tche tche!" Lakshmi was sceptical. "Then who will go to doctor? Who will buy medicine. Everyone will do *jigaree-pokaree* on hand."

"Vimla's jigaree-pokaree. It works," said Mehnaz.

"The relief may be temporary," I warn them. "But it is real. And of course, not everyone can do it." I guess I couldn't resist saying it.

Mehnaz, of course was not interested in all these qualifiers. All she knew was that she got instant relief and was thrilled about it. I was happy to be able to give that relief.

I found myself offering to administer the jigaree-pokaree to my room and batch mates. Inside me a secret effervescence: the thought that I had something quite unique to offer. This was strengthened with every successful 'healing' and the resulting surprise on the part of the 'healed'.

It was a small step from my roommates to the ward. It began quite dramatically one morning. One of the patients, a frail, middle-aged lady had a fierce bout of coughing. She had just been brought in from the ICU, having suffered a mild heart attack. The resident doctor was called in. He prescribed a cough syrup. It did not help in the least. She kept coughing. Unable to get her breath back as the spasms took hold of her. She would sit up and go into a violent coughing fit. One of the nurses would try and stroke her back to give her relief. One spasm followed another in quick succession. Leaving not just the patient, but everyone else in the ward breathless. The nurses knew that for a heart patient like her, this could be extremely dangerous.

I was at that time assisting with the patient in the next bed. I could not bear to see what was happening. On impulse, I went over to her bed. I took her right palm in mine. I began massaging the webbed portion between thumb and forefinger. She winced with pain, but continued coughing. The other nurse watched silently, not knowing what else to do. The RMO said he would have to phone the visiting consultant and ask for his advice. They may have to readmit her into the ICU. I continued pumping the other areas of her palm in desperation; then went back to the webbed portion again. I saw her wince, but she let me continue.

Five minutes later, I was giving up hope because the coughing wouldn't stop. I looked at her face and saw from her expression that she wanted me to continue. I decided to do so, if not for anything, to give her the comfort of touch. Two minutes later, the coughing subsided. Five minutes later, it stopped. I continued massaging her palm for five minutes more. There were no more spasms. We waited in her room for the next ten minutes. The RMO came in saying that the consulting physician had advised them to admit her into the

ICU if the fit continued. I left the bed and went back to the other patient. After attending to her, I left the ward. The RMO and the nurse stayed on to observe her. Fifteen minutes later, they emerged from the ward saying that the patient had fallen asleep.

That started it. Patients pleaded with me for my attention. Coughs, aches, stomach upsets and all kinds of real and imaginary ailments were presented as excuses for my palm massage. I acceded to a few requests, particularly when I saw that the person was actually in pain. With every relief offered, my services came into greater demand.

Am I getting puffed up with this success? I don't know. And then. I am beginning to sense an undercurrent of resentment and even antagonism towards me from some of the other nurses.

***

What's happening to me?
I see Confusion with a capital C.
Churning inside my brain.
Who am I?
Street-sanctified goddess with extraordinary powers?
Channel of a delayed outpouring of the Paraclete's gifts?
Fluke's dazed scapegoat? Freak?
Butt of some divine joke?
Come now Vimla.
But why do you agonize?
What's happening is not extraordinary.
Though you would like to think so.

Shake yourself out of this presumption.
Sister Matron is right. Intuitive TPR is unusual but possible.

I decide to write to Mother Superior in Delhi. About my experiences.
     Promptly, the response:

My *dear Vimla,*

     I am happy to know that you are comfortable in the BB Hospital.
     The episodes you related to me are not unusual. Don't be carried away by them. Without in any way belittling your natural abilities, I must tell you that acupressure or reflexology, though not part of formal medical practice, is being used by a lot of people these days because the relief that it offers is real. From what I have heard from my own acquaintances, the relief is instantaneous but not long lasting. In fact, they tell me that you do not even need to study acupressure to administer it. You of course, know all this and it is important that you try not to exaggerate its importance in your own mind. There are more significant, scientific procedures to which your training will expose you and to which you have to be receptive. You must look forward to that.
     I must caution you in applying all this in the hospital. It will not be looked upon favorably because it will interfere with medical procedures; with diagnoses and treatment.
     About the time when you helped to avoid digital evacuation: that too is not something out of the ordinary. It is the first and most instinctive pediatric trick a mother picks up when her child is

constipated. That of course is only as first aid. Very often it helps. But most of the time, one needs to treat the problem not merely with laxatives and suppositories or enemas but to get at the cause of the problem. I know this because of the basic training in primary health care that we nuns are given.

Even the episode with the high fever that you were able to bring down with a sponge is again not extraordinary. It is common knowledge that very high fevers can be brought down by ice sponges. The fact that you experienced the same symptoms as your patient could be a case of a very sensitive imagination, or it just could be that you are extraordinarily empathic. This is probably a case of what some call "compathy" – a step beyond empathy – the experiencing of another's physical condition. Most people have a little of it. In your case, it seems to be more pronounced, embracing everyone. From what you have told me of your past, I do believe that you are indeed made that way. If that is true, it can be a holy gift that you can put to good use, but it could also be accompanied by problems, the least of them being the pain that you will suffer every time you are with an acutely ill person.

Christina is studying Commerce. She is in the first year of her Graduation, that they call the Std. XIII. Doing fairly well. She shyly told me the other day that she thinks she has fallen in love with a young man in the same class. I wish that brings her some joy.

Preeti misses you, but Christina is doing a good job looking after her. She takes up her lessons at least for 45 minutes every day. Preeti is now in the Std. I.

In this letter, I know that I have put the brakes on some of your feelings, but I do that intentionally to caution you against doing anything that may get you into trouble, though I know that your motivations are all good. Try and find some time to pray, especially *about your work and your gift, but even better, make your work itself a prayer. It will be pleasing to the One who is certainly using you as an instrument of His healing.*

Enjoy yourself, Vimla and God bless you.

With love.
Sr. Angelina

Sister's reply was prophesy. Come too late!

Last week I received a summons from the Superintendent, Dr. Gorakshakhar. I was led into his room by Sister Matron. He did not even ask me to be seated. His look would have made a more faint-hearted person tremble. His pupils were fireballs aimed at me. He raised his already high-pitched voice to a level at which it sounded like that of an angry woman.

"You nonsense girl! What do you think you are doing? Nonsense girl, you! Who do you think you are? Some great doctor or what? A miracle worker or what?" He was screeching now.

I didn't say a word.

"Do you know what problems you can bring on us by your nonsense acupressure, or whatever it is you call that nonsense thing you are doing. You are interfering in the work of the doctors. We cannot allow it."

"It seemed to give them relief," I said weakly, "And they asked for it."

"They will ask for poison. Will you give it to them?"

Dr. Dinshaw had walked into the room. He is a senior consulting physician. Reputed to be one of the best in the city.

A darling of the nurses. Of patients and the resident doctors as well. Great bedside manner and a sense of humour. Teaches us Nursing Medicine. Excellent teacher. He had heard the earlier exchanges.

"Dr. Gorakhshakar is right. Let me explain why," he said in his best classroom manner. "I know you as a good student, and I am sure you will understand. You just said that the patients seemed to get relief from what you are doing, didn't you?"

I nodded without saying a word.

"That relief is a dangerous thing. It helps the illness to hide under that temporary relief. Let me tell you, my girl: I believe that acupressure and other such treatment may give relief. In fact, the next time I have a backache, I may request you to do it for me," he said laughing. "But here in the wards, it is as good as medical sabotage. You know what sabotage is?"

I nodded again, with my head down.

"Sabotage is a criminal offence." His seriousness was punctuated by little smiles that he inserted in between his sentences. "When you interrupt the prescribed treatment with the temporary relief that you are giving, it confounds the efforts of the doctor. It is like putting a thick veil in front of the patient. That is sabotage; a medical crime. But of course, I know that you are not a criminal. You are not even a saboteur. Sabotage is intentional; it is planned destruction. Your intentions were good." A big smile as full stop.

"Good or not good," shouted Dr. Gorakshakhar, visibly put off by Dr. Dinshaw's intervention. "This girl has to be punished. I cannot let her go just like that."

"I'm sorry," I said, trying to look at Dr. Gorakshakhar,

but my eyes resting on Dr. Dinshaw's face instead.

"I don't care for your sorry-vorry nonsense. I'm going to suspend you." He said with finality. I stood motionless, with my head down.

"Why are you standing there like a statue?" he screamed. "Get out of my sight."

As I left the room, I caught a glimpse of Dr. Dinshaw holding out a restraining hand towards the Superintendent.

I walked down the corridor, not knowing which way to go – towards my workstation or back to my hostel. What did suspension mean? I thought of Mother Superior and how she would feel. Looking back at Preeti's father's episode, I thought that she would find a reason to absolve me in her mind. But I was miserable. Head lowered, I walked towards my workstation. I heard behind me the clicking heels of Sister Matron hurry towards me.

"Vimla," she called. "Wait."

I stopped and turned around.

"The Superintendent wants to talk to you," she said. As I followed her back to the dreaded room, she said. "You're lucky that Dr. Dinshaw was there. He has requested Dr. Gorakshakhar to give you another chance."

As we entered the room, I could sense, almost physically, two contrary vibrations. Of anger and comfort. When I looked at the faces of the two doctors there was no doubt which vibration came from where. I looked down at the worn-out floor, which felt kinder than the face behind the desk.

"Look at me," Dr. Gorakshakhar ordered. Slowly I raised my head. "I don't know why I am doing this nonsense thing," he said, shaking his head as if he was annoyed with himself.

And everyone else in the room. After a longish pause, he pointed his finger at me and said, "Do you promise never to do this again?"

I was slow in answering him and I could sense his anger rise. "Yes," I said after a perceptible pause. "I won't do it again."

He looked round the room, at Dr. Dinshaw and Sister Matron and then at me. "I'm giving you one more chance. The next time we catch you doing any nonsense thing like this, you will not be suspended; you will be thrown out."

I knew that I had to thank him for this mighty favour, but I remained silent, head bent, more to avoid looking at his face than from any feeling of remorse or meekness.

Sister Matron left the room with me. As the door was shut behind us, she said, "You're lucky, Vimla. I did not think that Gorakshakhar would have let you go so easily. You better behave yourself now." I know I ought to have been grateful for having escaped the suspension, but I was depressed to the point of sickness, feeling an ache spread from the centre of my chest to my hands and feet and my head. I walked with Matron almost blindly to my workstation. I felt her hand on my shoulder and immediately I sensed a little of that ache melt away. "Cheer up, Vimla. You'll be okay," she said. I put my hand over the hand on my shoulder, grateful for that timely comfort and I said, "Thank you Sister."

Inside her stern exterior, Sister Matron was a kind person.

By the evening, everyone had heard of what had happened. In the canteen, at dinner, I had to listen to a litany of "Lucky you!". It only served to depress me even further. In my room at bedtime, Padmini and Lakshmi continued the "Lucky" chorus, the former with her exclamatory giggle and the latter with hands joined in sanctimonious self-righteousness. I could therefore have hugged Mehnaz when she said, "Bunkum, I tell you. That's all bunkum! that Gorakshakhar is a duffer, I tell you. *Gadhedu che.* He's an ass. Forget it, darrrrling," she said coming to me. Then her eyes lit up into a smile and she said. "Arre, but that Dr. Dinshaw!" She put her fingers to her lips and kissed them with a loud smack and a flourish and said: "he is a real darrrling. Total darrrling che! After all, he is *apro dikraa*, Dinshaw, no?"

Mehnaz's lively intervention helped for a while, but the episode kept me awake for more than half the night. Together with the inevitable resentment against the Superintendent, I found myself indulging in a brutal self-flagellation, emotionally digging into my past and blaming it on the way I was made. I had never been chastised like this before. Not in the convent, not in Mr. Kumar's sex studio and not even on the pavement. On the streets, we were driven away by baton wielding policemen and abusive watchmen, but we took all of that with near-glee, looking at all of it as a game of hide-and-seek. I particularly was a pampered child. Yes, I am a spoiled child shielded behind this questionable label of "gifted." I found myself doing what I hardly ever do during my waking moments – wiping tears streaming down my face.

The very next day we happened to have a class by Dr. Dinshaw. He started the session with a reference to the episode of the previous day.

"I know," he said, "that all of you are talking about what happened yesterday with Vimla in the Superintendent's room. I was there and I would like to clarify the matter for you. This should have been a personal affair, but since you all have heard about it, I would like to put things in perspective. Let's have a little discussion, shall we?"

On the blackboard he wrote two words: RELIEF and REPAIR. He went on to speak about the medical connotations of those two concepts and the importance of both in the treatment of disease. Antipyretics for instance relieve but do not repair, but they help. Many are of the belief that some pain is part of the process of repair and that it is necessary as a means to keep track of the disease. That may not always be so, he said. Then he went on to explain why my well-intentioned attempts to relieve pain were a serious obstacle to diagnosis and healing of patients. He repeated his "sabotage" angle of yesterday and posed a question to the class. "If this was a case of sabotage, what should we have done?" he asked.'

"You should have dismissed her," said Dina, one of the girls in our batch. He paused for more responses.

"You should have suspended her," said Urvashi.

"How many of you wanted her dismissed or suspended?"

He waited long, but no hands were raised.

"How many of you were happy that we didn't do either?"

All hands went up and everyone turned to look at me. Someone started clapping. It was Mehnaz. Soon the whole class was clapping. I sat feeling grateful but embarrassed.

"I see that everyone likes you, Vimla. I am happy about that. But that was not why Dr. Gorakshakhar did not dismiss or suspend her. What do you think was the real reason?"

"To give her another chance," said Padmini, with a giggle.

"Do you think so? Can a hospital take chances like this? Of course we cannot. We were not giving her another chance. We were only being fair. Why do I say so?" He looked round the room for an answer and when he got none, he said, "For the simple reason that it was not really sabotage, which is always done with the intention of damage. Vimla's fault is that she did not know the consequence of what she was doing. Now she does, and if she does it again, she will be expelled on the spot."

Mehnaz raised her hand and asked, "Does this mean that she also cannot do it for us now? She gave me real relief. I'm telling you."

"But of course, she can," he said. "But never in the wards. Now let's get on with our class, shall we?"

After class, I went to up to Dr. Dinshaw before he could leave the room and I thanked him for what he did. He kept his books down on the table and looked at me. He said, "Vimla, my dear. I have been hearing things about you. Not just the acupressure stories, but other things as well. You have a gift, my girl, and with something like that, you would find it difficult to curb the urge to use it. Use it. Not in the wards, but use it. As a doctor, I should be sceptical about all these other methods of healing, but I am not. Whatever helps people is good. You're looking very depressed, my dear. Cheer up. Everything's fine now"

All I could do was thank him again.

My interactions with the patients are electric. Every time I touch a patient, I feel a whirring inside of me. Like a machine that has been switched on. Plugged into the patient. I begin to be attracted in a strange way. Not to the whole person, but to that moving, system of flesh and blood hidden under all that skin. I have felt the same with patients who are difficult and even obnoxious. I relate to the body, not the person (that sounds inhuman, but there it is.) Paradoxically, I cringe a little at the thought of surgery, of seeing and handling all that flesh and blood under the skin. I have not yet assisted at a surgery (I will not be asked to do that for at least a year, I think.) I would rather scan than invade the body. When I am near a patient, all my senses are on alert. In communion with the other. Unconsciously I see-touch-smell-hear his or her condition. And respond to it. I almost cannot stop it from happening. Every day I go round giving injections, enemas and sponges. But more: I find myself experiencing the condition of the patients.

Sexuality is something that confronts us at all times. In many different, often contradictory ways. Nakedness is at home in a hospital. Most times, pain renders the body innocent. Neither patient nor care giver is sensually affected in the least. The pain of the patient and the professionalism of the caregiver are ironclad chastity belts.

Sometimes, however, we have to deal with the rush of uncontrollable arousal among the patients. We see the extreme embarrassment of some of the patients when that happens. They try to hide it from us, turning to the other side and even pushing down the indiscreet part with their hands; shame and remorse written on their faces. I have noticed that it is the younger ones, both male and female, generally teenagers who experience this embarrassment. The older men and women tend to make a show of it. They may even make sexual advances, pulling us down to kiss or fondle us or even worse.

In our nursing classes, we are told to expect this reaction from some patients. We learn to either ignore it. Or if the patient persists with sexually aggressive behaviour to discourage it with firmness – either threatening to report it to the authorities and to the family (this is a more effective scare) or to threaten the stopping of treatment, which in reality, we cannot make good.

We evolve our own methods of handling these situations. Every nurse has a stock of stories to narrate on how she was able to cool the ardour of some patient's gonads.

I was particularly happy, and amused in hindsight, with my first experience of this kind.

The patient was a middle-aged gentleman (I still give him the benefit of that term) admitted for inguinal hernia repair. This is a common surgical procedure and the patient can often be discharged on the same day. My patient however had developed a high fever after being admitted, which according to the diagnosis was nothing more than a viral infection. He therefore could not be operated on that day. He would spend a couple of days before the surgery. During the morning sponge time for the other patients, he requested for a sponge for himself. This would not have been necessary for a patient brought in for only a hernioplasty. He would be well enough to take a shower on his own. However, since he had a fever, I agreed to sponge him, after consulting with the matron.

I did the usual head, face and torso. When it comes to the genitals, we hand over the swab to the patients to do it themselves. Unless they are too weak or unconscious. I gave the swab to the patient and asked him to sponge his genitals. At which he exposed himself. He took my hand in his. He smiled mischievously. I pulled my hand away and gave him the swab again. He took my hand once more. This should have caused me no discomfort at all, and in fact, it did not. I had handled the male equipment as part of my work in the past. But this was a different situation and I had to decide what to do.

I smiled at him and said, "You must be waiting for the surgery to be finished. Aren't you? Don't worry. It is a simple operation, though of course sometimes things can go wrong."

Then I went on to describe to him the surgical procedure. I knew nothing about it at all, not yet having done any surgical nursing. I had happened to read a few chapters on the subject. And of course I had some idea of the surgical anatomy of the hernia in question. But I spoke as if I knew it all, ad-libbing like crazy, using anatomical and surgical terms quite out of context and which meant nothing at all.

"It will be done under local anaesthesia," I told him, "and you will be able to see the whole process. The doctor will even ask you to cough with force while the surgery is being done to see if there is any stress. If there is any stress, there could be problems. Have you ever watched a surgery? Very interesting, but scary. You get frightened just looking at the surgical instruments that cut into your flesh. They don't use big knives or saws or anything like that for hernia operations. They use these very delicate scalpels. Have you seen a scalpel? It is like those cutters you get in stationary shops, those cutters with handles and very thin blades, with sharp points that you break off when they get blunt. The surgeon picks one that is of the correct size and sharpness. Then, he makes a mark with it at the right place in the groin, near the scrotum. Using the right amount of force, he cuts at that exact place. If he cuts too deep or even a little away from the right spot he could cut away your seminal cord, and then, finished! You will not be able to have sex again. It is interesting to see how the cut is made. When the blade enters the skin and goes further down to the flesh, you will first see just a white line showing the fat layer and the flesh. A little after that, the line becomes red and then you see the blood flowing out as if a pipe has burst."

I was going to ad lib a little more–about lateral and cephalad misalignment of the internal ring, about the squeezing of the cremasteric muscle, the exposure of the external oblique aponeuresis and other scary sounding gibberish that I was making up in my mind – but I didn't have to. The fierce little warrior had already become a deflated balloon.

As I opened the curtained enclosure and left the room, I heard a sniffle. I turned around and noticed eyes filled with tears. This time I did not mind seeing a grown man cry.

In my hostel room that night I think about what had happened. Here was this man with a perfectly normal reaction to feminine touch. Aroused, he wanted urgent gratification. Catharsis not quite like Aristotle's, but catharsis nevertheless. I would have given it to him for a fee in Mr. Kumar's establishment. What's different now? Was this prompted merely by hospital ethics? Or had I changed as a person as a result of what had happened to me since then: my relationship with Mother Superior and my new Catholic catechism? Am I now walking blindly along this path just because I was pointed in that direction? Or do I truly believe in what I am doing? How will I respond, for instance, to a Mr. Kumar-type argument: the patient was asking relief. My duty is to give relief. Not from a headache or biliousness, but in this case, from an excessive sexual build-up.

In answer to that, my mind goes back to Mr. Kumar. His own fake tirade against prostitution's answer to excessive sexual build-up: Offering itself as a dumping ground for all that "sexual waste", as he called it. He presented his 'venereal theatre' instead as an aesthetic response to sexual need. That night, as I thought about it, I realized the speciousness of his argument. A diabolical twisting of sin into a rational sweetmeat. He had shifted the focus from a question of purpose and timeliness to one of manner and style, offering the latter as a legitimate outlet for what in reality was that same sexual waste.

Sin, if you must, but do it in style!

In her letter to me on the subject, Mother Superior wrote:

"Mr. Kumar has written his own fantastic gospel as have many others. These will have followers among those who find them attractive, convenient or (who knows?) even sensible. There are, we know, a variety of gospels according to societies, communities and nations and they have their adherents.

You and I have to make a choice, and hopefully we have, between these and the ones that satisfy the demands of your finite reason and those that appeal to the infinity of a lively and divinely inspired faith.

I know that though you have received grace in baptism, you still have to make decisions every day and that upon these decisions depends your physical, emotional and spiritual comfort. You have the filters of the scriptures to help you, and I hope they do.

You do not have to look too hard to see the jagged edges of a Mr. Kumar's sexual aesthetics, put together and held in place by the same slime that he pretends to rant against: the vulgar overflow of excessive sexuality. He is not alone in the justification of licentiousness; society is full of these seductive philosophies.

It needs no theologian to recognize these phonies; it needs plain human sensitivity and a healthy respect for the body as a divine gift. Aesthetics and ethics, goodness and beauty do not necessarily cancel each other out; in fact, together they lend each other an inevitability greater than if they were considered separately, particularly when you look at scriptural ethics.

You'll find a luminescent sexuality presented in the scriptures, right from Genesis 1 and 2 to the New Testament. You see a radiant goodness touched with beauty, the beauty of inevitability; the feeling in your bones that nothing else could be righter, more in place and more in harmony with human nature.

What could be imbued with more poetry and passion than Adam's song of joy at the sight of the first woman: "This at last is bone of my bones and flesh of my flesh." And the writer's comment, "So a man shall leave his mother and father and cleave to his wife. And the two shall become one flesh." Thus with the very creation of Man (both male and female He created them) was born this most wonderful thing, sex, a gift to humanity; this mystical big bang, if you will, that gave birth to all of history.

The conjugal act becomes then an extension of that first gift from the creator, a gift of self of one to the other, of man to woman and woman to man, thus to become an instrument of continuous creation. I find this extraordinarily beautiful, Vimla, because of that feeling of inevitability that it evokes in me. Nothing could be righter.

Nakedness was a glorious thing of which we were not ashamed until the serpent, foreshadowing the Mr. Kumars of all time, designed the logic that led to Shame and the fig leaf.

With that first shamefaced cover-up has sprung the shameless strip tease of subsequent generations, from big city cabarets and all that pornographic muck to the soul-numbing institution of prostitution; the sad abuse of a great gift.

This misplaced sexuality is (you are right Vimla) a gross misplacement, in terms of purpose, persons and time. We are handing it around for the wrong reasons, to the wrong persons at the wrong times; an explanation for unwanted pregnancies, infidelity, venereal disease and prostitution.

A wonderful and precious crystal wine glass that was given for us to use on very special occasions of celebration, we are handing around with soiled fingers to an inebriated crowd to be used as a spittoon. What we are witnessing today is the premature ejaculation of an entire generation, of a people who have not been able to hold their emissions for the right moment.

Nakedness is still glorious and you, Vimla see this

glory every day in the work you are doing with the body –
within the curtained privacy of the sick room, the surgical
theatre, the X-ray theatre and the labor room. You see the
resurrection of this naked body from near-death to
triumphant life.

Nakedness is still beautiful within the love-filled
bedroom of man and wife when the original gift is given
again in conjugal embrace.

As a nurse, you have been entrusted with the
nakedness of so many men and women with a purpose and
I know that you have a sense of a sacred mission for you.
I think you are doing well, my godchild.

I cannot suppress a smile while I congratulate you on
your cleverness in taming your priapic patient. You will
have many more challenges ahead of you, I assure you.

As for news from the convent: I thank God for the robust
health I hide within my frail frame. I am doing well.

Preeti is doing fine, but we have noticed a trait that
worries us a little. She seems to have become a compulsive
liar. She lies not to protect herself, but to entertain. We
have told her that she should not do it, but it is as if she
cannot help herself. And she is extremely inventive. She can
weave a perfectly credible story around the lies she tells, and
very often we do not know what to believe.

As if to perfectly complement her ability to lie, she has her
skill at copying handwriting about which I wrote to you the
last time. The other day, she wrote a letter in Christina's
handwriting to Brian, asking him to meet Christina on that
Sunday at 3 p.m. on the terrace of their college. The poor
fellow waited there in the sun for two whole hours before he

went back home. *He showed her the letter the next day. You couldn't tell the difference between Christina's writing and the letter.*

Say a prayer for the little devil.

I pray for you every day.

God bless you Vimla. And by the way, you will have to excuse my little sermon to you on sexuality. My letters to you are my only pulpit and, in a way my theological stimulus.

Affectionately,

Sr. Angelina

Mother Superior's letters: more than an exchange of news. They are my best counsellors. With little time for reading now, her letters are my literature.

****

Annual leave. I visit the convent.

Small gifts for Preeti, Christina and my godmother. Inexpensive. Dresses for Preeti and Christina from Fashion Street. Books for Mother Superior from the pavement.

Feels good to bond again. I absorb the affection, warm and wonderful around me. Glad to spend time with Preeti. She is doing very well in school. Bright girl. She has taken it upon herself to be the life of the boarding house with her mischief and her funny songs.

Evening. We are all having a pleasant chat session in the parlor with Mother Superior and the other sisters. Preeti limps into the room weeping. She shows us her knee. It looks badly grazed, with broken skin and specks of dirt in between. Blood trickles down to her shin. She holds her knee and cries. Her face twists in pain. Everyone rushes to her side to have a closer look. I dash off to my room, where I have my first aid kit. I quickly take disinfectant, cotton and dusting powder and a half-filled basin of water. I rush back to the parlor.

I find everyone with a strange expression on their faces. I bend down to look at the wound. As I bring the wet cotton to the knee, I see: painted wound! Preeti's masterpiece. Skin as canvas. Realism that would do well on the pavements!

Preeti bursts out laughing. "Fooled you! Fooled you! Fooled you!" she shouts jumping up and down. "You're a nurse now, no? Vimla Aunty. I wanted to give you some work, so you don't get bored." She cannot not stop laughing.

All round amusement. But I see it with concern. It is another form of the Preeti brand of lying. Harmless today. Watch for it tomorrow. My smile curls downward into thought.

Look! My body is a mirror of your body!

I have kept it to myself all this while. The strange experiences I had with my first patients. My body's spontaneous mimicry of their symptoms has continued. My body has become a virtual mirror of my patients' distress. It surprised me at first. I didn't know what was happening. I shared these experiences with only one person - my godmother, Mother Superior.

There were instances almost every day.

I was sponging this lady. She had broken out into an

angry red rash. From her neck down to her arms and chest. She was in utter misery. Kept bruising her skin with her continuous scratching.

Sr. Matron had made her wear gloves to prevent her nails from inflicting more damage. She said she didn't want the sponge. She could not bear anything on her skin.

I was told to add a disinfectant in the water. In this case it had to be cold, not warm. Cold water would at least soothe the bruised skin. I had to apply the prescribed ointment after sponging her.

I was taken aback when I saw her body. The rash looked alive. Ugly. Like tiny creatures on her skin. As I looked at her, I noticed my body slowly mimicking hers. My neck and arms began to get red and feel itchy. I was able, with some effort, to resist the urge to scratch myself. Instead, I went about sponging her. Ran my other hand over the parts just sponged. As I did so, I could feel the cold wet towel on the corresponding parts of my body as well. As if I was sponging myself. As the sponging continued, I noticed that the itchy feeling was gradually getting less on my own body. And so was the coloration. By the time I had finished, I could sense that the same thing was happening to the patient. There was visible relief in the lady's expression and as I opened the tube to squeeze out the ointment, she said, "That may not be needed now. I'm feeling better." But I applied the ointment anyway. The rash had not gone completely – both on her and on me – but it was much less. When I left the room, she smiled and said, "Thank you Sister. You have a very good hand. It feels very good when you do the sponging."

The moment I left her bedside, the rash disappeared

from my body completely and so did the itchy sensation. I was back to normal and continued with sponging the other patients.

The lady's rash came back. But with less severity. It lasted three days – much to the surprise of the doctors. They expected it to last longer. They were happy that the treatment worked so unexpectedly well. During those three days, I continued sponging her. Every day I went through the same mirror experience. But with reducing intensity, as the rash was getting better. I cannot say for sure what helped her to get better so soon. After every sponge, there was visible relief even before applying the ointment. It could be that the disinfectant in the cold water in itself was doing the trick. It could well be again that the ointment and the prescribed tablets agreed with the lady's condition. For the doctors it was one more success. So what if they did not know the cause of the rash.

I could not help feeling that I had something to do with the relief. I decided however not to let anyone know.

It seems like I cannot help myself. Every time I am with a patient, I tend to mirror his or her symptom. With almost the same intensity. This happens mostly when I am sponging them. As my swab goes over a body, my other hand senses irregularities as it passes over the organ under it. I sense changes in temperature and texture: warmth, heaviness, wetness, roughness, sponginess, prickliness; sometimes I even sense colours. At first I thought it was my imagination. Now, after all these months, I am not sure.

I take all this in my stride.

I go about doing my duties as a nurse: making beds, preparing bandages, recording temperature, blood pressure, respiration. Administering enemas, injections, glucose-saline, blood and other drips. Routine work. Maintenance workshop of flesh, blood and bone. But I see myself as more than body mechanic. The patient has now become an extension of my physical being.

***

I have started doing something else lately. A lot of reading. I have shifted focus from the general reading that I love to books on medical and paramedical subjects. I find that this reading surrounds my work with a depth it would otherwise lack. The nursing routine is important alright. But it is a very small cubicle in which I do not have elbowroom. That elbow is my restless mind. It needs more space than that little cubicle of my everyday work. The new reading has enlarged that cubicle for me.

We have a good library in the hospital. It stocks some of the latest journals on nursing and medical practices. Browsing one day, I picked up the Journal of Advanced Nursing. I glanced through a number of articles that I found engaging. I had it issued in my name and kept it for three days.

I see a smirk on the librarian's face every time I ask for one of these books or journals, almost reluctant to issue them in my name. She once asked me if I knew which side up I should hold these books.

Coincidence. I find an article in the Journal of Advanced Nursing that got me excited. It resonated with my personal experience as a nurse. An article on Compathy. A new concept in nursing and psychology. Physical empathy, in which the nurse experiences the symptoms of the patient to provide comfort.

I felt as if I had found my other self. I took down notes. Whole paragraphs in a separate notebook. With references to books and other authors relating to compathy. I remember Sister Godmother mentioning this in her letter to me.

Over the next few days, I was able to find more books on the subject. Other writers on the same subject. Some refer to "contagious patient distress" as a known phenomenon. A technique that can be used by care givers. I read with greed now: McCarthy, Randolph, Durufle. They speak of the transference of pain and the psychosomatic element of pain in general. Another article: a discussion on the approach to childbirth and labour pains. I read too about *courade*. An American Indian custom in which the husband suffers his wife's labour pains to make it easier for her.

It set me thinking.

What if we were all compaths? Born to share another's pain. You mine and mine yours. The mother hurts from the toddler's grazed knee. A whole room breathless with the suffocation of the asthmatic. But then.

Perhaps our bodies got clever. Created their own anaesthesia against the pain of another person.

I read in other books and journals: there are others like me. They experience the symptoms and the pain of others. It helps me feel less like a freak. Keeps me from that audacious presumption of being extraordinarily gifted.

I keep having those experiences of shared distress. Half-clandestinely behind the curtained sponging enclosure. Feeling once again, unreasonable guilt. As if I were consciously doing something wrong. Perhaps I am. I almost take them for granted now. Particularly with patients who are recuperating and whose symptoms are mild and not very painful. With my high threshold of pain, I absorb and repel those symptoms with not too much discomfort. The patient notices nothing. Except when there is a mimicking of external conditions.

More difficult for me to handle are the contradictions between the doctors' diagnoses and the feeling of certainty that my hands receive when they 'scan' the body. Most times my clandestine 'palm scans' correspond to the diagnoses – either initial or final – of the hospital. When that happens, I feel again that inner shower of glad confetti. Science corroborates my non-clinical verdict. Yippee! Clinical laboratory in the palm of my hand! Often, however, I have to smother the hurrahs when the two don't match. Happens. My verdict has turned out wrong. The patient has responded to the prescribed treatment. And still, the contradictions continue to torment me with that glad confetti, because, my 'diagnoses' have proved right most of the time. I use the library as reference guide. I relate symptoms and my scans to clinical conditions mentioned in the books. This is brash, I know. My secret sacrilege.

It has been happening all these months, so help me God.

The only person I could share this with was Mother Superior. This is what she wrote to me in reply:

My dear Vimla,

I have read with interest and I have indeed meditated about everything you have written in your last letter and in the letters before that as well.

I think you need help from a place higher and different from where you and I are standing right now. I really think you do.

Your life is a diamond cut out of the solid crystal of your unusual past. It has been cut uniquely into facets that are again truly rare. You may think that this in itself is enough. It is not. You need another facet, one through which will shine that ray of enlightenment that you need at this hour.

That facet is Prayer. You need enlightenment now, not advice.

On the natural plane, your sympathetic absorption of pain could be seen as nothing more than a psychosomatic condition in which your body gets carried away by a super-active imagination, or the other way around - your imagination gets carried away by a supersensitive body. Your ability to 'diagnose' with your hands is perhaps just a physiological translation of what we call insight, the ability to see or understand clearly what most people cannot, in this case, not with your mind, but with your body; it is a form of sensitivity that is perhaps a little beyond what is needed to feel body temperature, for instance or to note eye, tongue and skin conditions. That's only my guess, but it is the best explanation I can think of.

And yet, what you do might be considered amazing and even miraculous by some. I may call you differently gifted, while others may in fact look upon you as physically challenged, your 'freaky' traits seen as a terrible and tragic handicap. What person in her right mind would consider herself specially blessed to have to bear the sufferings of another's body and after being able to offer relief, not be allowed to talk about it or to be hailed as a healer?

I am telling you all this in order that you may not get puffed up with excessive pride or any feeling of superiority. It is human to do so, but at times like these you and I ought to reach for the divine.

You have an opportunity of raising this purely physical experience to a mystical level.

Only then will you be able to see a transcendental meaning in all this and come away from it every time feeling whole, holy.

Consider how the world has been viewing this creation called the body. The pious and the self-righteous have pointed to it as the seat of crime, heaping on it the "sins of the flesh": passion, adultery, gluttony, immodesty, brute violence and so many others. Subdue the body, we are told; it is the cause of all sin.

What an unholy rejection this view is of that first verdict, of the One who, after having created the Body, male and female said, "It is good"!

It is good, Vimla, gloriously good. When I see on television, for instance, the gymnast doing her perfect ten, the timing of the trapeze artist, the grace of the ballerina, the triumph of human muscle over perilous peak and heavy load, the speed of the sprinter, the endurance of the long-distance runner, the loveliness of the beauty queen... I cannot but applaud like a teenager at a concert and repeat: It is good.

I hear that chorus again in the Song of Songs' lyrical caress of the body.

You may see it in Hindu scripture and the magnificent temple carvings across our country.

I hear it in the mystery of the Incarnation when the Word chose to become – what else – flesh.

I hear it in the promise come down through scripture and enshrined in our Credo: the resurrection of the body.

The body is good. Glorious.

But more, the body has been a channel of grace: in the glory of the resurrection, but before that, in the pain of the Scourging and The Cross.

It is still a channel of grace: in the ecstasy of the conjugal embrace on the one hand and the cleansing pain of the penitent's mortification on the other.

Now do you see a place for your experiences, Vimla? Do you see your body and that of the others entrusted to your care as something truly sacred, a sacrament through which you can channel goodness, healing and indeed graces for your patients and for you?

You can view your situation as through a glass darkly, through the ground glass of the little knowledge and fuzzy science that surrounds the paranormal, or you can view it through the eyes of your faith. And then, who knows, you just might see a clearer picture of your role in the scheme of things.

That is why I began this letter with the need for prayer. I am not talking merely of those pious words that we squeeze in between folded hands on bended knee. I am not even talking about words. I believe, Vimla, that you have the gift of praying even in your silence, and even more in the work you do. Your hands that minister to your patients can be the prayer that will certainly be answered if only you will listen.

God bless you, my girl.

Your Godmother and your friend always,

Sr. Angelina

***

July, Six months later.

Life has been one nice, elongated smile.

Good feeling among all in our batch that earlier batches did not seem to have enjoyed. At least, that's what our seniors tell us. Warmth and sweetness spreads like honey on toast. Everybody is willing to help everybody else. We like each other; at least, I think, most of us do.

I have visited the homes of some of them who have parents living in the city. Mehnaz has a nice home in Jogeshwari, a suburb of Mumbai. It takes almost an hour by the local train to get to her house. She lives in a colony that they call a baug. Hers is called Malcom Baug, a colony of only Parsis, an island of comfortable and good living not far from one of the most crowded stations in the city, and neighbour to a number of buffalo stables or *tabelas*.

I meet her family and her neighbours. The neighbours walk in and out of the open doors of her home. And I begin to understand why Mehnaz is the way she is. All her neighbours are other versions of Mehnaz and her family. They are loud, lively, always laughing, fond of good eating, drinking and constant company. They all speak in the same way when they speak Parsi Gujerati, or what Mehnaz calls Gujirani. It is as if they are singing different verses of the same song. The tune of their speech goes up and down; the high notes almost sounding as if coming from a thin flute and the low notes like a cow's moo. They use almost the same bad Hindi words that we used on the pavements. But they make it part of the Gujirani song with an accent very different from the roadside language. They say Bean Shot and Marder Shot with plenty of Saala thrown in. As a result, they don't sound abusive at all. Rather familiar and affectionate. They are the pepper and salt, happily sprinkled over every sentence to gratify the tongue, so to speak. Mehnaz's uncle, a concert pianist, calls it "the musical appoggiatura to fit the tune of Parsi speech."

There is hardly a time when they are alone. At any time, you will find neighbours dropping in, opening the refrigerator and helping themselves to what there is in there, as if the house were theirs. It is not the same in the other houses I have visited. (The visits to homes of my other nurse friends that I have made in the past two years are my only knowledge of how people live in homes. Had I visited only Mehnaz's home, I would have thought that all homes were open houses like hers.)

"Meet my best friend." Mehnaz introduced me to her family and her neighbours.

Her father said, "Tch sala, bad luck. We wanted to meet her not so good friend. Her best friend will not tell us all the mischief that this *dikri* is doing there with the doctors. What do you say darrrling?" He said slapping his wife on the back.

Darrrling laughed and asked me in mock secrecy, "Any nice young Parsi doctors in the hospital? Any chaanas for Mehnaz?"

I told them about Dr. Dinshaw, but her father brushed him aside and said that he was married. "We don't want any divorce-bivorce *ka jhanjat*," he said.

"You don't worry about me," said Mehnaz. "I know how to catch my own *bakra*."

They don't always speak like this, however. When they sit

down for a serious conversation, they speak English in an accent like Mother Superior's and Mr. Kumar's when he is speaking English. One of their neighbours, Mr. Dhondi told me that there were mainly two kinds of Parsis: Baug Parsis like them and Bangla or Bungalow Parsis.

"We are the nicer Parsis," he said laughing, as if he were telling me a joke. "The Bangla type are the snooty ones, nose a little in the air, as if to smell the vultures before they come. We are simple. We eat hearty, good solid Parsi food with our fingers sometimes. "They eat the same food as we, five days a week, but on Saturdays and Sundays, when they invite guests home, their cooks will make French cuisine, with five courses of very fussy looking small servings with wines and cheese and they will eat with fork and knife. Of course, they are richer, with money that they have inherited from their grandfathers. But a lot of that is changing today. Many Baug Parsis are doing very well in big companies. Some of them have started companies of their own, but they still prefer to stay in the Baug because all their friends are here and they love the life here."

It was the first time I was spoken to like this by an elder. As an equal, and not like a junior. I felt a small shower of confetti inside me at that time.

I was invited to Petula's home as well. Her house was even farther away in the suburbs, in Orlem, Malad, almost an hour-and-a-half by train. Petula's family was different from Mehnaz's. Every one spoke only English, but it was a different kind of English, both in vocabulary and enunciation.

Petula too introduced me as her best friend. The first thing her mother asked me was: "Are you a Catlick?" My "yes" brought a beaming smile on to her face. "Good. At least, our Petula has good best friends," she said.

As you entered their home, there was an altar with pictures of the Sacred Heart of Jesus and the Sacred Heart of Mary. They looked like family portraits. A small electric altar lamp was constantly burning as in a church. The walls were covered with picture frames. There were pictures of St. Jude, St, Anthony and the Pope on the same wall as the altar. The other walls had photographs of the family. There was a picture of their great-grandfather in a coffin, dressed in an expensive suit. The rest of the family stood around it, all dressed in suits and black dresses. Next to it was the wedding photo of Petula's parents.

Petula's mother pointed out to people in the pictures and told me who they were.

"Dis is me and my husband here; dis is my bredder-in-law, he is the manager in his bank, doing very well; dis here is my faader-in-law and his wife. Dey had tree chillen and my husband was the last."

While Mehnaz's home served all meat – chicken and mutton – Petula's home was all fish with rice. Spicy fish curry made with coconut. They also served dried fish, which I had never tasted before. Neither in Mehnaz's or Petula's home was any vegetable served. After lunch, Petula's mother asked Ashley, the younger son to sing. He brought out his guitar. He asked me if I sang. I said that I sang a little.

"Do you know any Connie Francis number," he asked me. I didn't know what he was talking about, not knowing what Connie Francis or even number meant. I shook my head, feeling foolish.

"You don't know any Connie Francis number! What kind of Catlick you are, men? Any udder number you know?" he encouraged. I just shrugged with a smile.

"What do you sing, den?" he asked.

"I sing the songs they sing in church," I said, and he laughed.

He sang many songs. I didn't know any of them, but Petula and her mother joined in. Her father joined in as well. You could see that they were all very proud of Ashley.

We could only do these home visits on our off-days. We did not have fixed off days. And they were not common days for everyone. So only another trainee who had the same day off as I could invite me. I suppose I was invited because I knew nobody in the city. I often wished I could return the favour. Some of them just called me home to meet their parents and have a cup of tea, but every one of these visits made me feel special. For me it was a new experience.

Among a few others, I was invited to Anuradha's home together with Padmini and Lakshmi. Their food was all vegetarian – "pyoor vegetarian", I was reminded by Anuradha's mother, with an emphasis on the "pyoor". We sat on floor mats with our *thali* on a *paata*. Anuradha's mother, who did not eat with us, served us. She kept refilling our *katoris* with dal, *sabzi*, and *vatana* as we ate; frying fresh hot *puris*. Even before we could finish the ones we had, she would pile on more. When I stood up from the meal I felt fully stuffed.

Back home, I ruminate on paper.

Glad confetti, these visits; yes. But they bring on something else.

A fizz. Of Thought? Reflection? Desire? Longing?

Maybe all of that.

Little bubbles that come to the surface and disappear.

Remembered picture: my pavement of Mumbai's millions.

Mechanized marionettes rushing in all directions.

On the conveyor belt of that huge factory, my city.

Now they were freezing into single frames.

Family portraits. Each different from the other.

I step back to look.

I like what I see. Nice. Very nice.

I close my eyes to see my own longing.

Come on imagination.

Draw me a family portrait with me in it.

Blurred outlines and faces.

Is that Preeti, Christina, Monica, Sister Godmother?

And who?

Women, women all women.

I want a family portrait. Like Mehnaz's, Petula's, Anuradha's.

Husband, wife, children.

Husband. Husband?

Word without shape for me. A visual blank.

And then that rogue's gallery of faces from Mr. Kumar's studio.

No. I open my eyes.

I smash the incomplete photo frame against the blackness that fills me.

I write to Mother Superior.

My dearest Godmother,

In a few months, we will finish our training and get our diplomas. After that we will be full-fledged nurses. As you know we have to put in a full year's internship in this hospital as part of our commitment before we start our traineeship. I believe that we will be paid the regular nurse's salary for that period, which will be much more than the stipend I am getting today.

I would like to send you money every month for you to use in the convent in any way you wish. I don't need much money for myself; just a little for my toiletries and now and then, a new salwar khameez. In any case, we can talk about it when I come home for my holidays.

Speaking of coming home, I must tell you about how I have been feeling lately.

I have told you about my visits to my friends' homes. It has got me thinking about family life and my own home. I have been oh so happy with you in the convent, but after I have finished with the hospital, I am on my own. I know that I can always come back to the convent make myself useful. I also know that the convent eventually hopes that people like me have their own families.

I have been thinking. It may not be necessary for me to get married to move out and start a home of my own. After a while, with the money that I earn as a nurse, I would probably be able to rent a small room either in Delhi or Mumbai.

I would like to know what you think and what advice you would like to give me. I trust your judgment more than mine. Of course, none of this is something that will happen soon. There is still more than a year to go before I have to leave this hospital. We'll talk about it when I come home.

I love you, my Godmother.

Your Godchild,

Vimla

Her response:

My Dear Vimla,

You know that this convent, or wherever I am is your home at all times, but I was happy to read your letter. To me it is a sign that your vision is enlarging. Until now, you were under the control of your circumstances – even during the seeming freedom of the streets.

Your life has to have more facets than what the convent and your hospital have been able to offer you. Your relationships with people other than your godmother and your colleagues may turn out to be the most important sources of your happiness. You must cultivate and cherish them.

You also know that we will help you find a good husband for you if you don't do so yourself and if you want us to help you. We have done it for so many of our convent's daughters.

I appreciate your offering to send money regularly, but I would advise you to wait for a while, perhaps until you have finished with your internship. By then you will have a clearer idea of what you want to do and where you would rather live.

There is a possibility of my transfer sometime this year. I do not know where it will be, but wherever that is, you are welcome.

Preeti is turning out to be a very good artist. She still has a strong urge to tell lies. I have tried to channel that into story telling. I have encouraged her to design children's storybooks with her drawings. She has done some excellent ones and I am even thinking of getting someone to publish them. As a book written for children by someone *who is still a child, it could be an attractive idea.*

I hope that the success with her story telling will help in at least subduing the compulsive liar in her.

We are looking forward to your visit.

Affectionately,

Your Godmother,

Sr. Angelina

Seven months later. Vacation time. A nice deep breath after the hyperventilation of hospital work. I revel in the affection of my godmother, Preeti and friends. Christina and I exchange our life stories. Girl talk. We are at the same stages in two different places. She will be graduating soon. Choices pop up, asking to be considered. Her impatience now is for marriage. Brian, her man feels the same. His parents however think it is too early. He must multiply his finances and polish his prospects for the future. Life is different for me. I have one more year to go in the hospital and I do not have any romantic relationship. Christina is a little concerned.

"Don't you feel like holding a boy's hand?" she asked me. "Not any boy, but someone special, someone who is handsome and good. Have you never imagined a boy being nice to you, caressing you, running his fingers through your hair and neck, saying nice things to you, even kissing you?"

"Maybe I am not in the right place for all that. What romance do you expect me to have with patients, nurses and doctors?"

"Aw! Come on Vimla! You have seen nurses who have married their patients and their resident doctors. Not that I am asking you to do that."

"The truth is, Christina, I haven't even felt like it."

In the silence that followed, I could sense Christina trying to put her thoughts into words.

"I don't know if I should ask you, but do you think, it is because of your ... how should I say it?

"My past?"

"Has it made you hate men for ever?"

"I cannot say, but I have never had so much as a romantic heart-beat since then."

"Do you intend staying a spinster?" she asked me.

"I haven't even thought about it," I said. She was thoughtful for a long time. Then she said, "I hope you meet a nice fellow soon. I am so over the moon with Brian. I wish something like that for you."

In the last week of my vacation, Mother Superior was told that she would be transferred to Mumbai, where the Order had a convent and a home like the one in Delhi. I was thrilled. It would mean that I would be able to visit her more easily, on weekends, for instance. I could run to her whenever I needed her help or advice.

****

We are full-fledged nurses now, earning a nurse's salary

Return to the hospital. Same place, different feeling. As if the air we breathe here has changed. I imagine a spring in everyone's step. I see a pasted smile on even Lakshmi's face!

I am assigned to the maternity ward. I had worked here

earlier as a trainee nurse and I loved it. It feels even better now. Every childbirth I assist in is for me hugely rewarding. Outwardly I am just assisting the gynaecologist. We stand there directing the procedure, whisper-shouting "Push!" like enthusiasts at a school tug-of-war event.

Inside me, I find myself experiencing the feelings of both mother and baby. Of giving birth and of being born. I go through the pains and the joyous relief of the birthing process. I feel the pains of labour. Then I hold my breath as I am being pushed from inside the womb to the outside. When finally, the new-born is out, held up and slapped, I find myself gasping for breath at the gush of air being pumped into the baby's lungs - and mine. I hug the just-born bundle in my arms. I feel its tender softness under the wetness of birth, the comforting smell of the womb in my nostrils. I take the baby, wash it thoroughly and as I hold it close to my bosom, I feel the urge to feed it myself. I hand the baby back to the mother as if giving her my own very personal possession. A special gift from me to her.

The odour of innocence, the feel of infant skin on mine, the song of gurgle and cry are all wrapped in my gratitude. I gaze thoughtless at their soft crumpled faces, waiting for them to open their eyes or yawn or make their first movements of freedom. I am touching, smelling, hearing and feasting my eyes on the miracle of new life every day. Yes, I witness Caesarean sections and torn vaginas that have to receive sutures but I have been fortunate. In these three months I have not had to witness a stillbirth or any other mishap that otherwise is quite common in the maternity ward.

***

Short bliss, that. Three months later. I am placed in the drug detoxification ward: snatched out of heaven and hurled into purgatory. Purgatory it is for the ward's patients. The poisons have to be expelled from their drug-soaked bodies; a medical exorcism of chemical devils. An excruciatingly painful process. Deprived of their drugs they gasp as if for their last breath. They plead with tears in their eyes for just one 'fix'. Their withdrawal symptoms are terrible to look at. We see them writhing in pain, with the most painful form of muscle cramps. Violent shaking and tremors, vomiting and sleeplessness for days. They cry like babies. "Kill us," they beg between groans.

Purgatory it is for me, an involuntary mimic of their symptoms. I feel what they are feeling.

Most sad to see are the younger patients; many between the ages of fifteen and twenty-one. Many are from decent families. Their people come to visit them every day. There is an eleven-year-old picked off the streets. When he was brought in, nobody expected him to live. His breathing was hardly noticeable. His skin looked and felt like soiled newspaper. He looked not more than seven years old because he seemed to have stopped growing. It looked as if someone had scooped out his eyeballs and replaced them with glass eyes from some old plastic doll. His eyes were fixed and continuously watering. He was a 'crack' addict, though the others in the ward wondered where he got his 'crack' from.

Fortunately, Chintoo (that's what the others in the ward called him) got better much sooner than some of the older patients. He is still undergoing treatment for his withdrawal symptoms, after which the hospital wants to admit him in an institution that takes care of children like these.

There was a female detox ward as well, but I was assigned to the male ward. There were a number of patients who were foreigners, people who came to India as tourists and stayed to travel all over the country.

Part IV

REDEMPTION

Lachmi's Notebook

The hospital admits an important character in our story. A depressing case.

The senior nurses knew him well. This was the second time in three years that he was brought in. According to hospital records, he was 39 years old. He looked at least 55. He was picked up from the streets by policemen, who took him for dead. They brought him in on a stretcher. He was more a soiled rag than a human being. Skin on bone, he was caked with mud from head to toe. Hair and beard so filled with muck that they looked like clay sculptures attached to his face. His finger and toenails were long, cracked and dirty. He was totally lifeless and it was hard to tell whether he was dead or alive. There was no movement and very little respiration.

I was asked to prepare him for the resident doctor's examination. It was not an easy job. I got the help of the ward boys to clean him up. They laid him sprawling out on the bathroom floor and were going to hose him down with cold water straight from the tap. I stopped them. I asked for two buckets of warm water. The men splashed the water on him as if he were a thing. They had a hard time washing all that mud out of his hair and his beard. They moved his lifeless limbs up and down like levers on some machine. The two buckets were not enough; we needed two more. I need not have, but I helped a little as we dried him with a towel. But for the fact that there was no rigor mortis, this could have been a corpse. One of the ward boys had to sit on the bathroom floor and hold his torso up, while we wiped him dry. You could count every one of his bones.

They dressed him in hospital clothes and laid him on the bed. The doctor who examined him asked that he be immediately put on a glucose drip with electrolytes and be given oxygen to help him breathe. He would most certainly need medication and blood, but that would be given after the relevant tests were done. He recommended the usual blood, urine and stool tests for a start. The consulting physician would have to decide if something more had to be done. Normally, someone as bad as this would have to be admitted directly into the ICU and be treated under anaesthesia, but the hospital couldn't offer scarce and valuable ICU time for a street case like this.

Between the time that the doctor left the room and the drip and oxygen were organized, I stood by the patient's bedside with the curtain drawn. I observed him. His breathing was so slow that you had to wait at least twenty seconds and look intently to notice any but the faintest respiratory movement. As I watched him I began feeling breathless myself. I put my finger on his pulse and kept it there. I ran my other hand slowly above his body, without touching him. My hands sensed under his skin a cold deathlike stillness. I had never experienced anything like this before. At the same time, at almost regular intervals, I felt sensations in my muscles as if a thousand little ants were crawling under my skin. These sensations would come in slow waves while a mild smell of rotting flesh came to my nostrils. I ran my palm over his body again and took deep, deliberate breaths, slowly, consciously counting up to ten for every breath I took in and twelve for every breath out. I was doing a respiration of just three per minute; gradually I increased the rate of my breathing to six, then ten, then fifteen. The glucose electrolytes solution had not yet arrived and I decided to go and get them to hurry. I opened the curtains to go out, but before I left, I looked at his breathing again. He was doing a steady ten to fifteen respirations per minute. I almost did a high five.

When I returned with the glucose and the oxygen cylinder, I was disappointed to see that his breathing had slipped down again – to five per minute. I started the oxygen and inserted the drip in his veins.

The next day I went in to give him a sponge. He was still quite lifeless though his respiration had improved. The oxygen was obviously helping. I had to turn him on his sides without any help from him. The previous day's wash was an imperfect one and he had to be cleaned more thoroughly. He had long, but scanty hair, which now, after the wash could be seen as black with streaks of grey. His beard, scraggly and untidy had even more grey. He had a longish face with a slightly hooked nose. His face was gaunt and his cheeks drawn in.

There wasn't even the flicker of an eyelid as I swabbed his face and neck and the rest of his body. As I did so, I experienced the same symptoms as the previous day, slightly less. I ran my other hand over his body, imagining my energy being transferred to him. I imagined (or was it real?) that as my body was fighting his symptoms within me, his cells were beginning to come to life. I continued swabbing his body. Usually we hand over the swab to the patient to sponge his own genitals, but in this case, since he could not, I did it myself. By the time I came down to his toes, I thought I noticed a slight twitch in his right foot.

Life, I thought, was coming back into this all but dead body. And I had this feeling that it was coming from me. I felt rewarded and drained when I drew open the curtain around his bed.

As I went about attending to the other patients in the ward, I thought there was a change in me that day. I experienced the "contagion" of the patients' symptoms much less than on other days. One of the teenagers, called Brandon was writhing in pain. As usual, I went over to him to see if I could help, but I did not experience his pain with the same intensity as I did before. I think I managed to soothe his pain a bit, but I felt too drained of energy to do more.

This is a difficult ward. As I sat at my station, I told myself that I ought to take hold of myself and control the sympathetic contagion. I could not let it happen and hope to stay healthy for long. The doctors too may notice what is happening and I could get into trouble again. At this stage of my career, I did not want that to happen.

In the evening before I left the ward for the day, the ward boys handed me a dirty haversack. It belonged to the new patient. In it there was an old unwashed shirt and trouser. In the trouser pocket there was a broken rosary. I found a few other articles in his bag that surprised me. There was a ballpoint pen, a number of pencils of different kinds, brushes and tubes of oil paint and watercolours. There were four sketchbooks with drawings and sheets of drawing paper with portraits, nudes and landscapes. He had written with a bold hand his name on each of the books: John.

What was an artist like him doing on the streets, I wondered? As I dug into the bag, I found a couple of notebooks, a little bigger than the ones I use. I flipped through one of them not intending to read it. I noticed something peculiar. It was written in English, but there were no punctuations at all. The whole thing was one sentence with no full stops, commas or semicolons. It appeared to be a memoir because it was written in the first person. I began to read. It seemed like a collection of prayers. But the prayers were so personal, that I could see the person of this John peeping through it. You would have thought that the absence of punctuation would make the writing unreadable. On the contrary, it had a feel of racy spontaneity and innocence that quite fascinated me as a form of writing. I kept the notebooks back into the haversack, but I told myself that I had to read the whole notebook, if I had the opportunity to do so.

In our hostel room that night. I narrated my story. The soiled rag as new patient – about the haversack and what I found there. That was stimulus enough for the imagination of all three. Particularly Lakshmi and Padmini.

"Artist's material. Notebooks with prayers. Funny, no?" giggly Padmini.

"He must be robberman," offered Lakshmi. "These drug addict people will do what-what things to get money for drug. Even kill. You take care, Vimla."

"This is big mystery detective story," the giggle said.

"How do you know if all that work is his own – the drawings and the writing?" Mehnaz asked.

"I was able to just glance at parts of the writing," I told them, "and I feel pretty sure that it has been written by him."

"We'll know tomorrow." Said Mehnaz.

***

I become washerwoman of an enigmatic bag

John regained consciousness on his fourth day in hospital. The first thing he said on opening his eyes was a feeble "Thank you, sister." He spoke very softly and very little; just a "Yes" and "No" to questions, because with consciousness came his withdrawal symptoms. He seemed to have a higher threshold of pain than most others, because all you could hear was a controlled but continuous groan as he clutched at his stomach. At times he would have hallucinations and would talk to the walls. He would point to the door and say softly "Leave me, leave me now." Or he would join his hands and say, "Please, I do not want to see you here. Why have you come" Sometimes he would just laugh quietly to himself and sometimes cry.

His withdrawal symptoms became less acute after a week of medication. Though he was moving around, he had to carry his drip with him.

From the fifth day itself, he said that he did not need to be sponged. He would have a shower on his own. He wanted to be left to himself. Preferred to do everything on his own, except of course, the administration of the drip, the medication and the routine checks. The doctor would examine him – his eyes, reflexes, and weight – and prescribe changes in procedures and medication when necessary. After every examination, he would smile and politely thank him. Even during his withdrawal, he was the least troublesome of the patients in the ward.

A week later, after he had taken his shower he asked, "Where's my bag?" It was on the side table and I pointed it out to him.

"That's not mine," he said and then looked closely at it again to make sure. He did not recognize his own bag. It looked different. That's because on the previous evening, I saw the bag lying there, filthy as sackcloth rolled in muck. I thought of all those beautiful drawings and notebooks inside and had a sudden urge to have the bag washed. Like a response to an itch that needed scratching. My mind revolted at reconciling that dirty backpack with what was inside it. I wrapped the backpack in newspaper and took it to my hostel, washed it thoroughly myself and let it dry the whole night. There was a dirty shirt and trouser too. I removed the broken rosary that was in his trouser pocket, and wrapped the trouser and shirt up in another newspaper with the intention of sending it to the laundry. I brought the washed bag to the ward the next morning and when he was still asleep, kept it back on the table.

In the meantime, I read everything in the two notebooks. They were like the notebooks that I am writing. Very different in style, though. They were in the form of personal prayers based on what was happening in his life. Those prayers became for me a prism through which I could see his life story. An engaging story. This is what I saw: an extraordinarily brilliant young man belonging to a middle class Catholic family. Knowledgeable beyond his years. Far above the others in his class and in his age group. An excellent student. A good writer. A good speaker, winning prizes in elocution and public speaking. He had a gift for drawing and the visual arts.

Everyone expected him to collect a string of impressive university degrees and be a corporate leader or a rich and famous person. They were all disappointed when he decided to become an artist. He was totally caught up with the images that he said were swirling in his imagination. He just had to put them down on paper. He got himself an art degree after five years of study and later got himself a job. The turning point in his life seemed to be his meeting with an English hippie artist and his girlfriend. They introduced him to the world of psychedelic drugs and everything else that went with that culture – free living, free thinking, free sex and the spirit of peaceful rebellion. It was not merely an attraction. It seemed an involuntary happening, in which he did not have any control of what he was doing. He stopped going home to his family. He lived in the small, dark and dingy rooms rented by his hippie companions.

Inevitability. He earned the anger of his father, who in a fit of rage turned him out of the house. Later, his family seemed to have made a few attempts to bring him back home, but he was so swallowed up in his psychedelic madness, that he ignored all their invitations. His family had made plans to leave India and settle down in Australia and they were offering to take him with them. He turned his back on all their entreaties. He left the city for a while to be free of them. When he returned to the city, his family had already left the country.

He got hooked on to all forms of drugs, smoked, sniffed and injected. For years he roamed the streets with the hippies in that hazy state of drug-induced unreality. In time his addictive companions left the country for their own. He was left wandering on the streets of Bombay. He took shelter wherever he could, with pavement dwellers as his companions. To many of them, he was their guru. He was unable to give up his addiction. Picked up more than once by the police from the streets and brought to the hospital in an unconscious state.

The story was not narrated as I am doing it here. They peeped through from the prayers that he penned from time to time in his notebook. Intense expressions of his thoughts and feelings, mostly the latter. Sometimes devout, often angry. Prayers that beat his own breast and fought with God. The prayers were written in one continuous stream of passionate feeling, written without punctuation, sounding more like poetry than prose. As I read them, I felt the rushing emotions of this strange man of the streets.

***

It took him a little while to recognize his own bag lying there on the table where I had left it. Before he could say anything, I left the ward and went to my workstation. A few minutes later he walked over to where I was.

"Somebody has washed my bag." He said.

Guiltily I confessed. "I did."

"Then you saw what was in it. You read the notebooks." He said it as if he hoped that it was not true.

I nodded.

"I wish you had not," he said in a soft, pained voice.

"I could not help it. I glanced at a few lines at first, and then couldn't stop reading. Your writing moved me. I have never seen prayers like those before, and you write so very beautifully." I said, not merely to excuse myself and make him feel good, but because I really thought so.

"They were not meant to be read; not even by me," he said speaking slowly as if he was writing every word in his head before speaking it. "They were not even meant to be written. Those notebooks are my own private confessional between my God and me, and like a confession, not to be visited again. I wrote them out only to give some sort of form to the way I felt at that moment." He closed his eyes hard, as if he was trying to shut off the vision of something he didn't want to see.

He continued in the same soft, slightly pained voice, "I know that the hospital had to strip my body naked in order to wash me of my visible sins, but did you have to see my naked soul?" he asked with his eyes still tightly shut and a voice that was barely louder than a whisper.

I was dumb; no words coming to my mind. I could ignore his feelings. I imagine that most nurses would. To everyone he was nothing more than a beggar picked up from the streets. He ought to be grateful that he was alive and that we were taking care of him free of cost. What right did he have to fine and fancy feelings like these?

But I remembered his notebook and some of the sentiments expressed in his prayers. I looked at his pained expression. At that moment the words that came out of me were not mere words.

"I am sorry. I am very sorry."

He opened his eyes and looked at me. "Please," he said. "I don't want you to say that. More important, please do not feel sorry. I know that you did not mean to hurt me."

"I should not have read it." I said, with my head bowed down.

"Sister," he said softly and I looked up at him. "I want to tell you something that may surprise you."

He paused before he resumed speaking. He spoke slowly, softly. "I have been here before and I know what a hospital is like. I know its smells. I recognize the feeling in the eyes of the doctors and nurses. I bless them for what they are doing. But there's something about this time around that is different. I don't know how long I was in limbo. Or even how long I have been here. but at some time during that cloudy state, I felt a presence around me and I know now that it was yours. You may laugh at what I am about to tell you, but I felt as if this presence was absorbing all my pain and in exchange giving me my breath back. I could feel hands sponging me, and I think they were yours. It was not the usual sponge. It was life giving. I felt energy moving from you to me like warm milk. Do you believe me?" He asked.

I nodded.

"Do you believe that I was imagining things because of the state in which I was?"

"It could be, but I don't think so. I believe it was real."

"Why do you say that?"

Maybe I should have stopped myself, but it just came out. "Because that is what I experienced myself," I told him. "I felt your pain, the muscle cramps, the tremors and your lifelessness. After I had absorbed it all, I felt my energy move from me to you."

He looked at me for a few seconds before his eyes seemed to lose focus.

"Do you know?" he said, "this is more than just a physical experience; more than a bodily experience. It is an out-of-body, a mystical experience for me. I should feel thankful, but it is not gratitude... It is as if there is something..." he did not complete his sentence. He remained silent for a long time. Then he said, "I don't know." And he walked away with his head bowed down.

The next day, he came toward the nurses' station. Nobody else was there with me. He walked past me. And then slowly turned back.

"Yesterday you were telling me that you felt my pain and my lifelessness and that you also felt your energy move into me. Have you felt like that before?" he asked.

I paused to consider if I should tell him. Then I said, "All the time. It is part of my constitution, I think; a burden you could call it, or a blessing; I don't know."

"Do you know how or why it happens?" he asked.

"I don't know. But I'm guessing," I told him. "The first part - the sharing of distress - is what I have come to know now as compathy. There have been others who have experienced it. I have read about it."

"Have you developed this ... faculty consciously? Or...."

"No. I have always had it. It is the other part that has me confused. The part in which I seem to transfer healing and relief to the patient. It could be that it is just the result of my wishful thinking. It could be that the patient gets relief because of other natural reasons. And I attribute it to my interaction with him or her. A silly presumption. I don't know."

"It is no presumption, I assure you. I did feel your energy

seep into me."

"One thing I know. I have a very high threshold of pain. An unusually good immune system. I have an extraordinary ability to fight disease. I have never been sick. And even if I bruise myself badly, I never need to take medicine. My body handles it without help. And then, I suspect I have a crazy imagination. So strong, that the images in my brain get transferred on to my body. When I see a sick person, my body mimics that person's condition. When I take on the symptoms of another, I believe that my body fights those symptoms for the other person. I get healed of the transferred symptoms because of my extraordinary immune system. Then those healed symptoms get transferred back. At least, I think that is what happens. I am not sure. It's only my wild guess. I have not discussed it with a doctor or anybody else, except with my godmother, who is a nun."

"Incredible," he said. "Do you do it consciously?"

"I confess that I do. I will it to happen. I have to consciously pass on energy waves from me to the other person. Again, this is very presumptuous of me."

"Did you do it consciously for me?" he asked.

Shyly, I nodded.

He looked at the drip attached to his veins and then looked at me. "This drip and all the medicine I get is all very good, Sister," he said. "But the breath I breathe today belongs to you."

He walked slowly back to his ward.

***

Sister Godmother's letter: she has been appointed Mother General of her Order – the Myrrh Bearers or "The Marys of Magdala", or the MOMs for short. She will be based in Vasai, a suburb of Mumbai, where she will have her Generalate.

She has asked me to pray for her. Her responsibility now is even greater. She has charge of all the convents of the order in India. There are four of them – one each in Mumbai, Delhi, Aurangabad and Mangalore. She believes that her order needs to do much more today. She too spoke about AIDS and how it would call for much more love and service from the sisters of her Order. She sees a situation where there will be many more orphans, who themselves have a chance of being HIV positive and therefore with very little time to live. These are the children of sex workers, who need to be taken away from their mothers and cared for separately. They are children who will have to suffer for no fault of theirs. Even if they are infected and destined to die, they deserve the healing hand of God that the sisters have to lovingly extend to them.

She informed me that Preeti was doing well and that she no longer needed any supervision from any senior orphan or boarder. In fact, Sister Godmother believed that in a year or two, Preeti herself could take on the responsibility of looking after an orphan child. This would be good for her.

I felt those glad confetti inside me again. I was thrilled about Sister's transfer to Mumbai. I decided that I would visit her as often as I could, though Vasai is a long train ride from our hospital. I promised her all the help that I could give, particularly in the new challenge as she sees it.

Monica has moved to Aurangabad for her Postulancy. She assures me that I am constantly in her prayers.

***

A week later. Life in this ward is challenging.
I receive a most unusual letter

Difficult ward this. More than the others in which I have worked. When the patients are not writhing in pain, they are plotting to outwit us. A game of catch-me-if-you-can. Constantly thinking of clever ways of smuggling their addictive substances into the ward. They try to bribe the ward boys, or bluff them, inventing the most believable lies. Some attempt escape. They have to be strapped to their beds. After a few such episodes, they tend to calm down and try other strategies. The nurses have to work in tandem with the psychiatric counsellors on the one hand and the ward boys on the other. At times, it is necessary for us to keep an eye on the ward boys as well, who will, for a good enough incentive, give the patients what they want – from something as simple as a cigarette, which is forbidden, to injection drugs and needles. The more difficult ones are the paying patients, pampered sons of rich parents. They throw tantrums to extract money out of their visiting relatives.

The treatment and procedure for each patient differs according to the substance to which they are addicted and the length of addiction. Some of them, particularly the ones who can pay, might go through the Rapid Opiate Detoxification (ROD) process that is done under anaesthesia and sedatives if the patient is unconscious as was the case with John. If John could have afforded it, he would certainly have gone through the ROD, which makes the process easier and, some believe, more effective. He, of course, pulled through without the ROD. Many of the medicines given to control withdrawal are themselves made from the same chemicals that go into the addictive drugs. They must be given with caution and careful monitoring. We control the rate of flow of the drip. Particularly of medications like methadone because it can result in an overdose. Sometimes the patients slyly increase the flow themselves for faster relief. We have to keep a watchful eye over them.

After a week or so of withdrawal, the patients are able to move about with their drips attached. They may be kept in the ward for anywhere from three to six weeks after withdrawal. During this time, they are given counselling and psychiatric treatment. This may sometimes include ECTs or shock therapy.

***

One evening, last week, when I was leaving the ward after my duty, John handed me some folded sheets of paper. I saw that they were torn from one of his notebooks. I was going to open and read them there itself but he stopped me. "Read it in your room," he said. "It is the first thing I have written since I came to the hospital. You have read my prayers. This is not one of them. But it comes from the same font of feeling. I hope you will not be offended."

I couldn't wait to go to my room. I had a quick wash and dressed for dinner. Before I left for the canteen, I sat down to read what he had written. After the first reading, I felt I had to read it again, not just to get used to his unusual style of writing, but to take in its full meaning:

Here I sit asking myself how I should speak to the Breath I have borrowed and to the Channel of that life given to me today and I wonder how I should do all of that without being brash or irreverent or even without using the petty vocabulary of gratitude and selfish concern for health of skin and bone yes yes my own sickening skin and sickly bone and of the daily arithmetic of my wellbeing that others measure with calibration and mercurial numbers but You with the rhythm of your own heartbeat yes and of that warm Comfort seeping into my veins not via needles and tubes but from the aura of Your Presence while I pray to the diminishing cells in my body to remember and to pass on in their history books the story of how once upon a terrible time made holy they saw resurrection because You or was it He had chosen to scourge your own body in mystical imitation of Isaiah's prophetic Stripes by which we are healed Oh Sister Breath it is good that You do not count Your Gift as gift so that by His grace it becomes flesh and blood and respiration for those who need it so bless You and Your ignorance of self while I pray for my own self-control to resist an excessive wanting for a nearness of You or for a lingering of the moments when your daily fingers on my wrist read the messages of my ventricles while I wonder nervously whether systole and diastole can divulge the secrets of the breast together with those numbers that You have to record on a chart and when You walk away from my bedside I wonder if You can see that sentimental sinew stretching between my bedside and Your departing feet to breaking point as You leave the ward leaving me with my remembrance of who I am and where I belong and filling me with thoughts of worth and worthlessness and the poetry of Fate and the divine ditties of improbability that my life has had to sing from those first stanzas of half-forgotten innocence right up to today's verses of mystic wonder and hope because it is now not just the flesh that has risen from the grave but with it the spirit which now needs to be led into a new sunshine to celebrate His gift given through Your hands so now I vow from this breath and this word onward to walk away from the darkness of my addiction into the light of His kindness shone in my direction like a torch held by You yes Sister Healer I make this promise to Him and to You so help me God

It felt as if I had read the whole piece without exhaling. When I finished, I read it again. I smoothed out the folds in the sheets and kept them flat inside my own notebook.

In the canteen I had my dinner alone. Oblivious of what I was eating. The words I had just read streamed through my mind like a scroll in a movie. I read a hundred meanings into what he had written. I walked back to the hostel alone. Back in my room, his words kept scrolling in my head. I tried to imagine what he was thinking when he wrote them. Or was he thinking at all? Writing like that does not come from thinking, I told myself. Nor is it meant to get you thinking. It is as if the words had lost their way in a maze of non-meaning. Attached themselves to a cloud of sensations and feelings that could not be communicated, only partially expressed.

A disturbing thought crossed my mind: could it be drug-induced? Was he getting his substances secretly from someone? I dismissed the thought as an improbability. He was one of those whom nobody visited. He also did not show any signs of having taken any drugs. And then there was that very sincere sounding promise at the end of the piece to give up his addiction.

I was snatched away from my thoughts by Lakshmi's "You're very quiet today. There is something worrying you."

"Oh, nothing," I said, feeling as if I was caught doing something shameful.

"Khee-khee-khee, she's calculating her savings," said Padmini, who had a gift for the silly.

"Why can't you leave her alone?" said Mehnaz. "Just because we share a room is no reason for us to keep our brains open for everyone to see what's going on in there."

That night I lay awake composing a response to John's note, which I thought deserved a reply. I could, of course, just pass it off with a casual thank you, but I decided to write.

In the morning, before I left for the ward, I wrote my reply:

I started with a Dear John, but after having written the whole letter, I decided to cut that out. For a nurse-patient relationship, that seemed a little out-of-place. This is the final version:

I admire your writing, but even more, I appreciate what the words convey.

You show me too much kindness. What I did for you, I would have done for any other patient. It was perhaps because you were brought into the hospital in a condition that needed some extra care that I did what I did. I was only doing my duty. I do believe, however, and this is only my belief, that my unusual constitutional condition did help you recover faster. I say this because I could feel it while I was at your bedside. But then that often happens involuntarily even with other patients.

I must say too, that you are more than just a good patient. You are unlike anyone I have nursed before. I think that you are a good man. Everybody else here thinks so too. You have

something in you that makes me feel happy to be your nurse. I
feel strangely rewarded even when I do little things like taking
your temperature. So, please do not be grateful for what I do.
I am a nurse and you are my patient. I want you to get better.
I care for you.

Vimla

Even after I gave it to him, I was in two minds: should I
have deleted the last line. I left it unchanged because it
expressed how I felt. I thought there was nothing wrong in
that. I handed him the reply at the time I was doing the
routine recording of TPR. He asked my permission to read it
while I was doing my job. By the time I had finished, he had
read the note. He took my hand and gently kissed it. This was
something that many patients do. But for some reason, this
felt special to me.

The visiting consultant was happy with John's progress.
At this rate he could be discharged in another week or so. His
survival was a surprise in the first place. Now, having passed
that stage, he seems to be on the fast road to recovery.

My brain swirls with contradictions. Good news becomes
my depressant. His impending discharge turns into a cloud of
gloom. I try to shake off the feeling. John's quiet presence
during this short time in the hospital seemed to have done
something to me. His soft, stainless utterances have stayed in
my memory.

What's happening to me?

The next day, during the routine recording of TPR, I ask
what his plans are. He tells me that he isn't thinking about it.

He has decided about just one thing – he will not get back to his addiction. Just as he had promised in his note to me. He knows from past experience that it will be not be easy, but there is a feeling within him that this time around it will be different.

"Why do you think so?" I ask him. After a long silence, he says, "My motivation is different and stronger today."

"What do you mean," I ask.

"It may be difficult for someone else to understand this," he says, "but my motives for giving up my addiction until now were self-centred. It all had to do with self-pity, which is a soul-numbing experience, not enough to beat addiction."

"So, what is different today?" I ask, not quite seeing the point he is making.

"My motivation today stems from outside myself," he says.

"I still don't understand."

He smiles. Very softly, "I don't want to talk about it now, but I am putting myself and my resolve on trial."

***

I made the TPR entries in his chart and left his bedside, but it was as if I had left something unfinished. Like a puzzle I was not able to solve, an essay I had left half-written. But then, what business was it of mine? I asked myself. Why should it matter to me whether or not he went back to his addiction? Did I feel, at the back of my mind that it would be a waste of my personal contribution to his recovery? Would I feel the same for any other patient?

Later in the day, he himself came to the nurses' station when no one else was around.

"I hope I was not rude to you in the morning," he said. "I did not mean to be. It is just that I am truly feeling my way through the rest of my life. Perhaps that's the way it has always been. I have gone where my feet, my heart and my fate have led me. They have not always led me to happiness or even comfort, but they have taken me closer to what I am inside me. It is hard for me to explain this. My own family would not understand."

"I am sorry if I was asking you questions that were no business of mine," I said.

"On the contrary," he said. "If anyone has a right to ask me those questions, it is you. I meant every word in that note I wrote you."

"So did I, in my note to you," I said. "I do care for what happens to you now. Have you thought of where you will go after being discharged?"

"No, I have not given that a thought. I don't need to. I know that I will step out of the hospital and right out into my dwelling place of all these years, the pavements of this city."

If only he knew! The pavement was my home more than his. I had to keep myself from telling him that. I knew what life on the streets was like. In hindsight, I saw it all. The grime, the crime, the moment-to-moment uncertainty, the grab-and-run ruthlessness of relationships and transactions. And the freedom. To do what one felt like doing. The paradoxical availability of personal space, both horizontal and vertical. Not the claustrophobia of four walls and a roof. I had come out of all that, to a life that was rewarding. I am happy about the change, the feeling of personal achievement, of being able to read the great writers and to at least aspire to write like some of them. I believe that my life is better now. John's story is quite the opposite. A sad story. He ought to go back to where he once belonged, I thought and I said it.

"Isn't this the chance for you to go back to where you once belonged," I told him. "Not to life on the streets. Not to the same people, the same unhealthy living, the same addiction. All the time you spent here and all the good that may have been done will have been wasted."

"That will not happen. I promised you that."

"Look for a small room to live in? Find paying guest or hostel accommodation." I said as if writing a prescription that I did not understand myself. "With your talents, John, you could find enough work to pay for a decent life."

"I don't want to lead a decent life, as you call it, Sister."

He spoke slowly. He spaced out his sentences as if he were reading out from a screen on which the letters appeared one by one. I will write it down as he spoke it. Each line separated from another by feeling-filled silences.

"I want to live my life inside out.

Most of the life I see is being lived outside-in.

In which the outside, with all its tangles is forced into our insides.

Into our souls.

It is probably right for most people, but not for me.

It is a choice of inkpots and paper.

Do I want to use my inner spirit as inkpot or as paper?

Should I dip into my spirit and write on the ruled sheets of the world?

Or should I dip my pen into the sticky inkwell of the world to write out the script of my inner life?

I choose to live on the outside the life that's there inside me.

The only outside that will allow me to do that is out there on the pavements.

There may be other places in the world that could be right, but for now, the nearest outside for me is there on the side of the streets."

It was as if I was being shaken out of my sanity. I could hardly make sense of what he was saying. And again, that same worry crossed my mind: had his brain been affected by all those years of addiction? Was his mind losing its grip on reality? Yet amid these fears, I thought I saw through the mists. Contours of a meaning more luminous though more distant and blurred than the easily accessible shapes of common reasoning.

Not knowing how to respond to such a fuzzy line of thought, I asked: "Why do you think that the pavement is the right outside, as you call it, the right sheet of paper on which you will write out your script?"

He smiled as if he was now enjoying the conversation.

"You choose your paper depending on what you want to do with it.

I see what you call decent living as so much graph paper. Ruled sheets with blue and red lines to help you do the writing needed for decent living.

That's very good, but I choose the openness of the blank sheet, preferably handmade.

So I can write, scribble, draw or paint on it with pen and ink, with a brush, with my fingers or anything at all.

What matters is what's inside me.

The ink, the paint, the shades, the viscosity and the dilution.

The pavement is blank, handmade paper, very rough sometimes, but still for me, very liberating to work on."

"But then, John," I ventured to take his analogy further into a debate. "There other pens and brushes splashing their own colours and scribbling their own vulgar ideas on that same blank, handmade paper. Where does that leave you?"

"I don't know if you have played this game in school: you have one person splash paint on a piece of paper, or even do a shapeless scribble.

"Your challenge is to add a spot of colour or just a few lines to transform that patch of nonsense into something beautiful or meaningful.

"I used to enjoy playing the game. I still do, as you can see.

"In many ways it is a metaphor for the Incarnation. Think about it."

He indeed left me thinking.

***

Something is happening inside of me.

Like clear, clean water made turbid by a drop of spreading glue.

I shake off the thought of it.
Deny that it is happening.
Futile, the effort.
The turbidity swirls inside. Keeps me awake at nights.
Is this me? Vimla Lachmi?
I am not I. Not now.
Or else how could it be?
I have fallen in love.

Now I have said it.

How could I? I have never felt like this with any other man.

This John. Why is he on my mind?

Like an indelible stain on my brain.

In my bosom. In the way of my vision.

A translucence through which I see everything else.

John. John. John. John.

Why? And how?

I have never had feelings of any kind for any man. Neither emotional nor physical. Strange, given the life I have led. Men, many men have walked in and out of it. And that not very long ago. They walked in, scribbled on the ledger that was my body and walked out. Scribbles in stinky ink. A blur of featureless faces. Yellowing teeth. Nasal hair. Halitosis. Body odour. Sweat. Stubble. Biceps. Triceps. Abs. Bellies. Flab. Erections. Bodies more than men. Except, perhaps... Wait... this one very young schoolboy, Prashant Lobo. Liked him, yes. That too merely because of a mild appreciation of the sensitivity that set him apart from the others. Even with him there was no affection. Not the slightest feelings of sexuality.

Compathy? Did I have it then? With the men? I was not aware of it. But I was able to 'see' the extent of their arousal. Even before they unbuttoned. I could put a finger on just those muscles that needed to be relieved of their tautness. With the objectivity of a doctor. Ignored their inarticulate sounds of relief and animal pleasure. I did not need Mr. Kumar's persistent instruction: keep emotions out of the business. I had no feelings at all for the men we serviced. His pseudo-aesthetic brainwashing: we were engaged in a form of art. Not vulgar whoring. A form of theatre, a script we enacted. Much like any Hollywood actress opening her mouth in passionate invitation to the actor's hungry kisses. Making believe she is making love to him and to him alone. And then in another and yet another movie does the same with other actors, other scripted lovers. Giving audiences the impression of intense emotion, when in truth there is none. The kiss, more than fornication signifies passion.

Thus for me, my past encounters with men were just scribbled sheets of paper. A plausible explanation for my emotional and sexual numbness.

So, how can this be? I have fallen in love with John. I have tried in vain to tell myself that it is not true. When I see him in the ward or when attending to him during my nursing duties, I have to rein in my feelings to stop myself from doing or saying anything rash before everyone in the ward. I have not told anyone about it ~ not Sister Godmother or Mehnaz or even myself until this moment. Now that I have put it down in writing, I feel I have embarrassed myself. Like a boil I have just discovered on my person. Perhaps because at the back of my mind, there is a feeling of hopelessness surrounding the whole thing. The other girls like Christina, Petula or Mehnaz thrill to the thought of falling in love. Why don't I? Am I not entitled to the same joys of romance with which the others seem to be blest?

John was kept in hospital for a week longer than was intended. A couple of days before his discharge, Dr. Tambe, his consultant physician thought it would be a good idea to use him as a case study. His unusually quick recovery meant that the hospital was doing something right. It would be useful to extract out of this case, the factors that made for so much success. After a week of studying the line of treatment and the patient's response to changes, they were not able to see any significant correlation between treatment and response. It was decided that there was no point in keeping him any longer. John will be discharged the day after tomorrow.

John and I have been talking to each other a lot. I find myself wanting to be with him all the time. I look for excuses to go to his bedside or the bed next to his. Even that is not necessary, now that he can walk around without his drip attached. I am not sure if the other nurses notice anything going on between us. I am not even sure if John himself is conscious of my feelings. He never stops talking about how precious I am to him. About that very special "sentimental sinew" that attaches me to him. But never any show of romance. No talk of love.

This sudden wake-up of my slumbering heart is uncomfortable. These stirrings are new. Heartbeats gone berserk; beating inside a perplexed body that won't listen to my heart. I feel like grabbing his hand. Oh so often! Telling him what I feel. In those three trite worn out words. I love you. That I want to spend the rest of my life with him. I have not been able to work up the courage. Or even the line of conversation that could lead up to something as bold as that. My past work did not need that line of conversation. Prostitutes don't propose. But I am a nurse now. And I am in love.

Two days from now, he will be out of the hospital and out of my life. The very thought of it fills me with a hopeless depression. For the first time in these four years, my mind is not on my work. I have been doing my duties almost mechanically and that makes me feel terrible.

***

Two days later

John was discharged at noon. He went away taking with him his only possessions ~ his sketches and notebooks inside that haversack I had washed when he first came in. He wore the shirt and trousers I had got back from the laundry. So he looked more decent (I know that he would hate to identify with that description) than when he was brought in. Before leaving, he shook hands with his doctors and with all the nurses in the ward. He had designed small cards, half the size of his palm, to give each one, all expressing his sincere gratitude for what they had done. Small, minimalist line drawings representing various forms of resurrection. In one of them, for instance, the cover page showed a dead tree; the inside showed the same tree in glorious leaf splendour. In another, a half-dead bird in the palm of a hand was followed by the same bird in flight; simple almost obvious drawings ~ given another dimension of meaning by his surprising turn of phrase. He met me separately and gave me a sketch of myself, with the line at the bottom: With your breath, I breathe today. He kissed my hand as he handed it to me. I surprised myself when I did the same. I took his hand to my lips and kept it there for some time.

"I will miss you," he said softly. "Because I hope never to come here again."

"I hope you will never need to," I said, trying to find the right things to say. "But can you not visit us?"

"That I can. But I don't think I will."

I hesitated before I said it: "I would like to meet you some time. Can we?"

"You know, Sister. I do not have an address."

"That makes it easier, doesn't it?"

"It probably does," he said with his head down.

"Where do you think you will be from now on?"

"I don't know. Anywhere. That's my address."

"We could meet at the waterfront across Churchgate Station."

Hesitantly he said. "We could."

"Tomorrow evening. It's my day off."

As he left the ward, the nurses waved goodbye with much fondness. His little cards would be preserved more than some of the expensive gifts they received from the richer patients.

Two weeks later.

I really don't know what exactly happened in the following narration.

Make of it what you will.

I have been meeting John almost every day since his discharge. After duty hours, I rush through my dinner and take the bus to Churchgate. We meet at the waterfront and take a walk. Or just sit on the parapet wall facing the sea. On the first day, we just walked and talked as if conversation was all that we were after. Inside me however I was restless and impatient to express my feelings. I found myself wishing I had some past romantic experience to prompt me. How do I do all the things I feel like doing with him: reaching out and holding his hand? Or sidling close to him? Or even saying the things I feel like saying?

As we sat next to each other, I sensed his body wanting to touch me. I could feel the tension of his holding back as well. It was I, not he, on the first evening itself, who made bold to take his hand and keep it in mine. That was our first show of romantic intent. He let his hand rest in mine while we continued sitting in silence.

I would rush back before our hostel deadline. I would lie in bed and stay awake for hours. Going through the emotions of the evening. Imagining the things I would say and do when I met him the next day. I found it hard to go beyond the first day's demonstration of feeling. Even in the wild freedom of the nocturnal mind, I moved very slowly. From holding his hand to snuggling close to his body. To putting my arms around him. When in my imagination I kissed him ever so softly on his cheek, I had to shake the vision away as being impossible. I couldn't do it, I told myself. He might be offended. It might just mar the poetry of the moment, which I thought for him was the essence of that mutual experience. I went back to designing in my mind a whole new sequence. One that would lead to a tender, more intimate and sensual expression of my feeling for him.

For one who had learned to play a man's body like a musical instrument, I was as good as paralyzed.

I confess to lying awake then and thinking of those lectures of Mr. Kumar and Noor Jehan. Of sexual technique, and the specious art of his venereal theatre. His chart of erogenous zones. Of visual and dermal stimulation. Of male sexuality and our own personal experiences with men. The toughest of them being like wax flutes in our hands. Ready to melt if we blew too hot. When I could do it for so many, why could I not show the same mastery now with this one man in my life? That was when I shuddered at the sacrilege of associating that memory with the sanctity of what I was going through. I opened my eyes and looked around the darkness of the room to block any further thoughts in that direction.

The nurses and the doctors are now aware of what is happening. Sr. Matron called me to her room and spoke to me.

"Stop this madness," she said. "I cannot understand how a smart and sensible girl like you can lose your mind so completely. What's happening, Vimla?"

"I love him." I said simply.

"That's rubbish. How can you fall in love with a person you don't even know?"

"I know him, Sister. I feel I know him very well."

"How can that be? He's been here only a few weeks."

"He's an extraordinary person, Sister."

"Nonsense," she said, "he is from the gutters".

Strangely those words didn't hurt me. Nothing anybody said could stain my feeling for John. He held an inviolable place in my heart.

All the other nurses have the same thing to say. It is interesting to note the amazing similarity in everyone's thought and vocabulary. I listen to them in silence and in order not to prolong my own discomfort, I agree with them about my loss of sanity.

John himself is maddeningly passive in our romantic overtures. He lets me hold his hand. Never reaches out himself. Hands clasped in each other's. I sense in him a physical tension, a desire to go beyond holding hands. It is a feeling that fills me to the brim.

A whole week of my going out together. I could contain myself no longer. I had to steer this feeling towards something more palpable.

It was my day off and I was able to meet him in the afternoon, after lunch. I persuaded him to take a bus to land's end at Warden Road. Better known as Scandal Point. Popular venue for the city's lovers. Their point of public privacy. We spent a long time strolling along Warden Road, oblivious of its ostentatious stores of vulgar glitter. Towards evening, we walked towards the sea. As usual, I took his hand and kept it in mine.

The sun was poised to make its slow dive into the water. It blushed slightly as did the few clouds flirting with it on its descent. It was low tide and the sea had receded towards the horizon leaving a shimmering scribble of flaming sunshine on the wet sand. Jagged rows of black rock smudged the watercolour effect of the evening. Behind some of the rocks, there were couples borrowing a few moments of intimate privacy.

I held fast to John's hand. I led him towards the horizon away from the crowds. Footwear in our free hands, we walked some distance and sat behind one of the rocks. I sidled as close to him as I could to feel the warmth of his flesh.

We sat staring silently at the horizon as a wet, translucent crimson dripped slowly from sky to waterline and on to my consciousness, which was slowly fading out into a hazy reflection of the shimmering shore, blurring the borders between sleep and waking; the distance to the horizon becoming for me an infinite space in time - hours, days, weeks, ~ in which I experienced sensations, happenings that I wanted to go on for ever. That sunshiny scribble was sketching animated sequences for me in which I was playing a live-action role, sensuous, pleasurable, real.

Even now, as I write, I do not know if I was awake or asleep or what happened in that space and that time.

I realized that my eyes were shut. When I opened them, I was lying on his lap. The water had come right up to where we sat. We were wet up to our waist. I looked up at John's face and experienced a moment of blissful intimacy.

"Something happened," I said.

"You fell asleep," he told me, smiling.

"It was not sleep. Something else... something was happening to me ... to us..."

"The sunset was beautiful," he said.

I looked into his eyes as if I would find something there. He just gazed back into my eyes. I looked at the horizon then. Cloudy fingers, stained with sunshine were dipping a fiery wafer into the water.

"We have to rush. We're late!" he said.

We almost ran back to the road. I decided to take a taxi back to my hostel. I was late, a good ten minutes after evening bell. Sister Matron saw me enter.

"Where were you? she asked. "You're all wet!"

"I took a bus to Warden Road."

"Scandal Point, for sure. John was with you, wasn't he?"

I nodded. "Yes, he was." She shook her head in an attitude of frustrated incomprehension and walked away.

I changed into dry clothes to get ready for dinner. I was completely wet, waist down. More than wetness, I still experienced sensations in my body that left me puzzled.

Sleep came late that night, dodged by visualizations of the evening. I tried to recreate; to break up into clear-cut images the experience of that sunset. I felt sure that something had happened in that state of wakeful sleep on the rocks. Could it be that John had ... but no. How could that be? A terrible thought struck me then. Did he give me one of those drugs? Had he gone back to them? Would he have done that to me? They were all in the realm of possibilities, I thought; not probability.

We met again the next evening at the Churchgate seafront. We sat on the parapet facing the water. I wanted to ask him what happened the previous evening. He sat there, silent, not even holding my hand.

"Last evening..." I began.

"A slice of heaven," he said, not looking at me.

"What happened?"

"It was a heavenly sunset and you looked like divinity," he said.

"Nothing happened?" I asked.

"Everything happened. Inside me."

"I mean ... nothing happened ... outside?"

"Nothing but the sunset. And you. You fell asleep and I took you on my lap. It was beautiful."

"Was that all?"

"What more could I ask for?"

Still puzzled, I reached out for his hand. We sat like that for I don't know how long, saying nothing to each other.

Then, not able to hold back any longer, I said it: "John, I love you. I have never felt like this for any other man before and I love you with all the feeling that is in me. I hope you know that."

He didn't say anything for a long time. "John." It was as if I was waking him up.

He looked at me then. "That is what I feared," he said. "I was hoping that it would not be so; that you would not feel what I am feeling; that I would hold that feeling tightly within me and not let you or anyone else know my own love for you."

"But why would you want to do that?" I asked, surprised.

"I cannot bear to see you hurt," he said. "Look, Sister..."

"Vimla," I interrupted him. "I am no longer Sister to you. I have told you that, but you still persist...I am Vimla, who loves you, John, you should know that."

"I know. And yet... look at me. Look at where I live. I cannot drag you from where you are down to where I am."

After a long silence, during which my mind was in a whirl, I said, "Can we sit down and have a chai somewhere? I want to talk to you."

We walked to a small restaurant and sat near a window at a table that had only two chairs.

"What I am going to tell you, will shock you," I said. "And I want it to." We ordered our cups of tea. "You should know, John, that while you have come from a good and decent family, it is I who come from the pavements."

He looked at me as if the meaning of what I had said had not sunk in. He just looked at me with almost no expression.

I continued.

"I was born on the pavements of this city. I do not know who my parents are. Unlike you, I have lived my entire childhood on the streets."

When he still did not say anything, I told him my story, leaving nothing out: my life on the streets, my time in Mr. Kumar's establishment my escape and then the convent and the nursing course. We sat there for more than two hours, calling for more cups of tea, while he listened to the story of my life with a sense more of wonderment than shock. He did not ask any questions. He just sat there and listened. When I had finished, I took his hand again in mine and said:

"Don't you see? Destiny has written this script out for us. Just for us. You and I from opposite sides of life. We have raced towards each other all these years. Like those lovers in the movies. Now we find ourselves here at this point together. It is for a purpose. Don't you think?"

"It is for a purpose." He said, "But I don't see it as you do. I see it differently. I believe that you have been specially chosen; lifted up, like Moses from the bulrushes and taken to the house of the Pharaohs, where you have a mission. I think it is beautiful. I cannot interfere with that mission and drag you down to the streets again."

"Why should you think about it like that?" I argued. "I need not end up on the streets again; neither do you. Perhaps my mission is to take you out of the streets and into a life where you can use all those gifts given you." I paused to see what he would say. I could see that he was thinking and that he was uncomfortable with what was going on in his mind.

I continued: "I have a little money saved up now. We could

get married and move into a small one-room house in the suburbs, even if it is on rent. I think we could make a good life together. Think about it John."

"I am not going to think about it," he said, as I paid the chai bill. "Thinking will not help. I have to follow my heart."

We parted promising to meet the next day.

When I reached the hostel, I was exhausted; too tired even for dinner. Mehnaz, Padmini and Lakshmi had finished their dinner and were chatting away in our room. They knew I had come from my meeting with John. I spent a few minutes awake with them and excused myself, saying I was tired and that I wanted to sleep.

I don't even remember my head touching the pillow before I went dead to the world.

***

Now the somnambulant pen does some sleepwriting.
Breaking those tangled visions into verbal pizzicato

Sun streaming straight into my eyes
As we sit on that parapet wall.
A bright blindness that makes me hold up the question to the light?
Will you, John? I ask. Will you?
Yes, he says.
Yes, I ask?
Yes, he says again.
You said yes exclamation.
I said yes full stop.

Unmindful of sun in my eyes and the eyes of a hundred
strollers in the sunset
I kiss that Yes on the lips.
Say yes again, I plead and he says yes.
And I kiss that second yes and a third.
How many Yeses with kisses fly into the setting sun
I don't know
Because he said yes he will marry me
Yes yes yes he will marry me.
And I write out the happy ever after with my finger in the
clouds
We walk without talking
Only saying our yeses and then
when we have exhausted that
New one-word thesaurus of ecstasy
I say let's take a bus.

So we take a double-decker.
Sit in the upper deck holding hands.
Where? Asks the conductor.
Wherever we say and I pay the fare to Wherever.
This is where we will live, said John.
On Tomorrow's top moving deck.
And we will go where the bus goes, said I.
To the last stop, he said.
To the last stop I said.
But there is a first stop I said.
What's that he asked.
Marriage I said.
What'll you wear, I asked.

Will you trim your beard and comb your hair?
And will you wear a dark suit and black shiny shoes
And a bright cheery smile for a change, my John?
And he laughed
(I promise you, he laughed, for the first time, he laughed)
And said: that's another husband you are talking of.
Oh I said, then you can come as you are.
Or let me buy you a nice new *churidar* kurta set, ok John?
And I will wear my nurse's white uniform.
And who will be your best man and my bridesmaid? I
asked.
Can you be your own bridesmaid? He asked.
Can you be your own best man, so it will be you who kisses
the bride? I said.
And thus we nothing-talked right up to the last stop.
We did not get off there.
We kept sitting even after everyone else had gone.
Aren't you getting off? The conductor asked.
No, we said. We are taking another ride.
Another fare and we were on our way back.
Who needs a house? I said.
We have a double-floor moving roof over our head.
And then I stopped and grew silent for a second.

We need a house, John.
We will want to do more than sit and hold hands, won't we?
Oh there's so much I want to do with you!
And the thought picked up speed with the flying
lampposts and the first floor balconies that went past us at eye
level.

We looked inside them and wondered which of those
could be like ours?

And before long we were back to where we had boarded.

We unclasped our fingers as I went one way and John the
other.

I have to sleepwrite of the next day
When we meet at the Victoria Gardens, not far from the
hospital.

And within five minutes of being there I know
It was a dream place for lovers:
Cool, welcoming benches and shady lawns under clusters
of trees
Telling you: this is your own place.
So we sit down on the lawns near the monkeys' cage
Far away from the vulgar gaze of curious human eyeballs.
I lean on my right elbow, John on his left,
Monkeys in their cages in front of us.

And still those bright sunrays in my eyes.
We turn, he to the left, I to the right.
Find ourselves face-to-face. Lip-to-lip,
Victoria Gardens our Eden,
Loud chatter of monkeys.
Four pairs on their elbows in their cages
Face-to-face and lip-to-lip,
Show their teeth in mocking laughter.
And we, offended by that simian desecration of our
conjoined sanctity,
Pick ourselves up and move on.

From dance of peacock to roar of lion
Stretching their caged circumferences
To miles of wishful freedom.
All suddenly transformed for us
Into hardcover parables of what is and what can be.
Metaphors for madmen and mystics.

And so the somnambulant ink traces the bliss
Of many months of bus rides and waterfront walks and
chats in chai shops
Until that day when I walk down the aisle
In my nurse's uniform washed and ironed to bridal
whiteness
Led to the altar by Fr. Mathoor;
And John on Sister Godmother's arm
In white kurta and churidar and *kolhapuri* chappals.
And Christina and Monica and Preeti and Mehnaz
And Sister Matron and Dr. Dinshaw and
Padmini and Lakshmi
And Swami Mudaliar.
All in happy attendance
And the Magdalene choir singing the Magnificat
'The Lord has done marvels for me, holy is His name
And the Sanskrit, *Vande Satchitanandam*'.

The bright sunrays still in my eyes.

The thin wires of gold slipped into our fingers with soft
"I dos."
Beautiful. Very beautiful. And for me heaven.

All the way to when they had all gone home.
And we are left alone.
John and I in our little room made ready
With new bedcovers and soft pillows inviting us
To the embrace I dreamed of and longed for all these
months.
With trembling fingers I latch the windows shut.
An incense of unknowing fills the room and our senses.
Softly covering our slow nakedness
His hands on my skin and mine on his.
Fingers in my hair and on my face and neck.
Palms around my breasts, my back.
Hands down my thighs and legs.
And even now that sunray in my eyes
Breaking up visions of me and him and that incense cloud
What's mine and his lost in that cloud of ignorant bliss.
Whose hands are these? His or mine? Whose thighs?
Whose legs?
Where are my lips? My tongue? Where his?
My body is not where I am.
It zooms heavenward in a warm tunnel of unknown
pleasure
And comes crashing down again and up again
Sending thrills down a spine that's not even there.
And John; I feel his feeling and his flesh with mine.
Flesh and sinew melt and then float outward and then
inward
And then outward and then inward again.
Like a giant bubble that gets bigger and bigger
Filling up the nothingness that is me

Causing me to sing and shout in the tongue I do not have:

Shalyala mala gazula blanga shalyala glamula re

Shalyala mruna laka demba thralla mlazu mlazu rana re

Shamaleeshamaleeshamaleeshaleeshamalee

Yes yes yes yes yes yes yes!

And the giant balloon now bigger than I can hold within me

Bursts into a million droplets that move out into space

Catching the iridescence of some thousand-hued rainbow

Filling the universe

Looking like ten thousand diwali rockets gone crazy.

And blinded still by that sunray in my eyes,

I wake up with a start.

Right in front of me is the light bulb in our hostel room, still on, shining in my eyes. I look around and see Mehnaz, Padmini and Lakshmi staring at me with a strange look. Padmini looks as if she is suppressing a giggle but is holding her tongue.

"You were dreaming," Mehnaz finally said.

"You were making those kind of noises," said Padmini, this time without a giggle.

"It looked like you were doing it... with someone," said Lakshmi.

"What's the time?" I asked.

"It's just 10.15. You were asleep for five minutes."

"Just five minutes!" I was surprised. The dream seemed like it took months. My throat was parched. I got up to go for a glass of water, but Mehnaz, who had left the room, came in with a glass.

"Here," she said. "You must be thirsty."

"How do you know?" I asked as I took it.

"I know," she said. Then she whispered in my ear," I'm not a virgin like you are." And then she told everyone in the room "I think we better go to sleep now. *Batti band karo.*"

I was grateful for the sensitivity of my roommates in leaving me alone. They switched off the light a little after that and went to bed. I lay awake thinking of Mehnaz's last words. Virgin, she had said.

In many ways she was right, even in her ignorance of the Guddi part of my history. In all those years of "work," I had not experienced anything like this. If an or-gasm it was today, this was my first, with a man who wasn't there.

Next evening, I took the bus after duty hours to keep my appointment. When I got to the waterfront, I was met there not by John, but by a muscular hunk of a man who introduced himself as Dondu. He was waiting for me where John usually did. He had over his shoulders a boot polish stand. He handed me a sealed envelope addressed to "Sister Vimla". He informed me that John would not meet me today. When I asked him if he would meet me on some other day, he told me that he didn't know. He bowed as if to an employer and left almost running.

I tore open the envelope and read the contents of the letter.

I will not even try my dearest to unravel the tangles of my unreasoning heart that has me hanging on a cross of contradiction with my right hand nailed to your love and the other fixed to an unknown destiny to which I will not drag you my dearest and thus in this painful suspension between heaven and hell with earth nowhere in sight I leave you and go to a place where you will not find me and

I do not want you to try and God knows that on some day of redemption our paths may meet again for a grace filled togetherness and until then remember your own John whose love for you is strong and unending

I could hardly stand. I walked jelly-kneed to the parapet wall. Sat there with that note in my hand, enveloped in a blankness. Not a thought crossed my mind. I was without a shred of feeling. Just a blackness that became grey and turned to a glowing white as I sat, facing the traffic and the crowds but not seeing them. I don't know how long I sat. When I stood up to go, I felt as if it were an image of me standing up, leaving the real me sitting there on that parapet wall forever.

A week later

Letter from Sister Godmother. I had decided to write instead of talking to her on the phone. I told her everything that had happened.

My dearest Godchild,

I feel your pain. As I sat in the chapel and meditated on what you told me, it was as if I myself had fallen in love and had been hurt. It is hard to bear, I know. And to a questioning mind, it is cruel, unfair. But this is the madness of divinity. The pain that is given to you has to be tweaked to become your redemption. It is not easy to do this tweaking. But pray, Vimla and you will see the light.

John could not have been your husband or anyone's husband. He is a mystic and a monk though he may not know it, and the pavement is his monastery. His struggle with his own spirit has led him to this place that could well be his station of redemption. You and I have to find ours, and I am convinced that whatever is happening in our life

is going to lead us to it.
Prayerfully and with much love,
Your Godmother,
Sr. Angelina

Six weeks later. I think I am pregnant.

My periods are six weeks late. Morning sickness. I wake up retching. The whole day I am nauseous. My breasts feel tender. Something is growing inside me. I can feel it. John's resurrection inside me. A contradiction of feelings. Alleluia I feel sick!

I have never had a day's illness in my life. If I did have a fever or a stomach upset, I never suffered any discomfort from it. Even external wounds were nothing.

I was told this: one night, (and I vaguely remember this) when I was a little girl, just learning to walk, I fell against a thorny bush. I was extricated from the thorns, body very badly bruised. Bleeding profusely. I didn't let out even a whimper, they said. Just looked curiously at all that torn flesh. Wiped the blood away with my hands. It was late at night; no way of finding any medication. They just washed me and put me to sleep. The next day, the shock: my wounds had formed healthy scars and were already on the way to being healed.

This morning sickness is the first time that I am experiencing my own illness. Illness? Sickness? All these years as a nurse, I have only "suffered" the contagious distress of my patients. My body has fought the pain and the symptoms for them. This is the first time I find myself submitting to my own symptoms. Not severe, but they are there the whole day. More in the mornings.

Nothing. All that's nothing for a person with a very high threshold of pain.

The real discomfort is in my head, not my womb. In my mind not my body. I find myself struggling to reconcile my joys of pregnancy with my unspoken idealism. Confusion.

I desired to give me body totally to John. On the day we were married and not before that. It would be my wedding gift to him and his to me. Something too precious and special for us to have before our day of commitment. Any pre-nuptial "giving" of my body would have ugly associations. With my work in Mr. Kumar's establishment. And therefore a sacrilegious devaluation of the gift. I do not know if I would have felt this way if I did not have the whorehouse written into my flesh's memory.

I am expecting a baby and I do not know how this can be. I try to remember if anything happened to result in my pregnancy. Was that night a dream or was it a reliving of something that actually happened? That sensuous sunset at Scandal Point. Did it happen there? Did he in fact drug me and take me? Improbable. But then, how do I account for this impossibility - my pregnancy? Suddenly the past few months seem a blur to me. I am unable to differentiate between the real and the imagined. I am strangely happy and confused at the same time.

Everybody in the hostel knows what is happening. They are shocked. Not just my roommates. Our entire batch of nurses and the resident doctors and interns cannot believe that I could "do such a thing". Some of them take me aside and advise me to get rid of it before it gets difficult. Six weeks is no problem, they tell me. It can be done here itself and everything will be fine.

Mehnaz too cannot believe it. She was absolutely convinced that I was a virgin till this happened. "I could believe it of anybody but you." She said. "In any case, it has happened and nobody but you should decide what to do about it. Don't listen to all these people. Do what your heart tells you to do and if you need any help, remember that I am with you."

The hospital administration has not said anything yet. I am sure that I will not be allowed to work beyond a certain period of pregnancy. Until then I should be fine. In any case, there are only three months more for our internship and after that some of us will leave for other jobs.

I had told Sister Godmother that I would like to work in the hospital at Magdalene Home. I could help in the maternity and general hospital and I could help with her plan to care for the children of AIDS affected mothers.

She is happy to have me. The hospital may not be able to pay me as much as other hospitals. But at least, I will have accommodation. I tell her that money is the last thing on my mind, now that marriage and family life is out of the reckoning.

I do not know how to break the news of my pregnancy to her, but I have to do it. I have never kept anything from her and I know that, whatever I do, her response will be prompted by her love for me. I will not speak to her about it. I have decided to write and tell her everything, but I will wait for a while.

A week later.

Earlier this week, Sister Matron called me into her cubicle.

"Shouldn't you be doing a pregnancy test?" She asked.

"Maybe," I said and added, "All the symptoms clearly indicate pregnancy, Sister.

"It is better to be sure," she said.

"You ought to do a proper gynaecological check-up, which would include a pregnancy test. As an intern attached to this hospital, you will not be charged for services and even for medication. "

She arranged for me to see Dr. Mrs. Patkar, of the obstetrics department.

"Do you want to go ahead with the pregnancy if the test is positive" the doctor asked.

"Yes." I said.

She gave me a list of dos and don'ts and an exercise chart.

Sister Matron has moved me back to the maternity ward.

I wrote to Sister Godmother, telling her everything.

A month later.

My pregnancy is now showing. Showing off. My uniform is uncomfortably tight for me. Need to have new ones made or alter the ones I am using now. Patients ask me when the baby is due.

Sister Matron wants to see me.

"Hello Vimla. How's he or she doing?"

I cradle the balloon with both hands.

Caress the tight uniform.

"Good. I've had no trouble."

"Very good," she said smiling. "I've got good news for

you."

"What's that?"

"Mrs. Pinto."

Mrs. Pinto was the hospital counsellor. Why Mrs. Pinto, I wondered.

"Why Mrs. Pinto?" I asked.

"The obstetrician is taking a special interest in your case. Wants all to go well."

After a pause, "You're going to be a single parent. Not easy to go through it alone."

"So?"

"A little pre-natal counselling. Don't worry, you won't have to pay for it."

I am surprised and grateful. The hospital is taking an interest in my pregnancy. Not charging a paisa for anything.

Mrs. Pinto is eiderdown. A gentle and warm personality. When I entered the room, she stood up from her chair and came towards me. As if I were a friend.

I would put her on the plump side of healthy. On the fair side of a wheat complexion. She has a roundish face and the beginning of a double chin. She enveloped me in a warm embrace. She then held me at arm's length and looked at me as if at a painting she admired. Gently she put a hand on my stomach as if patting a baby's head.

"Nice." She said. "Must be a wonderful feeling."

"It's one of the best things that has happened to me," I told her.

"Please make yourself comfortable," she said, offering me a seat.

"I ask a lot of questions," she said with a ringing laugh.

"My husband says I talk too much. But that is my job."

She did ask a lot of questions. I did not have to answer all of them she said. Only the ones I was comfortable with. She spoke to me like an older friend. It was almost like girl talk. How did I meet John? Was it love at first sight? How long was the romance? And about the pregnancy. Quite naturally she shifted from girl talk to concern. She talked to me about my plans after the internship and of how I would manage as a single parent without the child's father.

After a few sessions, I found myself talking very freely with her, almost as I would have done with Sister Godmother.

"I am in touch with Dr. Mrs. Patkar," she told me. "She wants to be a little surer about the maturity of the pregnancy."

She made me do little breathing exercises and some exercises in visualization.

"Try to think back," she said gently. "Did you have intercourse more than once? Do you remember if it was close to ovulation?"

Patiently she guided me backward in time. Helped me visualize each event as I went along. Every meeting with John. I told her about my strange experience at Scandal Point. The extraordinarily coherent and vivid dream. Of plans for my marriage. The nuptial ceremony. The conjugal act. My very first orgasm All of it so real. I told her about my disappointment the next day when I found that John had gone away leaving me with the letter. She asked me how I felt about him. I told her that my feeling for him had not changed in the least.

As these sessions progressed, I found myself feeling strangely unsure of myself. Mrs. Pinto was very sensitive to my feelings and gentle in her approach. She kept saying "how beautiful!" and "how sweet!" Even telling me that my love was a gift that I should cherish. I spent hours at night going over the events of the past few months in detail. All of which left me feeling terribly confused.

After the last session, which was yesterday, she told me that Dr. Mrs. Patkar wanted to do an ultra-sound imaging of the uterus. Just to make sure that everything was all right.

Tomorrow has been fixed for this ultra-sound imaging.

***

The Next day

Life has been sucked out of me. That ultra-sound was cruel. Displaying the swollen void that was my womb. Pseudocyesis. Hysterical pregnancy. False pregnancy as truth. Hysterical laughter at my gaping ovarian emptiness.

My last day in the hospital.

Keep churning, you big, ruthless cement mixer. Pulverize all thought, feeling and sensation within me like so much crushable rock and rubble. I weep no longer. You've used all my tears in the churning.

I come to know the truth now: it was Sister Godmother who asked the hospital authorities for the test. She, the all-knowing didn't need ultra-sound to see. My womb was in my head. And it lied to me. Deceived my body.

Clever she. And kind in her own way. She didn't want to tell me herself, because she knew it would depress me greatly.

And so: enter Mrs. Pinto, the counsellor to prepare me for

ultrasonic truth.

Evening. I walk over to the Gloria Church. Submit my knee to the last pew. I utter no prayer. Vaguely remember.

My tears a cataract down my cheeks. My mind a blank. My eyes shut.

Hours of blinding bright white, lachrymose vacancy, nothingness. Two. Three. Four.

How many hours, I don't know.

"It's late, my child." A hand on my shoulder speaks close to my ear. I look up at the cassocked face, smiling down at me. "The sacristan wants to shut the doors."

It is dark outside.

I stand up and smile at the priest. I thank him and leave the church.

Peace like a balloon, envelopes me as I walk past the traffic.

Our last day in the hospital. Internship over.

Bittersweet bubbles of emotion burst at the farewell party. Excitement of going out as full-fledged nurses. The pain of parting. Exchange of addresses and promises to keep in touch.

Some have decided to take on a job here in this hospital itself. Some have got jobs elsewhere. Nurses from other cities have got jobs in the hospitals there.

Mehnaz will join a group of paramedics doing work in the villages. She plans to work there for at least three months before doing something else. Padmini and Lskhsmi have got jobs in the Middle East. Petula is getting married to a distant relative who lives in America. She will get married and leave with him to live in America.

I will work in the hospitals of the Magdalene Home in Vasai, I tell them, tripping blindly on an uncertainty. Just to be able to give them an answer to their questions. The way forward is lost in a misty swirl of thought and emotion. I, a mind and body person find myself overnight blinded by a heart that I have never really encountered before. Days and nights have become a continuum of cloudy opacity. I seem to be moving about and doing things unconsciously like a sleepwalker. And yet I sense a hammering out of another future in my brain, a feeling that something is being given shape even while I do my sleepwalking.

Late one night I find myself at Magdalene Home. Did I sleepwalk to this place? I think not considering the determined steps I took to get here. Sister Godmother must have had a premonition of my coming. Or did she eavesdrop on my mind? She has a room ready for me. We sit and talk until midnight. The misty swirls of all these days dissolve slowly into a new openness. I see faintly, but getting clearer a different horizon.

I go to bed exhausted. Hit the pillow as if it is Sleep itself.

The next morning. After the Eucharistic Celebration, I go to see Sister Godmother in her office, the Office of Mother General.

"Godmother," I say as I sit in the chair in front of her. "I have come to tell you that I want to be a Myrrh Bearer, a Mary of Magdala. A MOM. I want to be a nun."

Part V

THE PEDESTAL

Sr. Angelina's Notebook

Why? Why? Why?
Why am I so sceptical?

VIMLA'S DECISION to become a nun was a thunderbolt. Not just the shock. It troubled me. It falsified my understanding of the girl. I would never have thought of her as an escapist, and this from all outward appearances, at least, seemed like a running away from reality. The motivation for her decision seemed out of character, spurred mainly by John's decision to go away. Of course, there have been countless "vocations" as a result of broken love affairs, but I did not see Vimla doing such a thing.

"Why?" I asked her. "Why are you doing this?"

"I don't have a simple answer," she said. "I know that you are looking for motivation, Godmother and I understand that it is important for you to know."

"Is it because of John's decision not to marry?"

"Yes and no."

I waited for her explanation.

"If John agreed to marry me. I would never have even thought of becoming a nun. More than anything else, I wanted to be with him. I feel that I am married to him even now. I feel like a widow who does not want to marry again." She paused to see if I had something to say.

"Is this then a form of escape from a hurtful reality."

"I don't think so, Godmother. On the contrary, I am embracing reality."

Again, a questioning silence.

259

She said, "Now that marriage is out of my future, I have two choices: to stay single or be part of a community. I would be comfortable with either. But I have chosen the latter because I think it will help me use my gifts better. I think that this is the best way for me to spend my life. It is a studied decision."

"Do you think you are answering an inner call?"

"If you are asking me if I am being spiritually motivated, I must be honest and say no, Godmother."

"There are a whole lot of welfare groups that could use your gifts. You could join them and still be free to do whatever else you want to do."

"I could, Godmother, and I probably would, if I found one that gave me what I am looking for."

"What are you looking for?"

"It is hard to explain, Godmother. It is not spiritual. If anything it is physical. It has to do with my body. I wanted so much to give it to one person. After all those who thought they had it earlier. They didn't, you know. This I know now. The body is nothing without the mind. Now if anyone will have it, it will have to be divinity."

I didn't know what to say. And I said so: "I don't know what to say." She smiled.

"What do I do now?" she asked.

I told her that in her case, we could do away with the period of aspirancy and move straight on to postulancy. After six months as a postulant, both she and the convent could take a decision on whether she should continue with her novitiate and the vows. As a first step, she would have to make a formal request to be a postulant.

Looking back, I began to see that in many ways, my own decision to join the convent was more intellectual than spiritual. Even today, I ask myself how much the spirit leads me. I try; heaven knows, I try. Those bended knees and folded hands in the privacy of my room are not proof, to me at least, of an outpouring of grace and the spirit.

Vimla's Notebook

Chapters. They turn for me with a mere flip of impish fingers dipped in divine mischief.

The asphalt pages of my childhood's documentary turned, first to the soiled sheets of a lascivious theatre. Then the ruled, neat handwritten narrative of the boarding school and the hospital. Now they have me reading my present continuous biography from the assiduously illuminated pages of this postulancy.

4. 45 a.m. Today as every day.

The convent rooster – the morning bell ~ rings.

Stale night saliva rinsed out into quiet washbasins.

Mentholated mouths readied for praise, worship and the holy wafer.

Skin soaped and washed.

With hands forbidden to transfer sensation

                    to this fleshy vessel of concupiscence.

Original sin must die of atrophy without stimulation.

5.25 a.m. The brass rooster rings again.

The chapel receives the soft steps of nuns and postulants.

Simplicity: the chapel.

A rectangular floor covered with mats.

A sloping roof with Pinto & Co. Mangalore tiles.

From the roof hangs an oil lamp that is alive at all times.

A large wrought-iron cross on the wall in front.

Below that the tabernacle that houses the ciborium with the holy wafers.

A sturdy rectangular table covered with white lacy fabric.
Two vases with flowers adorn the table. Two candle stands.

One by one the feather-footed nuns and postulants float
in. Genuflect.
Bow before the tabernacle.
Sit cross-legged on the mats. Listen to the hum of silence.
Signs of the cross.
Voices in the upper register sing the entrance hymn in
perfect unison.
Yesterday's practice was good.
Fr. Trevor at the Eucharistic table.
From the Lord be with you to Go the Mass is ended.

We will return to this chapel seven times in the day.
Two better than our Islamic sisters.
The shape of my utterances have changed.
The visceral vocabulary of once upon that time
watered down to the grammatical thinness of propriety,
functionality and now piety.

I kneel with the other postulants and pray, rather, declaim.
Those antiphons, canticles, lessons, versicles, responsorial
psalms, pious ejaculations...
those syllables sprinkled with holy water and sanctified
with the censers of liturgical flourish.

Hail city of refuge!
Hail David's high tower!
With battlements crowned

And girded with power.

The inspired metaphors and the prosody
of the Little Office
send me to a literary not religious ecstasy,
giving me goose bumps with those corns on my knees.

Hail Gideon's fleece!
Hail blossoming rod!
Samson's sweet honeycomb.
Portal of God.

Hail garden of pleasure!
Celestial balm!
Cedar of chastity.
Martyrdom's palm!

They swallow me whole. The aesthetics of ritual and
rubric; the form and structure of Time as it is laid out for us:
Matins. Lauds. Prime. Terce. Sext. None. Vespers. Compline.
The very décor and decorum of the convent are cleverly
designed for the transportation of the potential mystic.
Beautiful.

But I must shake off this awe of form and give in to the
simple religious fervour and worship of the devotee. Bride of
Christ I must be. Not easy.

I try. I try.

In my room, I pick up the Bible gifted to me by my
godmother.

Shun the literature of the world. Embrace the literature of

the Word.

Whip the flesh to find the spirit.

I open the Book at random. The Song of Songs.

Pure delight.

As the apple tree among the trees of the wood,
so is my beloved among the sons.

I sat down under his shadow with great delight,
and his fruit was sweet to my taste.

He brought me to the banqueting house,
and his banner over me was love.

Slay me with flagons, comfort me with apples:
for I am sick of love.

His left hand is under my head,
and his right hand doth embrace me.

I read and I have to fight off the sensuous pictures of me in John's embrace.

Was that the devil's finger as bookmark?

Other pages of the Word wash over my slippery pebbled mindscape. The red-lettered lines of the Galilean's utterances burn themselves into my heart.

I keep the Book slowly down, walk to our common bathroom and change into my nightgown. No changing in our rooms.

Three other narrow beds at arm's length. Three other

postulants kissing holy pictures, family photos and crucifixes.

Whispers hiss across the room to cheat the hours of required silence.

Lights out.

A whispered good night from the bed next to mine stretches out a hand towards me. I respond. Stretch out my hand as well. Our fingers just about touch. Good night Aruna.

I lay my body down to sleep. Not my mind.

Morning. I read a news item in the Hindustan Times.

ARTIST AND WIFE HELD FOR PAEDOPHILIA

The Delhi police late last night arrested well-known socialites, Mr. and Mrs. Kumar from their posh South Delhi residence. Mr. Kumar, an artist, has held frequent exhibitions of his paintings and sculptures in Delhi, Bombay and Calcutta. Mrs. Kumar also runs an elitist beauty parlour in South Extension.

The arrest is in connection with a raid carried out six years ago in Greater Kailash in which a number of women were caught in flagrante delicto as it were. Many of the women were of foreign origin, in India on tourist visas. They have been allowed to leave the country since there were no charges framed against them. There were also a couple of minor girls, only one of whom was apprehended. The other escaped.

Mr. and Mrs. Kumar have applied for bail. Their story is that they had established an experimental theatre group, which was misconstrued by the police as prostitution.

The past stares at me like a ghost.

Letter from Preeti

My dearest Sr. Vimla Aunty,

It feels so good for me to call you in this way. You were always special to me. Now you are extra special. Mother General says that you are a good nun and that you pray lots and try very hard to be very good.

You will feel proud of what I have done. I put my paintings in the school exhibition. Four of the paintings were sold. I got two thousand rupees, which I gave Sister Superior. She says she will open a bank account in my name. So that if I have to do more studies I can use that money.

Please pray for me.

I love you.

Preeti

***

Around me, piety is a performance that begs from me wonder and secret envy. Knees hinged for genuflection. Eyes raised heavenward. Palms squeezing a wishful holiness to the breast. Lips atremble with the words of the Catholic prayer book. Polyphony of many silences.

When will I stop being a mere spectator? I go through the motions with the others. I pray and I hope for grace.

It is not an empty piety, I can tell. The postulants are earnest in their espousal to Christ. I know that it does not come easy. They try. Like I do. But I lag behind, I think. I feel inadequate. Sinful even.

I speak to Sister in Charge about how I feel. She laughs and then suddenly is serious.

"You are looking at their piety, Vimla. That's only a mask," She said. "A beautiful one. It hides the tremendous effort behind it." I see shades of Sister Godmother in her.

"I know, Sister...'

"The mask hides the sadness of the clown."

"Am I your sad clown without even that mask?"

"We are all sad clowns. We are all hiding the hard face of our efforts. Hoping for holiness."

The postulants, twenty in number come from simple backgrounds. Most of them have just passed their 10th standard board examinations. There are two Science graduates among us. One of them is my bedside neighbour, Aruna. The one whose fingers say "goodnight" to mine every night. The other two, Rose and Mary Ellen seem to be the happiest girls in the convent. They speak as if they have nothing to hide.

"I had one only boyfriend when I was in standard ten," Rose confides. "He was in 12. He left to become a sailor."

"I never had a boyfriend, baba!" confesses Mary Ellen. "When I was in the eighth standard, we went for a retreat and after that I decided to become a nun. To give myself to Jesus."

"You must have had many? You went to college, didn't you" Rose to Aruna.

"No. No boyfriends. I concentrated on my studies. Science is not easy."

Aruna then turned to me. "And you? Did you have a boyfriend?"

I hesitated. "He was no boy. But yes, I did fall in love with a man."

"What happened?"

"He went away."

"Like mine." Said Rose.

"Is that why you decided to join?" Mary Ellen's question.

"No." I said simply, not wanting to go into the complex reasons that I shared with Sister Godmother.

Later that same evening, Aruna spoke to me while we were doing garden duty.

"Do you still think about your man?" Aruna's question. I was not sure how to answer her, but I did.

"Yes. In fact, I allow myself to think about him."

"But isn't that wrong? Shouldn't you give yourself completely to Jesus?"

"Do you think Jesus would mind if we loved other people as well and thought about the people we loved?"

"I don't know. There is so much I don't know. I want to be a good nun, but it is not easy."

Vimla's notebook

I must be honest to myself.

I don't know if I can continue as a postulant like this. Or if I should. Am I living a masquerade? The escapist as devotee. The jilted lover as mystic. Where is He to whom I want to give my body? My mind. My soul? I need to see and touch Him in the same way I saw and touched my patients. I saw and touched John. I felt their feelings. I felt their pain. I was one with them.

I must be honest. I must leave.

***

Just back from a talk with Sister in Charge. Everyone's confidante. Easy to talk to. She looks the comforter she is. Big round softness. Santa Claus face without the beard. Santa in a sari. The shabbiest nun in the convent. A continuous twinkle in her eyes. Her cheerful exterior hides a perceptive, intuitive mind. The postulants' best friend, she knows how to send them away with some of her own smiles. I decided to talk with her.

She greeted my entrance into her room with a hearty "Vimla! I was just thinking of you." She laughed as if she had cracked a joke.

"I don't think I should continue here, Sister." Again that laugh and then a sudden seriousness, which I have come to recognize now as her manner. The laugh as think-time perhaps.

"Every single one of us has felt like that, Vimla. You're doing well."

"I came here to give myself to Jesus. Now, I feel I cannot do that."

"Why do you say that?"

"How can I give myself to someone I cannot see?" That laugh again, but before she could get serious, I said, "John I could see. Touch. Know he was there. Where is He for whom I joined this convent? I do not see him. It is all a big lie. We have all been fooled, Sister. You. Godmother. Fr. Trevor. The convent. I am fooling myself. I cannot go on like this."

"The eyes of the spirit," she said.

"I don't have them."

"You do."

"How do you know."

"I know. Because I see your earnest struggle," she said with complete seriousness. "You will stay, Vimla. You will stay."

***

I punish the flesh

UNWORTHINESS TRICKLES like a sticky sap down my consciousness. And doubt with it. Does one put on holiness with a religious garment? Sanctity with a vestment and a mouthing of vows? Was He listening to the words I uttered that day, just a week ago? Rather, was I listening to my own lips? The enunciation of my wish: To reject the attractions of the world? To give myself wholly to God. To minister to his body seen in the sick and the needy around me.

I accept with gratitude Veronica's veil of compassion. Beautiful ritual.

Uplifting ceremony, yes. The whole church strung with white ribbons. Flower arrangements looking like gardens sculpted in white. Lilies. Roses. Carnations. All white. The simple symbolism of our rubric. The elevated aesthetics of Holy Orders. The feeling of near-levitation. It is real and rare. The congregation of nuns of our order. Others as well. Overdressed parents, close relations and friends. Preeti is there. Paid for her own train fare from Delhi, she tells me. Mehnaz and Petulia. Surprise invitees of Sr. Godmother, who couldn't attend. Mehnaz works with an organization looking after street children. Said she was tempted to bring a few of those adorable urchins along. Resisted. Petula doesn't practice nursing. Wished she had done a course in running a household instead.

The guests are a picture of decorum. You can almost feel their inner tremble as if a miracle is expected. Like perhaps the Holy Dove appearing above our heads on cue with the sweet equal-voiced unison of *Veni Creator Spiritus*. My own senses, swollen with expectation, could burst. Or so I feel. Into an effervescence of spirit-filled gladness. And then the *Veni Sponsa Christi* weaving its velvet polyphony into my emotions. Stirring up a near-conjugal excitement. My marriage to Divinity.

Come Bride of Christ
Accept the crown
Prepared for you from eternity.

I am at this station of unknowing now. Behind me those two years of the novitiate. Successfully completed from all outward appearances. Six years preparing for my First Profession. Done. Behold: the picture of a good nun.

Sr. Mary Vimla of the Marys of Magdalene.

How do I feel? Do I feel anything at all? I don't know. In my mind I am all there. A nun. With very high spiritual hopes. But how do I touch the spirit?

It's this body. I touch only this body. Flesh-heavy. Warm and alive. A strong pulse of 68 bpm. Dictating my every move. Prompting my mind. Smothering the spirit. Villainous body. The Serpent uncoiled. What can I do? What should I do? Answer me from above.

***

I feel the pain all right. The pain and the empty space in my belly. The pain in those portions hidden by my clothes. They hurt. My torso. Back and chest. Breast included. Excruciating. Blouse and sari, covering those instruments of self-inflicted torture. The pins and paper clips that I have secretly sewn into the course sackcloth underneath my visible clothing. I have placed them front and back. Sharp points directed towards my flesh. The sackcloth is wrapped tightly around my torso. Cruel corset. A continuous lashing of the body. The additional invisible layer makes me look a trifle broader. The other nuns tell me I have put on weight. The wows were good for my health, they say. Joke. A whole month now of this torturous lingerie. My secret. Not easy to keep. The pain should not show on my face. A month and a few days, I think. I cannot see all the bruises. I feel them. Claws of a fierce animal. Penance. I feel hopeful. The mortification of the flesh must work.

At table I hardly eat. Feigning fullness. Sister-in-charge recommends a bitter herb as system cleanser. To sharpen my appetite. I take the bitter herb. Not my food. The mortification must work for me. I want it to. I want my spirit to break out of this heavy layer of flesh. Just peep out and I will be in ecstasy. I plead with the spirit.

Go to sleep, Body. Rise up, Spirit.

***

Penance. I'm in tears. I speak to the crosshatched image behind the confessional. Father forgive me. I don't see the Bridegroom's face. I cannot feel His touch. I cannot hear His voice. Is He there? Doubt has become my faith. My faith is being crushed by my senses and my intellect.

Comfort comes in soft, understanding, consoling tones. You cannot see him, He can see you, says the crosshatched image, his lips almost touching my face across the confessional's netting.

Halitosis as pre-penance?

You cannot hear him. He can hear you. He loves you. What you cannot, He can.

I go back to my pew comforted. Not comfortable. Not convinced.

Back to my pins and paper clips. I notice my body while bathing. My skin is like a torn fabric. As if whipped by a cat-o-nine with sharp bladed points. Blood oozes from the wounds even as the water and soap cause them to smart.

One more month of clandestine penance.

It's no use. Pain and an empty stomach are no mortification for this body. It can take it. Has taken it. Has known how to take it. This is my curse. This high threshold of pain and hunger. That's my cursed blessing. It's no use. Pain only makes me more conscious of the body I want to put behind me. Pain for me is spiritual self-abuse. Pornography of the spirit.

It's no use. I put an end to the self-inflicted mortification. A week later the wounds have healed. Not a scar. Just smooth skin. Even I marvel at this.

***

Circular from Mother General.

My dear sisters in the Lord,

I see the work you are doing in your various centres and I feel elated. I have also had opportunity to see our new MOMs in their ministry and I know that the Lord's vineyard is blessed with good hands.

You and I need to be reminded, however that our ministry must be imbued with grace. There is the need for spiritual exercising. This being Lent, this is the right time.

I have taken this opportunity of organizing a three-day Lenten retreat for the new Marys of Magdalene. At the Motherhouse in Vasai. The retreat will be given by Fr. Lobo. He is a young priest, ordained just a year ago, but he has already been noticed for his sermons. This will be his first retreat, but I am sure, it will be good.

Yours in our Lord,

Sr. Mary Teresa

***

CONSTERNATION. The ghosts of yesterday have a way of reappearing. O God, why?

What a day!

Morning. We assemble in our motherhouse chapel, Vasai. The altar has been stripped of all drapery. The windows are darkened by black curtains. Behind the bare altar table, a projection screen. Half-way down the room, a projector.

We all arrive the previous evening. Twenty-two of us. Spend the night in our rooms.

Mother General introduces us to our retreat master. The young Fr. Prashant Lobo.

Prashant Lobo!

Prashant Lobo. I stare through the imagined splash of cold water in my face. Blankness.

Then I see him as if in an apparition. This boy of so many years ago. His face tortured by guilt. His reluctance to take what he had paid for. His trousers down. His clean, innocent face, looking pained.

I look up at his face today. Hair cropped short. The jaw has squared but only slightly. His eyes are bright. Confident. Quite unlike the boy of then. I lower my eyelids to avoid a meeting of the eyes. Through that small crack in my vision, I see him. Black cassock draping a slim body

His thin, only just discernible smile spreads across the room like spilt honey. His eyes pan across his audience. As if speed-reading their features one by one. The smile gets broader now. And in that slow sweep of his vision, his eyes rest on me. No escape for me. Or for him. The slow head swivel stops. His jaw drops a little. His lips pronounce an inaudible "You!" Quick recovery. The swivel continues as if nothing has happened. Like a movie passing over a glitch. From the corner of my eyes I try to catch any ripples of attention among the sisters. I notice none. Yet I am not sure.

I would not like this part of my past to make a splashdown here among these nuns. It would be uncomfortable to say the least. More for him than for me.

His expression changes. He closes his eyes. In a voice that seems like a passionate whisper in each one's ear:

"Let us pray."

As one body, we all kneel.

He turns towards the front of the chapel. His back to us. Kneels. Joins his hands in front of him. Tilts is head up to the crucifix and says:

"Lord. You see us all here today.

We will spend the next three days not in this chapel

but in your heart and in your mind.

May your spirit come down upon us and enter every single pore of our beings.

So that we may be infused with your grace, your life. "

And then, do I notice a quiver in that resonant whisper?

"First, Lord, I bring myself to you with my past; with all my failings.

I bring to you everything I have done of which I ought to be proud and of which I ought to be ashamed.

And then I bring you the deeds and thoughts of every single person in this room. Only You know them as they are.

You have seen their deeds and they have hurt your goodness.

And yet you have let us come this far.

To this day of grace.

As we meditate on the body of Thy son, who gave his blood for us,

may we be filled with a new life,

so that when we leave this chapel after three days,

we leave as resurrected people.

We ask this in the name of Jesus."

Unbidden chorus: "Amen."

Then he turns around and speaks to us all. Never once again does he look directly at me. His eyes take the entire group in their vision. He speaks slowly, intensely. Pausing after each line. As if waiting to see it sink into our consciousness.

"We all need to go through a Passion, an intense body, mind and heart experience; of pain, degradation, uncertainty, suffering, sin. We need to go through a Death, a giving up, a surrender of the body-mind-heart experience and finally, a Resurrection, a rising up to a life of enlightened bliss. All of life needs to go through those three stages.

"For the next three days, we will try to do just that. There's no more appropriate time than now. The season of Lent. The season of prayer, fasting and penance. The season when you do the Stations of the Cross. We will do none of that. We will spend three days studying an old piece of cloth. A fascinating old piece of cloth. I promise you that you will not be the same after that. We will try to keep silent for these three days. We will speak only what is necessary. Even what is necessary we will express in the least possible words. For these three days, your thoughts, your feelings, but most of all your silences are going to be more important than words.

"We will now have a 30-minute break during which time you can try and finish all the talking that you need to do. Empty yourself of speech and bring your store of silence when you assemble here again."

In that 30-minute break I see him making contact with the retreatants. Short one-line conferences among two or three. Almost casually, he approaches me.

"Guddi. I know that's not your name," he says quietly.

"I'm Mary Vimla," I tell him.

"Mary Vimla," he repeats. "Rare combination of names. But nice."

Silence.

"I don't think you and I want to know how the two of us have come to this place. Do we, Sister?"

"No, Father."

"We'll keep it at that. And thank God for the path of miracles that He has laid down before us. "

He moves on to speak to the others. He has a pleasant, easy way with the nuns.

We reassemble. Hear that pin drop. Or is that a feather of the Holy Dove? Fr. Prashant Lobo switches off the lights.

Further draws the curtains to block off the sun's rays. But there is still light in the room. His face a sepia rendition of some old classic photograph. Very sombre now. Turns on the projector. The first slide appears. The title slide: *The Shroud of Turin*. A simple title with no embellishments. Like a title on a school textbook. With no promise of excitement. But between Fr. Prashant and the images on the screen something happens. There's a thick, homogenized presentiment in the room. One big piece of pious expectation. A shared trembling of the nerves. Something is going to happen inside each one of us.

The first slide after the title: an image of a long piece of cloth. The measurements are given: 3.7 feet by 14.3 feet. Looks like a dirty long rag.

My thought bubble: What a gift-wrapping in which the Son of God was handed back to the Father!

Fr. Prashant, with cue in hand is scientist-professor more than Catholic priest. The projector screen becomes the mysterious cloth. Woven, we are told in a three-to-one herringbone twill composed of flax fibre. A yellowish stain stamped across the length of the cloth.

The scientist-professor is now hypnotist. That stain. Look closely. The back and front of a man's body. Naked. In negative. Now see the negative of the negative. The positive image. Black-and-white photograph. Is that the Son of God with his hands modestly in front of his nakedness.

The cue moves across the screen. Pushed, it would seem by Fr. Prashant's voice.

Fabric becomes flesh. Transmutation in front of our eyes. Of stains and marks on the cloth into open wounds. We are looking only at the back and chest now. Just the back and chest. Semi-colons. Commas. Full stops. Hyphens. Exclamation marks. Punctuations with no sentences. Only blood. They start to bleed in our minds. In my mind. Count those commas. Ten eleven twelve. Of the same intensity. Written by that one lash of the cat-o-nine. Other punctuations written with differing intensity. 160 marks in all. More. As voice and cue point to each of those marks I shudder. Feel the excruciating pain of those punctuation marks. My back is one big hurtful mass now. More pictures of the shoulder. The neck.

Next slide, the front torso. More marks made into wounds in my mind, as voice and cue point to them I feel the lashes. I hear sniffles around me. Some of the nuns are crying it seems. Do they hurt as much as I do?

And then the big gash on the side. Deep. Between the fifth and sixth rib. I feel it. The pain shoots up my body and I think I am going to scream. I hold myself back. God bless this high threshold. My gaze is fixed on the body in front of me.

"Vimla!" a loud, frightened whisper in my ear.

Sr. Mary Violet touches my shoulder.

"You're bleeding all over! Your blouse is stained with blood."

The others around me have heard. They look at me as if at a ghost.

Fr. Prashant stops. Turns to the sisters who have gathered round me.

"What's the matter?"

"Sr. Vimla is bleeding." They say in tones of concern and consternation.

282 **Saynt Lachmi**

"How? What happened? Is she hurt?"

The sisters shake their heads clueless.

He comes over to where I am. Looks at the bloodstained blouse.

"Good Lord!" he exclaims. "How did this happen?" Looks around for answers. None. Puzzlement all around. Sr. Mary Dominica and Mary Violet have joined their hands in prayer.

The reverend is at a loss as to what to do.

"We'll break 30 minutes early today," says Fr. Prashant. "We will reassemble tomorrow morning."

Mother General is called. She takes me to her room and examines me.

Sister Godmother joins us.

My back and my chest are a mass of wounds.

My shoulder region lacerated.

In front between the fifth and sixth rib is a big fresh gash.

"What happened?" Mother General asks.

"I don't know." I tell her truthfully.

She looks at Sr. Godmother as if sharing a secret. An unspoken "do you think what I am thinking?"

Sr. Mary Teresa walks in with a first aid kit.

"I asked her to come with some disinfectant and surgical dressing." Says Sr. Godmother.

***

The next morning. The antiseptic treatment and dressing seem to have worked amazingly well. The wounds feel less painful. They look almost healed. Sr. Mary Teresa examines them early in the morning.

"Can't believe it," she says. "They looked frightening yesterday."

"But that's me." I tell her. "My body heals very fast. And then, you did a good job, Sister."

"Amazing. I can't believe it."

Much attention from the other Sisters as we assemble for the day's session. Fr. Prashant asks about my condition. Does it hurt? How am I feeling? Around me the visible signs of more than care and concern. Something else. I feel myself an object of .... not suspicion. Not awe. Not envy. Something else. A combination of all three? No. something else. Whispers. Muted conferences despite the rule of silence.

Self-conscious isolation. A descent into blankness. Or is it an ascent?

Fr. Prashant celebrates Mass. Makes it a happy get-together. Much singing. Clapping of hands. He's hardly at the table. Moves around like a restless brat not able to sit still. Throws in some sermon-time humour. Stimulates talkback and dialogue. Superimposes the Last Supper on to breakfast time. Breakfast of spiritual champions he says. The paten and chalice. The Body and the Blood. Energy for the rest of the day. A refilling of our jug of grace for the next 24 hours.

Lights out. Windows darken for the second day's session. We study the crucified limbs today. Bruised knees. The shoulder again. the thumbs locked against the palm. The pierced wrists and ankles. Cue and voice prod my senses. I don't know what's happening. The same sniffles around me. My limbs begin to ache. Now I am conscious of it happening again. Sympathetic contagion. Mind spins into incoherence. Madness. My body is Veronica's veil. Vimla Simon of Cyrene

Veronica. Take on His pain and heal it through my body. The compathetic nurse. It is excruciating now. I think I will cry out now. I look down at my bleeding wrists. Blood around my feet.

Sr. Angelina's Notebook

Is it Good Sense versus Religion now?

I FEEL A LITTLE MORE ASSURED TODAY. Our talk with Bishop Rodney stayed within the boundaries of reason, at least. He had summoned me together with Mother General to his office to discuss the matter of the 'stigmata'. The news had got to him on the third day of the retreat, when Vimla developed fresh wounds on her forehead and on top of her head. He had rushed all the way to Vasai to see for himself. Besides the bleeding head and face, he could see the faint scars of the previous day's wounds on her wrists and her feet, which we had covered with surgical dressing.

The three days of the retreat were a challenge of faith for me. The entire convent, including Mother General was excited at having a stigmatic among us. The sisters had in their minds already canonized her saint and were clamouring for the stigmata to be made known to the archbishop and even to the Vatican.

I was the lone wet blanket. For once, I did not agonize about my own faith. I felt that I ought to put things in perspective. Nobody knew Vimla as well as I. Not for a moment did I see Vimla's 'stigmata' as a supernatural or even mystical phenomenon. In fact, I looked at it as virtually an inevitability considering her physiological and mental make-up. I tried to convey this to brains totally numbed by an excessive religiosity. I narrated Vimla's past experiences in the hospital, but nobody was really listening.

I presented the same case to the bishop. He listened

without interrupting, taking down notes as I spoke.

"So, you think there is a perfectly natural explanation to what's happening, Sister?"

"Yes, I am sure of it." I said.

"You know that that does not take away from the possible spiritual and mystical dimensions of Sr. Mary Vimla's experience."

"Yes, of course. I grant that."

"At the same time, a stigmatic may not always be a religious person. The question is: can we give her the benefit of the doubt. Do we feel that her stigmata were caused by an intense feeling of oneness with the suffering Christ?"

"From what I have seen, I think I can say so." Said Mother General.

"I know that she was plagued by doubt and that she had this overwhelming desire to feel the presence of the Lord." I told him. "Yes, there was strong religious fervour."

"What do you suggest we do? You must remember that if we make this publicly known, the media will pick it up and your convent will become virtually a shrine overflowing with miracle seekers. More than that, it will seem as if we, the Church are endorsing the sanctity of the person and of the stigmata. As you know, we do not do things like that lightly without approval from Rome. Matters such as these require much investigation and proof."

"I think we should wait and watch," I said.

"Has there been a recurrence of the phenomenon?"

"Yes," said Mother General. "But her wounds heal quickly. Within a couple of days."

"It happens every time she goes into meditation now," I

told the bishop.

"I agree with Sr. Angelina's suggestion," said His Lordship. "We wait and watch. Try to ensure that this does not get outside the convent."

"That will be difficult," said Mother General.

"I would like to suggest one more thing, if I may," I said. "Can we have a scientific investigation into all this? A panel of doctors and psychologists to examine Sr. Mary Vimla? They could tell us something."

Mother General looked uncomfortable. With head bowed down, she ventured. "Your Lordship, can we not for once see the hand of God without the help of Science?"

"We see that hand every day, Sister," he said. "But at times like these we need to demonstrate good sense."

Sr. Mary Vimla's diary

Accused of sainthood, I plead innocent.

Yes. I wouldn't mind being a saint. If wishes were halos, behold one like a thought bubble over my head. I promise. But I am not a saint. Why do I say that? They ask incredulous, impatient. Didn't you bleed in the same places as the Lord? The stigmata. That's a sign from above. Heaven's canonization of the living. Sr. Mary Vimla, why don't you see?

I know me, I tell them for the hundredth time. I am a compath. A kind of sick person. Not a saint. What's happening to me is physiological. Not supernatural. I tell them in the simplest terms what they do not want to hear. They want a saint right there in their convent. Sleeping in the same room with them. Why won't I oblige?

General confessions after the retreat to prepare for general communion. Fr. Prashant sits in the cubicle that reconciles heaven with earth. I stand with the others in the forgiveness queue. Churning memory of commissions and omissions. Porous faith and slippery doubt. The rutted maze of the intellect. The mirage that is holiness. I want to pour it all out through that confessional sieve. A hand taps me on the shoulder. Whispers: "why are you here? You don't need to Vimla. Not you!" Sr. Mary Pauline will not think of a stigmata-blest sinner.

Cross-hatched behind the privacy of the confessional, Fr. Prashant is a figure I do not know, nor remember. He is not even there. I see not his history; merely his face, darkly. Behind the crisscross of the confessional. He makes tangible the mystery of absolution. The waterless lavabo of guilt and the grime of every day's consciousness. I see a murky mirror. With my image faintly there. Every whispered question and answer blows across that reflection. Like a breeze sometimes harsh sometimes gentle. Dispelling the blackness. Making that face clearer.

"Father, forgive me, Father..."

The words do a spin in my subconscious. Taking me, I don't know why to Gethsemane. The agony in the garden. The chalice of pain. I weep. My fingers entwine into a tight knot. I tremble. The past ricochets with the present. The fleshy days of Mr. and Mrs. Kumar and after. The hospital and my compathetic sharing of distress. My days of slender intimacy with John. My misty years as postulant and novice. There's no thought of sin. No feeling of guilt or remorse for what I had done. Sinless confession. And yet a need for reconciliation. Of what I am and what I want to be. An intense pain coming out of an emptiness within. My body is drenched in sweat. The crosshatched face pronounces penance and the absolution. I bow my head and catch sight of the sweat on my hands. Droplets of water. And blood. Oozing from my pores. I rise. Try to cover my hands and my face with my *pallu* to hide the bloody sweat. Head bowed I walk to my seat in the chapel.

***

Report of an Investigation On Sr. Mary Vimla's Stigmata

The investigation was conducted by a panel of doctors, psychiatrists, pathologists and a theologian appointed by the Archbishop.

The participants were:

Dr. P. G. Nadkarni M.D (Hematologist)
Dr. G.K. Govekar M. D. (Immunologist)
Dr. Ralph D'Souza (Psychiatrist)
Mrs. Letitia Gomes (Counselor)
Mr. L. Shirodkar (Pathologist)
Monsignor Francis Crasto (Theologian)

The investigation consisted of interviews with the subject conducted by the entire panel. There were two sessions that lasted a whole day.

Individual sessions with the psychiatrist and the counsellor. Pathological investigation consisting of
    blood tests and urinalysis
    MRI and brain scans
    Duplex Ultrasound Doppler Test

The stigmata play peekaboo with my meditation sessions. I contemplate the sacred wounds and they are there on my person. I am not uncomfortable with them. Only with the pious buzz around me. One nun has to see it, and in minutes I am surrounded. Wide eyes. Genuflections. Folded hands. I don't know how to handle it. Feel like an unwitting fraud. Stigmata becomes stigma.

The archbishop is pure ecclesiastical caution in his statements to the archdiocese and the press. Despite all attempts at secrecy, the news has spread.

People visit the convent but are not encouraged to see me. Letters pour in from all over the archdiocese. Some from other parts of the country. Petitions for prayers. Give us a miracle they plead. By the blood of Christ that is in you. By the passion of the Lord that you have borne. Pray for my son. My daughter. My husband. I go to sleep trying to resolve this sacred scam in my head.

The people are not interested in the findings of the expert panel, which confirm normalcy. All pathological tests show a remarkably healthy and normal body.

***

We are assigned our centres. Scattered all the way from Virar and Vikhroli right up to the Fort area in the South of the city.

Four of us join the older nuns in a centre near Girgaum. Shuklaji Street. We are six in all. Our duties involve helping with the Health and Well-being Centre in this area. This, I am sure is Sr. Godmother's idea. Putting me here. Amid sex workers and their children. They come to the Centre for treatment, rehabilitation, counselling.

Just up my street, as they say, Sr. Godmother.

I go to my work like a starving beggar to a feast.

***

I see: midriffs, thighs and raised cleavages as painted signboards, advertising their sad looking wares. Skin. Flaked and sickly, caked over with cheap talcum powder. The colour chocolate trying to look at least like burnt sienna but managing little better than ash grey. I pass them on my way to the Health and Wellbeing Centre and back to our little convent apartment on the second floor of an old building on Shuklaji Marg.

They call them politely, workers. Sex workers, but their workplace won't be called an office or even a factory. Long, narrow balconies leading on to small dingy rooms. The cages. Structures imitating the flaked, sickly and caked look of their occupants.

The public march past on this famous street is in itself immensely watchable. Housewives, eyes front, bazaar bags in both hands, hurry past in quick purposeful strides, necks rigid in their contemptuous refusal to look left or right. Well-dressed men, young and old slow down to half their earlier pace. Cast sidelong glances. Or even do a full 'eyes right' or left depending on which way they are going. Curiosity. Nothing else. To see what saleable flesh looks like. Just curiosity with just a little tingle somewhere, maybe. Schoolboys and teenagers do the same at a slightly faster pace, afraid that they will be seen. Worse, that they will be propositioned. The painted girls do so only to tease. Innocent but scared erections under their shorts. Truck drivers, who have parked in the nearby lane, do the slow, sideways march as if in an art gallery. Hands below to push the insistence down for a while. The girls respond with invitations, vocal and gestural. Pouts, flying kisses and a slight hitching of the already short skirts.

I want to go into one of those rooms. Sit on their *palangs* and talk to the girls.

Memory stretch. I did what they are doing now. Without the advertising and the make-up. Pretending that it was theatre not prostitution, while society now pretends that this is 'work' not whoring. Political correctness is incorrect; dead wrong. Hypocritical. It gets away with the idea that euphemism rectifies social disfigurement.

Our health centre with Dr. Pednekar in charge has just opened its doors. Already we have queues. It is a clinic and counselling centre. A ten-minute walk from our apartment.

One morning, I smile at a badly painted young one as I pass by. She looks confused. Next morning, I add a gentle wave to that smile. Hesitantly she waves back. Sr. Mary Ellen who walks by my side looks askance. On the way back the young one blows me a kiss. I imagine those bruised, smudged lips flying smack into my face to meet mine. I wave back instead. Must learn how to blow kisses. The next day, she walks down to us and accosts us with: "You people are Sisters, aren't you?" in Hindi. I smile and say, "Yes. Your sister. Everybody's sister."

"My name is Mehrunissa," she volunteers.

"Beautiful name. Mehrunissa."

An older woman from among the group yells, "KuumKuuuuum!!! What the hell are you doing? Your customers are here. Holding. Come quick!"

Mehrunissa makes the famous fornication sign to the lady. Forceful forward thrust of the back of her fist. Turns to us to explain. "Here they call me Kum Kum not Merhrunissa."

Smiles and says, "Okay then. I'm off for now." And darts off to her waiting client.

Sr. Mary Ellen looks at me. "Know your neighbour." I say with a smile.

***

It's happening, I think. The stigmata have stopped appearing.

Work envelops my being. And the Bridegroom is beginning to be more visible to me now. My work in the clinic is making that happen. I think I am getting a glimpse of his body. Not the body of the Shroud. A new body with fresh wounds. Lacerated, sickly, fevered, bleeding, pus and mucous-filled, crying out in pain. I sense the pain. Not as much as I did then, during the retreat, or even as much as I did with my patients in the hospital. The contagion of physical distress happens in a few cases. With the regulars. Not so much with the ones who walk in with casual ailments. Which is most of them. Coughs, colds, fevers, diarrhoea, urinary infections, wounds. Mostly children, sent unaccompanied by their mothers who are busy with their clients. Happy faces oblivious of the HIV virus they are hosting. Smiling through the gonorrhoeal marbles that were meant to be their eyes. Mothers come when the discomfort down there is unbearable. They hurl abuse even as they enter. On themselves, their god and the brutes who couldn't find another sewer to dump their filth into. Kill the pain they beg. Or kill me.

Dr. Pednekar is a diamond. Caring. Gentle. Just

wonderful. He is kind, respectful. To him they are as good as nobility. And the abuses melt on their tongues to words of thanksgiving. Dactar sahib is god.

Some of these become regulars. With them it happens. The compathy. The sharing of distress. And relief. Did you feel the relief, my bridegroom? I feel like asking. As much as you did it for the least of my brethren... He had said. Did it hurt then and does it hurt less now? I ask.

Must talk to Sr. Mary Agnes. Secretary and administrator of the Centre. Not much direct contact with the patients. Just paper work. Yet her discomfiture with the patients is a little too apparent. She cringes every time one of them approaches her table. Gentle Sr. Mary Agnes. Gentle but scared.

Sr. Mary Aruna is a wonderful counsellor. The ladies are able to confide in her.

She is empathetic. Her special gift. The sharing of mental distress. As against my peculiar particularity with physical distress. Yes. It is happening.

***

This morning: Mehrunissa runs across the street to meet me. Distraught. Angry tears have cut rivulets through the thick, dark layer of make-up that covers her face. Her friends, Nazura and Dusnumbri have been clapped in jail. False charges of indecent exposure. That sonofaswine policeman. Just because he didn't get his daily dig-in. The pig! Nazura was too tired that day. He dragged her by the hair. Handcuffs on her hands. Dusnumbri had run to her aid. She kicked and scratched the sonofaswine. So she was taken as well... She, Mehrunissa would not take this lying down. She was getting together her friends. 30 of them. Storm the police station. Demand justice. They were going to do it tomorrow morning.

"Just you watch, sister. See what I will do tomorrow."

Sr. Mary Ellen tugs insistently at my sari. "Let's go from here," she says. "Quick. Let's go."

I put my hand on Mehrunissa's shoulder.

"Fear not," I tell her.

***

News item in the Times of India

NUN ARRESTED ALONG WITH 30 SEX WORKERS
Demonstration outside Foras Road Police Station
(There's a photograph of the demonstration with an inset of Sr. Mary Vimla)

Thurs. 21:

Sr. Mary Vimla of the Marys of Magdala order, better known as MOMs, was among those arrested by the Foras Road police station for allegedly disturbing the peace and for unruly behaviour. She was with a group of 30 sex workers of the neighbourhood who had come in force to the police station to demonstrate and seek justice for their co-worker who was arrested two days ago.

On being asked why she was part of the group, she said that these were her sisters. She did not mind going to jail with them.

Handwritten posters in Hindi demanded the punishment of Havildar Ram Gopal Sahani, the release of Nazura Ahmed and Dusnumbri and justice for sex workers. A mild lathi charge preceded the arrest. All 31 of the demonstrators were under lock-up up for a night in the police station.

To date no FIR has been lodged either against the sex workers or Havildar Ram Gopal.

***

Lord! What a day! What a day!
I meet my long lost Parvati. And how!

Sr. Mary Ellen and I walk to our workplace, the health centre. The route is a path of contradiction for us two. For Sr. Mary Ellen it is a strip of burning embers. She hurries past the 'cages' like a firewalker. For me it is Friendship Road. I slow down to catch a few eyes along that corridor and blow some kisses. I have learnt how to do that now. Passers-by turn round to look at us curiously, diverting their attention for a while from the fleshy advertisements along the corridor of cages.

This morning Merhunissa runs across towards us with two other women. She introduces them. The ones just released. Nazura and Dusnumbri.

Dusnumbri. Wrinkled skin on bone. Even the paint on her face cannot hide the sickly pallor of her skin. I stare for a moment and before I can whisper a shocked "PARVATI!" she says hoarsely, "Lachmi Devi!" I run to embrace her but she moves away from me.

"No Lachmi. No! Stay away from me, devi."

"Parvati!" I call again and grab her into my arms.

"Not Parvati," she says. "*Dusnumbri*." Meaning Number Ten.

Mehrunissa, Nazura and Sr. Ellen look on, not knowing

what is happening. The corridor is abuzz. The painted faces stare at what is happening there in the middle of the street.

I look toward Mehrunissa, who says, "Yes, Sister. Her name is Dusnumbri."

"Why?" I ask of Parvati.

"I am Number Ten. Just Number Ten." Spoken with the finality of the clenched teeth and fist.

Parvati is a sacred name, she said. Like Lachmi. A holy name. I don't fit that name any more. I am a number for fornicating men to identify, she said.

Why? How? When? I asked.

It's a long story, she said.

Sr. Angelina's Diary

Archbishops can be gentle, you know.

THE MEETING with the Archbishop went off better than I had anticipated. He had summoned Sr. Mary Vimla together with Mother General and myself to talk about the arrest and the initial embarrassment to the archdiocese. I had expected the usual ecclesiastic sternness from him. Vimla had experienced some of it within the convent itself. With the aura of the stigmatic still surrounding her, she got away with a mild reprimand and a holy harangue about prudence and modesty and the virtue of invisibility. That, together with a contextual reminder of that poverty of spirit, the meekness that inherits the earth and all those beatitudes so nicely suited for sanctimonious scolding.

The archbishop's mildness surprised Mother General, but in that quiet maze of my Machiavellian mind (Oh Angelina! Angelina! Blessed indeed are the clean of heart) I could sense a more tactical reason for this leniency.

After the initial headlines were devoured, the media had slipped into righteousness mode, pillorying the law enforcement machinery. *"Trust MOMs to teach our city fathers a lesson in courage."* Giggled one eveninger. *"Sisters Act. Police don't"* squealed another. Social activists joined the chorus. They held meetings to denounce the police and stress the need for individual courage. The Marys of Magdala in particular and the archdiocese as a whole attracted some good press. The Archbishop was not unhappy after all. Mother General and I were surprised and not a little impressed with the way in which he conducted the entire session. No rough admonishment. Just a few emollient question marks.

"I am intrigued," he said with a smile. "Why did you do such a thing?"

With not much hesitation, Vimla said, "I don't know, Your Excellency. I do not have a reason. I just had to do it."

"That is a little hard for me to understand, Sister," said the archbishop still smiling. "Why would a nun like you feel that you just had to do it?"

Throughout the questioning that followed, I saw beneath the seeming softness of Vimla's responses a subtle mock-piety that disguised what to me was a certain belligerence.

"Those sweet ladies were our acquaintances. We met them every day on our way to our Centre. We smiled at them and they smiled back."

"Was that the only reason?"

"They called us "Sister". Yes. Perhaps, that could be the reason. We are called "Sisters", Your Excellency."

"And so..."

"I did what a sister would do."

Abruptly he changed the topic. "By the way, Sister, have you had any more of the stigmata episodes lately?"

"Yes, your Excellency, but differently."

"What do you mean by that?" the archbishop asked. "I work now in the health centre. There I meet people with rather serious wounds and ailments. They are terrible to look at and excruciating to bear. I know because I experience them ~ just as I experienced the wounds of our Lord." And then after a brief pause, she said with a smile, "We are all part of the body of Christ. Aren't we Your Excellency?"

Sr. Mary Vimla's Notebook

My moment of infamous fame

LETTERS FLUTTER in like currency at a *nauch* session. Leaving me feeling like just that. A nauch girl who has executed a provocative pirouette for lascivious eyes. They only send me deeper into myself. I had only taken orders from my heart. I am now paying the price of my emotional self-indulgence. I must be fair, I tell myself. These are genuine expressions of admiration. Epistolary applause from people who care.

The one from Mehnaz is pure Mehnaz.

Vimla dikri, I am proud of you. Send me your autograph, darling. I will cast it in stone and garland it every morning. I never liked convent sisters. Sala mutlabi log, all of them. But you have wiped that slate clean. Khachaak. Just like that.

Love you, dikri.

Mehnaz.

Preeti sent me her shortest letter to date.

Dear Aunty Sister,
You are my new heroine.
I love you.

Preeti

Fr. Prashant wrote:

Dear Sister Mary Vimla,
You have shown me that the Shroud is not in Turin. That
the image of The Body is infinitely larger than those 3.7 by
14.3 feet. Thank you, Sister.

Prashant

***

O Parvati! My Parvati!

I see my footsteps in the dust of the air.
Moving towards where I have not yet been but will go
tomorrow.
I spy predictions. With Yesterday as crystal ball.
My life gets written in the never drying ink of the past.
Like Parvati, lying there;
bone bundle loosely wrapped in skin.
Glazed, watery eyes.
Eyelids blinking at you like lips articulating some deep
emotion.
I have been seeing her every day in our hospital.
I had her admitted a week ago.
I come to her bedside every morning.
Watch her fade away with every cough and struggle for
breath.
AIDS. Full-blown and in the final stages,
dragging her through phlegm and blood to the precipice.

I begin to share her pain and fight to block the compathetic exchange of symptoms. I suddenly feel unable to
transfer healing from my strong immune system to her dying
body. Where is that force gone? Where the force? I feel within
myself the panic of death. I must be strong. I must not
succumb.

Every day I pick up the pieces of her broken narrative.
From the pages of her paradise, our pavement to other more
soiled chapters. Here is a gist of what she told me.

They fooled me. Our dadas of the roadside. Remember
them? They raped my mind. You were lucky to be stolen away,
she said, holding on to my hand. But they got me. They
ruptured my happiness.

They told me that I had worked well for them. That now
I should have my reward. Savitri chachi had found a good
husband for me in the village, they said, those dogs born of
slime. They took me to a village outside the city. They showed
me this boy. Very young. Just getting that fur over his lips.
Good looking. A real chikna. Brown skin, not black like
mine. If I was looking for a bakra for myself, he would be it.
I was thrilled. My heart was a drum on which his looks were
playing a thrilling beat. I was expecting plain chawal, this was
biryani. Mutton biryani. His name was Prakash.

It was a quiet marriage. No dhoom dhaam. There were a
few other girls of my age and a few grown up women from
the village. No men. Only the dadas of our pavement.
Prakash and I did the saath pheri – the seven circles round a
fire. Today I know that the pandit was a chor, sala harami,
but at that time I thought he was real.

On the first night this bakra pretended to not know what to do. He sat there with his pants on and did nothing. It was I who showed him how to use his popat.

The next day he was out of the house till late at night. He came back and slept. Did nothing. Didn't even look at me. In the morning, he woke me up, and before I was fully awake, did it in his half sleep like a bicycle pump, washed his face and went out of the house.

He didn't come back for over a week. When he did, he stood at the door and asked me if I had menstruated that week. I told him I did.

"Damn!" he cursed loudly. "All my effort wasted."

He left without even entering the house. Half an hour later he was back with another boy of about the same age and almost the same looks. He asked the boy to wait outside the house. He came in, threw me on the ground, did his bicycle pump thing without saying a word. When he had finished, he joined his companion outside. I asked him where he was going. He said that he had more work to do with a few more and went away.

We lived in a hamlet of about twenty houses. Small one-room mud houses in the middle of a rocky place where nothing grew. There were a few trees and shrubs along the river, a small stream about 15 minutes' walk away. We cooked and slept on the floor. We washed our clothes and bathed on the banks of the river. Here I met with the other ladies. They were interested in how things were going for me. How was my pregnancy going? Did I have morning sickness? Girl chatter. They never spoke much about themselves. Occasionally I thought I noticed them exchanging glances as if they were keeping a secret from me. Of course, they were. I came to know much later.

I didn't see Prakash throughout my pregnancy. For the nine months he was away, I was visited every week by a woman who asked me to call her Jamunabai. She would bring me meager provisions – dal, rice, potato, salt, oil – and taught me to cook. I had never cooked before when we lived on the pavement, remember? She too would hardly speak to me. The dadas came regularly. They said that they wanted to make sure I was comfortable. The dirty dogs!

It was a healthy baby. A boy, delivered in the house itself by Jamunabai. A day after the baby was born, Prakash appeared. His companion was with him. The dadas came too. Prakash was pleased.

The dadas in one voice: "You've done a first class job, you hero!"

I nursed the baby for a week. Then the dadas came and took him away. They said that they had to have him vaccinated and inoculated but I knew that it was a lie. I screamed and tried to grab the baby back from them, but they slapped me hard and threw me on the ground and left.

The next day, they came with the boy who used to accompany Prakash. They said that he was Prakash's brother, Prasad. They told me that from that day on, he would do the job. They said that they wanted no trouble, or else it would be very bad for me. One of them took out a knife and ran his finger across the blade to frighten me.

I was frightened. There was nobody I could turn to. Everyone here seemed to be part of a devilish plan and I felt trapped.

It was then, one day that Jamunabai spoke to me.

"There is nothing you can do", she said. "You had better cooperate with the dadas. They are powerful people. Above them there are even more powerful people with a lot of money. They have the police and the government itself in their pockets.

"Can you not help me?" I asked her. "What about the other women?"

She shook her head. "Most of them here are doing the same job as you."

"What job am I doing here?"

"You are making babies.

She told me that these babies would be taken and used in the cities.

"Look at me, "she said. "Can you tell me how many babies I must have made?"

"You tell me," I said to her.

"I've lost count. Fifteen. Twenty. I don't know. One every year. Sometimes just nine months apart. I was a baby-making machine." "Do you meet them?" I asked.

"Never," she said. "If I meet them now, I may not even recognize them. They were all taken away after a week of nursing."

She looked at me and smiled. "Who knows, you may well be one of my daughters" she said quite seriously. "Prakash could be one of my sons."

She told me that she had started this work very young. "I couldn't have been more than fifteen or sixteen," she said. Her sons would now be old enough to father children and may even now be in the employ of the dadas for the purpose.

She shuddered at the thought that one of her sons could have fathered one of her later sons. But that was her job, she said. She had stopped thinking about it. It was good that she was past the childbearing age now.

I was in a cage. I knew that I was being watched closely by men and women kept in the village for this purpose. To make sure that none of us ran away.

I made two more babies. One with Prasad and one with a man who was old enough to be my father. Each time I had to give away the babies, I fought and screamed though I knew it was of no use. I had lost all feeling, but I wanted desperately to escape. Not because I thought I was doing anything wrong. I just wanted to get away from these rakshasas who frightened me so that I spent many nights imagining the most terrible things happening to me.

One late evening Jamunabai came over and said that she knew I wanted to escape. I thought she was warning me of dire consequences; that she would tell the dadas about my intentions. But she surprised me when she said that she wanted to help me. I was still young, she said, and I could still do something with my life. She would try and help me. She said that the man who carried watermelons in his cart from the neighboring village to the nearest station was a friend of hers. She had done him a few intimate favours in the past and she could persuade him to take me to the station. I could hide among the melons. She asked me if I was willing to take the risk. I could ride ticketless to the city. She gave me the name of a lady, who she said would help me.

And that's how I came back to the city. But look where I ended up! That's when I decided to drop my name. Parvati was too good a name for what I was doing. I became Dusnumbri.

After her staccato narrative, she looked to me for a response. My tears were my only articulation at first. But speak I did. I told her that she was my first idol. Her face had always been in front of me all through these years. Clearer than a photograph. Framed in my heart. I thought there was nobody like her. She was my heroine. And Sr. Mary Angelina was my guide and teacher.

She wanted to know who this Sister was.

One morning I introduced Sister Godmother to her. I had given Sister a quick summary of Parvati's narrative.

Sister sat down on the bed next to Parvati, took her bony hand in hers and patted it gently. She said.

"Parvati. Tu Parvati nahin. Tu Pavitra hai." You're not Parvati. You are Pavitra, meaning 'holy."

She told her that what she had gone through was a kind martyrdom and that all that suffering had purified her in the eyes of God.

"He is very cruel. Isn't he? This god of yours." He asks a lot for our purification.

Yes, Sister agreed. But only from very special people like you, she said. Ordinary people like us do not have your strength.

***

Later, Parvati wants to hear my story. I see that my narrative is a form of life-support system for her, keeping her pulse and breathing going. She opens her eyes after long periods and that too for a few seconds. Then she closes them and says. "Keep talking. I'm listening."

When I had finished, she opened her eyes and asked: "Does it mean that you will not get married now?"

I tell her that as a nun, I am a bride of Christ. Her eyes close again. She asks me if this God of mine would accept the body of a one-time prostitute? We are all precious, I tell her. Then will he accept my body as well? She asks.

Parvati's eyes meet mine. Do I spy a hint of mischief there? "Back. Itching," she whispers.

"Will your God scratch my back now?"

She tries to turn on her side to give me her back to scratch.

I turn her over and part the hospital gown in the middle to bare her back.

I don't use my nails. I imagine them tearing skin and clawing at raw bone. I use the tips of my fingers instead, gently moving across her back. From one spot to another.

"Aah!" She groans with pleasure. "Aah! You got that brother-in-law of the devil," she says. "There! He's running towards the right. Catch him. Good. You've got him. Look! He's running again. Catch him. Catch him. Ahh! There!"

My fingers traverse the ridges of her back. Feeling her ribs like rumblers on a road.

"Oooh! Aaah! Lachmi. You are magic. How do you know where to scratch. Lachmi. Lachmi. You goddess. You devi."

"That is God scratching your back," I tell her. "I am only his hands."

"Then tell your god that he has very good hands."

I continue for I don't know how long. My fingers counting her bones like another kind of rosary.

"Ooh! Ooh! Lachmi. Devi Lachmi! .... Yeh swarg hai. This is heaven. This is heaven. This is heaven!"

**

Love, Grief and Friendship coagulate at the cremation. Though women are not usually present, there are about 30 of us. All of them, Parvati's Foras Road friends. And there's Sr. Angelina and myself.

There, in the flames, I see her body taking on its original and its final form. Ash.

Sr. Mary Vimla's Notebook

My new status does not sit comfortably inside my head.

Sister Superior! Me? How could they do it? But they did. They have given me the title. I feel inadequate. A wingless bird would feel more self-confident. In obedience to my new title, my hair has decided to turn colour with flat-brush strokes of silver across my full head of hair. It happened almost overnight, as if I had sleepwalked to some nocturnal hairstylist for my silver crown. Looks just right, say the sisters. The colour of dignity, learning, hard work, trustworthiness, sanctity, modesty and even aristocracy. The wimple of old would have hidden it from vulgar view. Our saris show off our hair or lack of it.

Sister Superior. It takes me a moment or two to realize that I have been addressed. Did they have to stick it on to me at all? Could I have declined? Should I have declined? It does not suit my being. It is not I. "Sister Superior". Feels like a mask; a little too heavy.

Authority does not sit well on my shoulders. I see it now. Decisions get stuck in that web between brain and tongue. The sisters wait to get orders from me and I look at them blankly; then with as much humility as I can muster, I ask, "What do you think I should ask you to do, Sister?" And with even greater humility, they offer a suggestion – if it is all right with me.

I've tried praying for wisdom. It comes, I believe, in the sobering realization that I am no commander of people. I never was one. My concern for others is a butterfly net, not the fishing net of the leader. Mine is a one-on-one mission. I sit across a sick person and I feel her pain. I ease it if I can. A relationship of bodies, more than of mind. A Sister Inferior if there was one.

I resign myself to a task for which I know I am inadequate. The devi's ego has to take a beating.

I spoke to Mother Superior about the way I felt.

"There are others better suited to this title." I told her. "I feel ... like... like a butterfly trying to roar."

"That's just what we need today in our convent. A butterfly, not a lion. I want you to go from flower to flower, spreading the pollen of ..."

"Holiness?"

"No." She smiled. "We've tried that. It ends up as empty piety, a veil behind which we can hide. Let's try a little realism, the flesh and blood stuff of life as we see it."

"What do you want me to do?"

"Be yourself. None of us has seen life the way you have. You have taken your unique experience and sanctified it with your new life."

"I don't know about that, Sister."

"You have, Sister Vimla. And it is precious. I want you to use it for our convent."

"How?"

"You will know."

***

A clatter of dissent confronts some of the programmes I have initiated. The Principal of our school, Sr. Mary Joseph comes to my room, agitated.

"The parents are disturbed," she says. "Yesterday I met a group of them protesting against the sex education we intend to start for our higher classes."

"I will speak to them," I say with hesitation, knowing how tentative I am with groups. "Why don't you call a parent-teacher meeting and I will talk with them?"

I know why I started the programme. As a matter of fact, I expected the parents to be happy about it. Other schools were doing it. Sex education and counselling. I was not prepared with any rationale or arguments in its favour. As I sat down to make notes on what I should say, my mind went blank. I stood up from my table with not a word written on that expectant blank paper.

At the meeting, I find myself unable to address the group. As I write about it now, I unravel for myself the 'singular' quirk of my personality. I can speak to only one person at a time. Someone asks me an angry question. I look at him and before I respond, I sense the cinders inside his brain and belly and I mirror his feeling inside myself. Then I begin to speak. I tell him and perhaps through him the rest of the group that the class is not about sex. It is about the body. Instrument of human potential. Vessel of amazing strength, Of elegance, intelligence. Of peace and joy and possible glory. The near-infinity contained within it. Infinity within reach. I hint at the body as a channel of grace. Sex is part of it. An important part, I tell him. So is compassion, empathy, love, endurance. The entire spectrum of the human experience. It ought to be an essential part of our education. I look at the man. I sense the dousing of the flames inside him. I pick out other faces, other eyes and I see varying degrees of calm. Not everyone is convinced, but the meeting ends with a general agreement that we can go ahead with the programme.

Elsewhere, we have had problems. Three of our nuns were very badly roughed up by street dadas. Fortunately, their bruises were not serious. They were slapped and dragged by the hair across the street. It's part of the cost, I tell the nuns. The cost of our programme for street children. It aims at providing holistic help within a realistic framework: basic nutrition, medical attention and early schooling. The reality is that it is not always possible to extract these unfortunate children from their present situation.

I was personally involved in the programme, as would be expected. Things have changed since my time on the pavements. There are many more families to be seen on the streets. The underworld has got a tighter grip of the begging industry. Any intervention here would be fraught with danger. An investigative journalist, who was attempting to trace the top of this pyramid was found murdered. Next to him was a note that promised the same fate to anyone who poked a nose into their affairs.

I knew that this was no idle threat. There was no point in being foolhardy here. I helped the sisters pick the areas which I thought would be relatively safe, but I was proved wrong.

I've decided to be more involved. We will confine ourselves to children who know their parents. At least the mother. Her cooperation will be necessary. There are more of these in the suburbs; mothers and children not part of a begging network. We have no option but to leave for the time being those floating babies and children, flesh-and-blood begging bowls designed by the dadas. We need to look at other ways to rescue them. This may have been a job for the police if they were themselves not a part of this inhuman machinery.

This work on the streets has got me in touch with my old friend, Mehnaz. Together with a doctor ~ a Parsi ~ she has set up a mobile clinic for pavement dwellers. I believe our nuns can work together with her. I have watched her pavement mission. She is not just nurse but entertainer, her Parsiisms providing her patients with more than relief – laughter.

***

Another ghost from the past.
And what's a thermometer doing in my mouth?

Note from Mehnaz sent via one of our Sisters. Information. Stripped of Mehnazisms. She has spied John on a pavement in Churchgate. This in the course of her work with street children. He appeared to be in excruciating pain from an ugly looking sore on his ankle.

Destiny is an elastic band that binds me to my past. I've decided to go and look for him.

He has aged. His long unkempt hair, thinner now, is fully grey. Emaciated. Gaunt of face. He lay there on the pavement with pain chiselled on to his features.

The sore on his ankle is a miniature garbage dump with maggots and flies hovering greedily over it. Paralyzed with pain, he let himself be carried into our hospital van. He did not resist. He couldn't.

He didn't speak. I did. "Why did you wait so long? This is

bad."

No answer.

"This could get gangrenous," I said to a face that tried vainly to hide the pain. "We'll have to attend to it immediately."

Had him admitted. No bed space. Had to keep him on a mattress on the floor. The resident doctor, Dr. (Sr.) Mary Thomas attended to him. Ordered blood and urine tests. Check for diabetes.

No diabetes. That was a relief. She prescribed antibiotics both internal and external.

I did the first dressing. I focused on his ankle. Felt a searing pain in my own. As I drained the pus and swabbed the wound, my ankle became a cauldron, bubbling over with a strange mix of fire and thistles. I moved my gaze from his foot to mine. I half-expected to see the same festering wound appear on my foot. Would I, the stigmatic be the bearer of John's stigmata now? I paused. Looked up at the ceiling for a good minute to blank out my mind. I applied the ointment on his ankle as if it were my own. Kept my hand on his foot for a while. Willing the healing forces of my own body to flow into him. Felt the energy flow from me to him. Or was this my imagination?

That was a week ago.

The sore is healing well. Visits to his bedside every morning. Like devotions to a sacred wound. I record in my memory the changing colours of the skin. Day by day by day. So now I can play back in slow motion the wonder of the healing process. Speeded up, I would like to believe, by my healing touch.

"How are you feeling?" I ask him, as if I need to.

"Better. Much better. The pain is much less."

"The wound is behaving itself."

"Thank you, Sister."

"Vimla to you. Not Sister," I wanted to correct him. But I didn't. I am a nun now. Sister Superior. Sister to everyone. To my lover as well.

Is he my lover still? Can he still be?

I have requested that he be admitted into our Home for the Aged in the building next door. He will resist this, I know. Must do it before he can use his feet again. His immobility manacles him to my will.

I examine my feelings for the only man I have loved. What do I feel for him now? Concern? Tenderness? Pity? Affection? Love? Passion?

I am propelled to his bedside more often than necessary. I finger his ankle with a tenderness that goes beyond mere nursing care. I more than sense the churning inside me for this man. I do nothing to hide or curb them.

My religious garment did not ask me to strip myself of feeling, surely.

***

I have been feeling feverish for the past two or three days. Strange. I cannot remember having a fever ever. A sniffle on rare occasions. Sometimes a cough that would come and go. Warrior body, mine. Fought the microbes of street and pavement. A battlefield more killing than a convent hospital. But a fever? I had only experienced it as a shared distress of my patients. I had never wholly owned this thing called a fever. Why now? It is quite high too, I am sure of it.

In a corner, unseen, I stick a thermometer in my mouth for the first time in my life. I do it clandestinely. As if committing a sin. Fahrenheit 102°. That's what I had expected it to be. Ignore it, I tell myself. My body can handle it. I do nothing. Take nothing but a glass of warm water.

Two hours later, the fever has vanished. The warrior triumphs again. Hurray and Alleluia for good measure. The spirit smiles. I go about my duties.

The real me is out there in the wards, sharing the distress of patients. Doing a healing sponge. A bandage. Administering a dose of medicine. And now, these past few days, tenderly fingering a one-time lover's ankle.

I have no appetite for food today. I eat a few morsels to appear to be eating. Something doesn't feel quite right inside me. My body has never behaved like this before. I know that. By late evening, I feel the temperature rise again. I am disappointed with myself. I am letting my body down. I sit down to write my notebook. To spite the fever. I will fight it with my pen. With my mind.

I write this with a fevered hand.
Febrile brain.
The battle rages but I will win.
I will win.
That warrior, my body has never lost. Never.
But why, Oh why?
I feel a rigor coming on at this moment.
I shiver uncontrollably.

Malaria? I know you.

I recognize your poisonous footprints in my veins.

Your hideous face.

You cowardly brood of Satan's offspring, you!

Will this warrior body be beaten by a tiny anopheles' proboscis?

Write, Pen. Write. Never mind the enlarged, trembling running hand.

Plasmodium Vivax. Falciparium.

I dare you. This is Vimla... Lachmi.... Lachmi Devi. Remember?

I cannot go on.

My pen does a saint Vitus dance over my notebook.

For the first time in my life, I will secretly commit this personal sin:

I will go and swallow two aspirin tablets. So help me God.

Sr. Mary Angelina's Diary

Finally, is this senility?

Or is this a huge cloud of happy indifference that has enveloped me? Nothing shocks or even offends me to any great extent now. I hear of one of our favourite girls eloping with a lover and I smile, while the whole convent seethes.

"After all we did for her!" Righteous voices articulate their pain.

"You prepared her for it," I say.

"Prepared her for what, Sister?"

"For an independent life of love as it should be lived today. Aren't you happy for her? I am."

"What will happen to her?"

"She will be happy. Isn't that what you want for all our girls?"

As I approach my eightieth year, it is as if I have walked out of a rainforest of engaging sights, sounds and experiences into an open meadow of light and free spaces. Blue skies beckon, smiling. I hear the birds chirping in my new brain. It is a wonderful time of life.

I am happy.

The Sisters were recently agitated about a couple of paintings that John had done in his spare time in the Aged Home. It was Sister Vimla who had started him on them after having nursed his ankle back to health. I was there when she gave him a sketchbook and pencils and a couple of canvas boards.

"You must have something to do," she told him, patting his head.

Her particular affection for him was apparent to everyone in the convent. She did not even attempt to hide it. Though it was only a pat on the back or a look of endearment every time she was with him, it was clear to all that there was a special feeling between them.

"Do you think that's right?" Sister Mary Louise spoke to me in private.

"Do I think what is right?" I quizzed her.

"What we see going on between John and Sister Mary Vimla."

"What's going on, Sister?"

"Oh, you know. Their love affair."

"Their love is not an affair. It is a feeling. A beautiful feeling. I wish I had it, particularly at this age." I then turned to her and said, "Don't you wish you had it too, Sister?"

She reddened. "But is it right. Sister?"

"It is not right. It is beautiful."

"In a convent?"

"It could lead to problems, I know. But in this case, it is just there, like two candles burning silently on two personal altars."

She was not convinced, nor was I intending to change the way she felt about it.

The two contentious paintings were nudes, done on canvas. The nuns were horrified and wanted to put them away where nobody would see them. They were even more horrified when I said that I would display them in my room. I thought they were theologically evocative in execution and design.

Both paintings were surrealist depictions of the body.

The first, rendered in luminescent warm colours ~ ochre, orange, crimson and sunshine yellows ~ had two bodies, male and female twisted into one to form the bark of a tree that reached up to heaven. The arms stretched out into branches that were covered with leaves of different hues.

The second canvas was a pieta in reverse: a woman's half-covered body, limp in the arms of a man, invisible except for his hands and feet. The entire canvas was painted in white and soft greys over a white background, rendering the figures barely visible. The hands holding the female body were pierced at the wrists. The woman's body had the marks of the sacred wounds – on the head, the side, the wrists and the feet.

Later, I asked John if someone had told him about Sister Vimla's stigmata experience. He said he knew nothing about it. He had just painted his personal image of her; a person who borrowed the Lord's wounds through those of her patients. I believed him.

John, an intensely introspective person spoke very little with those around him. He spent most of his time writing in his notebooks and sketching. Sometimes he would do a portrait of a fellow-inmate and gift it to him or her. There were a number of these, mounted on card paper displayed next to their beds. He wouldn't be speaking to anybody about Sr. Vimla.

***

Of a sudden there's a crumpling of those blue skies. Dark clouds have appeared. Sr. Vimla, my godchild is unwell. Until now this was an improbability. She has never fallen ill. Even now I see her, visibly incredulous regarding her condition. Nonchalantly she attended Compline, after which. I spied her rushing back to her room. I followed after her as she ducked under her bedcover and went into a violent rigor that had the bed itself shaking. All the signs of malaria.

We'll have to find out: Vivax or Falciparium.

Extract from John's Diary

Kyrie Eleison
Why do you dry up O fount of mercy when one of your little sprinklers herself runs out of that life-giving water O tell me O tell me why did she who went from aisle to aisle all these years distributing the cool droplets of your love have to now burn with a fever so high it scares the very mercury and her senses O Lord I seethe with angry questions looking for reasonable answers and then within the impotence of my being today I ask if will you not look mercifully now on this hidden spouse of my heart and spirit whose love has lifted me out of the stony bed of years past to these cushioned days of tenderness which I know are just the shapes of those droplets from your fount O Lord and shall I sit here healed while she is tortured by a ruthless enemy within O Lord for though I have not been to her bedside yet or touched her fevered brow as I would want to yes Lord I have heard frightened whispers flutter around me in corridors and in our meeting places I have heard words that I wanted to wipe out of the ether because they told of the grim pronouncements of the doctors and care givers and I watch the sisters get down on their knees

and I hear litanies of petitions go up in prayer to their source of hope and then from out of the blue I have this vision of the Vimla I knew who shared her patients' wounds and Yours knowing that she could overcome them and come out victorious which she did and now I ask the seen and unseen whether syringe and tablet can substitute for your mercy O Lord will you not once again sprinkle with your own hand some drops from that fount on this your handmaiden I pray.

Part VI

Ten years later.

THE HALO

From Sr. Angelina's Diary

Be warned: this is not going to be happy reading

TIME, THAT NAUGHTY OLD IMP has stopped teasing me with surprises, leading me, particularly in this last decade to accept the inevitability of events as they plonk down on to my calendar of moments and days. I expect the unexpected.

My 80th birthday drifted quietly by. The sweet sisters baked me a small cake to show they remembered. Bless them. But the mood among the MOMs was decidedly subdued, if not downright despondent.

Vimla.

Her deterioration has been slow but painfully visible. For the first time in years, I am experiencing a sense of hopelessness. It has taken more than eight years to come to this. She had ignored her first symptoms of illness. Didn't tell anyone about her fevers; just kept it to herself. That was the first time she had known sickness, being seemingly immune to everything that attacked everyone else. She was confident that her body could handle the fever.

Her first bouts of fever turned out to be malarial: plasmodium falciparium. It could most certainly have been fatal because of her recalcitrant attitude to treatment and her unshakeable faith in her body's capacity to heal itself. By the time the test results had come in and she was told, the fever had raced her to a delirium. With arms raised she would scream: "Come now Falciparium. Show me your worst. This is Lachmi devi." The doctors had given up hope, nevertheless had administered the chloroquin – or was it primaquin? ~

intravenously. Her recovery, surprising to the doctors, renewed her faith in her rare immune system.

But other symptoms followed soon after, mainly respiratory. Severe coughs, stubborn colds and bronchial attacks; they didn't seem to leave her. We all watched her as if in a tragic soap opera, consciously trying to fight the menacing microbes in the attitude of a Joan of Arc doing battle. Reluctantly she agreed to the prescribed medication. She responded well, bouncing back to her daily activities. But the symptoms kept coming frequently, necessitating medical treatment. One could sense her intense disappointment with herself. How could her body let her down? She made brave attempts to appear cheerful; took part in more activities than she formerly did, joining the choir, cooking classes, yoga sessions; but all of that was but a transparent film over her growing depression. In a weak moment, she mentioned to me that she had always been certain that she would go through her whole life without having to take any medication. She felt let down.

Her now chronic illness made it difficult for her to work in the hospital. That, for her was like a cruel and unfair sentence passed against her.

The real sentence came two years ago. Much against her will, we insisted on conducting a battery of tests. One of them, the most dreaded proved positive. HIV. Already at a fairly advanced stage then, it is now the full-blown thing.

It was something I feared even before her symptoms began to show. As a nurse, she has always been carelessly selfless in her care giving. Emboldened by her rare constitution and her compathetic nature, she tended to be indifferent to the care she had to take of herself. This took on a frightening aspect (for me at least) when she was looking after Parvati. There's little doubt in my mind that it was during this episode that she contracted the dreaded syndrome from her best friend.

Strangely, the verdict seemed to affect a change in her attitude. Her depression seemed to give way to an inexplicable acceptance of her condition. It was almost as if she knew whom she had to thank for her condition and was actually doing so. She was bearing Parvati's cross. Rather than looking at this as admirable I could not help but look upon it as a morbidity such as I would never ascribe to Vimla.

She lies there now in the hospital in what is certainly the last stages of the cursed virus. Propped up on pillows, she quite cheerfully welcomes visitors. John was there today. Before he entered the room, he stopped by the nurses' station and checked about her condition. Then he came and stood by her bedside. She was awake. He said not a word. Just looked at her as if in a daze. It was she who put out her hand and held his.

"Don't look so serious," she said. "You look as if you are going to write poetry." He smiled. She held his hand a little longer before letting it go. He waited for a few minutes, bowed to me and left.

I don't know how Mehnaz heard about it, but she was there too, trying to cheer up her friend with her Parsiisms.

Preeti has been visiting her every day. She is in the city, participating in an international calligraphy exhibition. Some of her fonts and calligraphic designs are on display and she is rightly feeling proud of her achievement. She is doing well, this girl; working for a publishing firm and doing a great deal of personal research on calligraphy.

And of course, there is the usual stream of nuns from our congregation.

I stayed by her bedside late last night until she fell asleep. When I came back to my room, I got down on my knees, wordless.

Sr. Mary Vimla's Notebook

The last entry

I BREATHED MY LAST at exactly 6.37 this evening. I noticed the time as I was dying.

The fever didn't leave me the previous night like it used to. It was high right up to the morning and for the whole day. The headache was bad. I groaned with the pain. They gave me tablets. It was no use.

I saw the sad faces of the people around my bed. There was Godmother, Mother Superior and Mary Ellen and Aruna and a few others. Preeti was there with tears in her eyes, poor thing. And John. And Mehnaz. Dr. Warrier had his fingers on my pulse and when it stopped beating, he looked around at Sr. Godmother and shook his head sadly.

I could see myself leaving my body. I saw my body on the bed with all the people around it. Then suddenly it was as if I was being pulled up inside a blue tunnel. As I flew upwards, I had a nice warm feeling. I flew higher and higher into the tunnel until I saw at the far end a bright white light. Before I could enter it, I said to myself, "My God! Is this heaven?"

Letter from the Auxiliary Bishop Trevor Gomes to
The Mother General, Sr. Mary Constance.

It is with much joy and excitement that we read your letter about the possibility of starting the procedure of raising one from your congregation to the altar. The road to canonization and sainthood is a long and arduous one, as you know, and the process may not even by completed in our lifetime. However, we must make a beginning with the hope that we will be able to give to Holy Mother the Church a new saint from our archdiocese.

The life of Sr. Mary Vimla was certainly unusual. From the time she received the stigmata, we had the feeling that she was being chosen by our Lord for holiness, and now He has chosen to give us a sign even after her death. We must be grateful.

The miraculous writing in her notebook after her death is certainly one of the evidences that we can list in our appeal to the Vatican. You did right by enlisting the services of the police's forensic department to verify the handwriting. Their letter confirming the authenticity of the handwriting is a good and valid document.

You have also mentioned two cases where near-impossible favours were granted to members of your congregation through the intercession of Sr. Mary Vimla.

We must not rest there.

Please get your congregation to put together all instances, big and small that would strengthen our case.

I pray that our efforts may bear fruit.

Yours in Our Lord,

Trevor Gomes,
Auxiliary Bishop of the Archdiocese of Mumbai

Sr. Mary Angelina's Diary
My motives are being suspected.
And please note, a twist in the tale

IT'S CURDLING NOW - my relationship with the sisters of my congregation. Mary, Mary quite contrary I hear them sing in my sleep. They think I am being unduly obstinate and intellectually rigid. I sense that undercurrent of their impatience with me. First, it was my insistence that Vimla's stigmata had natural causes. Now it is my resistance to their mad rush to canonize my godchild. In not so many words, I am being accused of coming in the way of them owning a saint. Nobody was closer to Vimla and nobody knew her as well as I did. God knows too how much I loved and admired her. All I am asking from them is a little sanity, a little deliberation, a little patience, for heaven's sake.

I will not speak to them about my personal views on sainthood and this procedure of raising a saint to the altar. I do believe in the communion of saints as enunciated in the Credo, but my personal communion of saints may not find place in the Church's calendar. Many of my saints are still alive in the quiet corners of their anonymity. I see the work they do and the little miracles they perform in the lives of people around them. I construct my own halo of awe and respect for them. There are others too, those that have passed on to another life, who find place in my prayers. I say a little prayer to them as much as I do to some of the saints on the Church's pedestals. These include little known and even ignored individuals whose lives struck me, even in my childhood, as holy. My father was one. I pray to him. There was a gardener, an asthmatic, who when he was not digging and planting was ready to help anyone in our village with physical work. He struggled for breath while he performed his tasks and he took with happiness whatever was offered to him as payment. I have seen him take that money, collect a few urchins around him and share a meal with them. A circle of happiness, that. I was a little girl when he died, but I saw him as a saint who was called up to his reward.

What irks me is this clamour in our congregation today to rush things; to push our candidate ahead of the queue for Vatican consideration.

My private meeting with Mother General was hurtful, to say the least. She accused me of being inordinately intellectual.

"You of all people should know," she said "that even science has to bow down before the Lord. Can you not for once submit your stubborn will to the will of God?"

I gave this a long pause before I said, "It is precisely that for which I am making a case, Mother. For God's will and his divine plan. Can we give Him a little time instead of rushing to push through our own demands of religious gluttony? In the final analysis, Mother, does not the real canonization come from above?"

I could see her jaws harden. Her eyes narrowed as she said, "Do you know what the sisters of our congregation are saying about you, Sister?"

"I don't want to know, Sister, because it would make no difference to the way I think."

"They are saying that you are envious of Sr. Mary Vimla. You cannot bear the thought that your protégé will be canonized a saint and not you. "

"If you intended to hurt me, Mother, you have succeeded. But if you intended to change my mind, you have not."

She looked at me like a mother scolding a difficult child. "Why are you being so hardheaded, Sister?" she asked.

"I just want the congregation to behave more prudently. I believe that Sister Mary Vimla was a most unusual person with gifts of body, mind and spirit that were rare. I haven't met anyone like her. Much of what we have seen in her borders on the mystical. And yet, I would spend much time in putting together a case for her beatification and canonization without any trace of emotion or congregational bias. In any case, Mother. I am a lone voice. I don't matter. You can go ahead with your campaign regardless of what I think. I appreciate the fact that you even stopped to consider my differing point of view. You have the entire congregation on your side. Please do what you think is right, Mother."

"I get the feeling that there is something troubling you?"

I took my time in answering, speaking without emotion.

"Mother, this is just my personal point of view, and you may take it for whatever you think it is worth. I believe that we are going about this with unseemly haste. Like the push and shove in the local municipal office. Everyone seems desperate for it to happen. We could, in this mood, act with more emotion than good sense. We may be overlooking important issues."

"Like what?" she asked.

"I am not altogether comfortable with the very "miracle" that prompted us to consider her sainthood ~ that last entry in Vimla's notebook. The one that she was supposed to have written after her death."

"The handwriting expert has verified it as genuine.'

"I have seen it. The handwriting is the same. I am not sure of the writing." I said.

"I don't understand."

"There's something about the style that does not ring true." I told her. "I would be happy and we would have a more watertight case if you asked the same forensic department to check the notebook for fingerprints."

Mother General looked at me with a confused expression.

"And one more thing," I said. "Please have someone check on the whereabouts of that charming young girl, Preeti, on the day of Vimla's death and on the next day. This is important before you go any further on this matter, Mother."

No, I could not ignore Preeti. And her extraordinary gifts!

Glossary and translations (Mostly from Hindi)

baap re baap!, Good Lord! Literally 'Father O Father!'

jaadoo: magic

shabaash: congratulatory term, well done, good job

harami: wicked, no good

kachra: dirt, rubbish, waste

dhobi: washer man, launderer

so ja: go to sleep

chalaki: cunning

fugree: a game in which two girls do the whirl

sevia: Very fine Indian noodles, generally eaten sweet

Choo-mantar: abracadabra

Fuljadi: a spinning fire-cracker

Gaalee: a bad word, abusive language

Sala: Literally brother-in-law, often prefixed as a mild abuse

Gupchup: idle chatter

Maramari: fisticuffs, scuffle, fight

Chaali: tenement like

Dada: mafia don

Khusspuss: secret chatter, whispered gossip

Bhel-puri: a snacky mixture

Theeka: Spicy hot

Meetha: Sweet

Chatpatta: Tangy

Kulfi: a frozen dessert, thick ice-cream

Chacha: Uncle

Ja-ja: Go fish

Bakwas: balderdash, bunkum

Hool: a threatening move
Booth: ghost
Kamaal hai: Amazing
Jagmag: glittering
Agarbatti: incense sticks
Kumkum: red powder applied to ladies' forehead
Bhajan: devotional song
Mithai: sweets
Pagli: madcap
Khel katam: the game's over; and that's that
Mazaa: fun
Peekha: bland, tasteless
Tadka: seasoning
Nangi: naked
Paaketmar: pickpocket
Tamasha: street performance
Randibaji: prostitution
Chachi: aunt
Kujli: the itch
Woh harami kujli. Pakdo saleko: catch that wicket itch
Arrey, ab bhaag raha hai: Damn, he's running away.
Swarg: heaven
Satchmooch: truly
Sandaas: excreta, stool
Kaise ho? Sab teek tak: Howdy? Everything OK?
Apsara: mythological, heavenly ministering maidens
Bulbul tarang: a stringed instrument
Banjaran: gypsy
Guddi: doll
Paani: water

Bahut jaldi ayee tu: you've come very early

Pehele baar kya: Is it your first time?

Aur ek ghanta lagega kilas ke liye: It will take another
    hour for class to begin

Undher aaja na: why don't you come in.

Nashta: breakfast

Kuchch khaya: Had anything to eat?

Upma: a savoury dish made from semolina

Arre kya hua saali: Hey! What's happened? (saali is used
    as endearment here.)

Tu ab medam ban gayi: You've now become a lady
    (Madam)

Aao mere saath: Come with me

Shaitan: demon

Khopdi: brain (colloquial)

Aapro dikra: a very Parsi phrase, meaning 'our guy'.

Tum sister log hai, na?: Aren't you people called sisters?

Ha. Tumhare sister. Sabka sister: Yes. Your sister.
        Everybody's sister

Sundar naam: beautiful name

KuumKuuuuum!!! Kya kar rahi tu saali? Girhak yaha
pakadke khada hai. Aa ja jaldi!: Kumkum what are you
doing? The customer is holding his own thing here.
Come soon.

Yaha mujhe KumKum kehte hain: They call me
    Kumkum here.

Achcha. Main ja rahin hoon: Ok. I'm off.

Dekho, sister. Kal main kya karoongi: You see what I will
    do tomorrow!

Darna nahin: Be not afraid

Ek pavitra naam: a holy name

Sala hero ban gaya, hamara bachcha! Kya?: Our child is
    now a hero. Wow!

Fuss klaas kaam kiya, tu sala: You've done a first class
    job!

Bahut Kattor hai. Yeh Ishwar tumhara: Very ruthless,
    your God!

Main sunn rahi hoon. Bolte raho: I'm listening. Keep
    talking.

Kya ab shaadi nahi kroogi tu? What then, won't you get
    married now?

v